T0243208

Lavender Lane

By Anna Jacobs

THE LARCH TREE LANE SERIES

Larch Tree Lane • Hawthorn Close • Magnolia Gardens
Lavender Lane

THE PENNY LAKE SERIES

Changing Lara • Finding Cassie • Marrying Simone

THE PEPPERCORN SERIES

Peppercorn Street • Cinnamon Gardens • Saffron Lane
Bay Tree Cottage • Christmas in Peppercorn Street

THE HONEYFIELD SERIES

The Honeyfield Bequest • A Stranger in Honeyfield
Peace Comes to Honeyfield

THE HOPE TRILOGY

A Place of Hope • In Search of Hope • A Time for Hope

THE GREYLADIES SERIES

Heir to Greyladies • Mistress of Greyladies
Legacy of Greyladies

THE WILTSHIRE GIRLS SERIES

Cherry Tree Lane • Elm Tree Road • Yew Tree Gardens

THE WATERFRONT SERIES

Mara's Choice • Sarah's Gift • Paula's Way

⁓

Winds of Change • Moving On • Change of Season
Tomorrow's Path • Chestnut Lane • In Focus
The Corrigan Legacy • A Very Special Christmas
Kirsty's Vineyard
The Cotton Lass and Other Stories
The Best Valentine's Day Ever and Other Stories

Lavender Lane

ANNA JACOBS

Allison & Busby Limited
11 Wardour Mews
London W1F 8AN
allisonandbusby.com

First published in Great Britain by Allison & Busby in 2024.

A CIP catalogue record for this book is available from
the British Library.

First Edition

ISBN 978-0-7490-3009-4

Typeset in 11/16 pt Sabon LT Pro by
Allison & Busby Ltd.

Printed and bound by
CPI Group (UK) Ltd, Croydon, CR0 4YY

Chapter One
Australia

Nina Thomas was walking back to her flat, when she saw a slender, silver-haired woman standing in a garden further along the street crumple suddenly and lie motionless on the tiny square of immaculate lawn in front of a pretty cottage. A quick glance round showed her that she was the only person out in the street, so of course she ran along to see if she could help.

By the time she'd reached her, the woman was stirring, so hopefully it wasn't anything serious. Nina helped her to sit up.

'What – happened?'

Wow! People really did say that after they'd fainted, Nina thought. 'I was walking along the street and saw you fall suddenly. I think you must have fainted.'

'Oh, drat.' She rubbed the side of her forehead, looked round and asked, 'Can you help me to get up and sit on the end of that little wall, please?'

'Of course.' She did that then asked, 'Can I fetch someone?'

'No!' It came out sharply and she looked ruefully at

Nina. 'My late nephew's wife is in the house, but please don't tell her I fainted when she brings out my mug of tea. She's looking for an excuse to move in with me and take over what's left of my life and I'm not having it.'

The woman looked to be quite elderly, possibly in her late seventies, but seemed to be in full possession of her senses now and had a healthy colour. She had a lovely smile when she relaxed a little but it was no business of Nina's what she did about her problem relative.

'I won't tell her if you don't want me to. I'm Nina Thomas, by the way. I live in a flat further along the street, Number 7A, and have just moved in after I sold my own house. I inherited the flat from my parents, but now am trying to sell that too so that I can move to England. So I'm only here temporarily. Are you one of the permanent residents?'

'Yes. Laura Chadwick. I grew up in this house.' She waved one hand towards the pretty detached residence then looked pleadingly at Nina. 'Look, I know this is rather cheeky but would you mind pretending to my niece that you're a friend as well as a neighbour? I'd be so grateful.'

'You sound as if you are having a problem with her.'

'Yes. She keeps going on and on about me having no one to turn to if I need help and saying she could be here for me. Only I don't need her or even like her. Why my nephew married her I never could work out, because she didn't make him happy, I could tell. Perhaps if she'd looked after him better, he might not have died so young. Would you do it? It won't take much of your time.'

'I'd be glad to pretend to be your friend, Laura, or even

to become a genuine friend. I don't know anyone round here yet, so why don't you come and have tea with me tomorrow and we can see how we get on with each other for real?'

Her companion's face lit up at the invitation. 'How kind of you! I'd love to do that. If you come inside with me now, I'll suggest she leaves us alone to catch up on our news.'

'Good idea.'

As they walked into the house together, Nina realised that Laura's obvious happiness at that invitation had made her feel better too. It was a technique that usually worked, she'd found before. If you didn't feel happy about life and did something to cheer someone else up, their pleasure could make you feel better, even if it didn't solve your own problem of the moment.

A middle-aged woman came into the entrance hall from what looked like the kitchen at the rear carrying a steaming mug. She stopped and scowled at Nina. 'Who are you?'

'What a rude way to greet one of my friends,' Laura said. 'This is Nina. Nina, meet my nephew's widow, Susan Jones, who comes round occasionally to check that I'm all right. Which I always am.'

The woman ignored that. 'I've not seen this person here before, Laura, so how can she be a friend?'

Even her voice was harsh and ugly, Nina thought. No wonder Laura didn't want her to move in.

'I've been living in another part of Australia for a while, but now I'm back and really happy to catch up with Laura again.'

'Which part of Australia?'

'That's none of your business, Susan.' Laura had completely lost her smile now.

The niece set the mug of tea down on the end of the kitchen bench and scowled at Nina. 'I'm afraid my aunt is getting tired now, so perhaps you can come back another day. If you give me your phone number, I'll let you know when she's feeling better.'

'I'm feeling fine, Susan, and even if I weren't, when my friend should come round would be none of your business.' It was Laura who was speaking sharply now and scowling at her niece. 'And as I've told you before, I'm doing fine living on my own and I definitely don't need a carer.'

'The doctor is worried about you.'

'No, he isn't.' She glared at her niece. 'And if I find he's been discussing my health with you then I'll change doctors.'

'He knows I'm trying to look after you. That's what relatives do when someone needs help.'

'You're trying to rearrange my life and I don't want to do that, thank you very much. And you're only a relative by marriage so I'm not really your business now that my nephew is dead. Please leave me alone from now on and get on with your own life. In fact, I'd rather you didn't come to my home again.'

The woman's mouth dropped open in shock at these blunt words then she snapped, 'I can't leave you to muddle through on your own at your age. You're already getting forgetful.'

'No, I'm not. Nina dear, will you please see Susan out? She won't need to take anything but her handbag with her.'

The woman hesitated, then stayed where she was until Laura yelled, 'Go away! Now! And don't come back!'

When Nina went back into the kitchen, Laura was sitting at a small table mopping her eyes. 'Sorry for that outburst. She won't leave me alone and it's getting me down. She's trying to gain control over me. Um, she didn't take anything with her, did she?'

'No. Just her handbag. Why do you ask?'

'She's pinched a few small items from me recently, some quite valuable. It can only be her who's taken them because no one else had come into the house on the days they vanished.'

'That's shocking. Perhaps you should consult your lawyer about her and get a restraining order to keep her away.'

There was dead silence then Laura slowly began to smile. 'I never thought of that. You don't think it'd be a bit drastic? Her husband, who was my nephew, died a few months ago and I felt sorry for her, so invited her round to tea a couple of times. Only, she kept saying I was failing and needed someone to live with me. I don't need or want anyone, least of all her.'

'She certainly sounds to be trying to take over your life. It's the first time I've met her and it's obvious that she wants to keep other people away from you. Some folk do that to elderly relatives and then go on to take over their finances too, so be careful of her.'

She waited a moment then added gently, 'Do you have a car?'

'No. I'm no longer able to drive because of a health condition.'

'Well, if you want to see a lawyer and arrange to keep that woman away permanently, I'll be happy to drive you to his or her rooms.' She grinned and added, 'And for the record I do not wish to move in with you afterwards.'

Laura chuckled. 'Thank goodness for that. I actually like living alone and have a good cleaner so I don't need anyone to help me in the house, though I would like to catch up with some distant relatives before I die. I lost touch years ago, sadly, when they moved to the UK.'

She continued to look upset, eyes brimming with tears again. 'You're so kind. I don't know what I'd have done if you hadn't helped me today.' She grimaced and pointed to the mug. 'Even the coffee Susan makes tastes awful.'

'I'll pour it away then, shall I?'

'Please do.' She sat down on a kitchen stool. 'I still feel a bit wobbly so if you'll kindly fetch me the phone and the index next to it from the hall table first, I'll sit in the dining area and ring up the social worker. Luckily for me, the council employs social workers to help oldies with emergencies. I went to a talk about personal security for older people living alone and the woman who gave it said she was employed specifically to help people like me. She gave everyone her card and I kept it even though I didn't think I'd ever need her help – only I do need it now, don't I?'

'Might be a good idea. I won't always be walking past when you need rescuing, though if I am, don't hesitate to call me in.' She brought the phone and index and gave them to Laura, then said, 'I'll pour the coffee down the sink, shall I?'

Before she did that, she took a sniff out of sheer

curiosity and grimaced, then sniffed again and frowned. What did it smell of? Not coffee, that was for sure. There was an underlying sickliness to whatever it was.

On impulse she put the full mug in a wall cupboard. When the social worker came, she'd ask her whether it smelt strange to her and if the woman laughed at her for being too suspicious, she wouldn't mind. It was just – well, you couldn't be too careful in some situations. She'd found that at various times in her life.

She couldn't help hearing the other woman make the phone call, and Laura's voice grew shaky as she explained the situation. When she ended the call, she looked across at Nina. 'Ms Gray will be here in about an hour and she'll take me to see my doctor then a lawyer. I can't thank you enough for your help, Nina, and for nudging me into doing something.'

'My pleasure. Look, tell me to butt out if I'm being too pushy, but do you want me to stay around until this woman from the council gets here?'

'Would you?'

'Happy to. I've nothing pressing to do now that my house is sold. I'll just nip back to the flat and change into something more respectable than these scruffy old clothes I use for my exercise walks. They're all rather sweaty now. I'll only be a few minutes.'

At her flat she quickly washed and changed, getting back to Laura's house in just under seven minutes.

To her amazement, that Jones woman was there again, hammering on the front door with a clenched fist and calling, 'Let me in, Laura. You really do need help.'

Nina marched up the garden path and called, 'Hoy!'

She watched the other woman jerk in shock and turn to glare at her, so asked sharply, 'Do we have to call the police to get you to leave her alone?'

'It's the other way round. It's you who won't leave my poor aunt Laura alone. And you're not a friend or I'd have recognised you. You're a complete stranger. What are you after?'

Nina could see the curtains at the side of the front room move and guessed that Laura was watching out for her and mustn't even have dared open the door when her niece turned up again.

She went and stood in front of the big living room window where she could be seen clearly from inside and called, 'I'm back, Laura.'

'Oh, Nina! Thank goodness!' She stepped from behind the curtain, beckoned her across and pointed to the top part of the window, which was open, saying in a low voice, 'We can chat here, if you don't mind waiting outside. I've called for urgent help.'

'Of course I don't mind.'

A car drew up before the house shortly afterwards and a policewoman got out. As she reached the front door Susan stepped back a little, then stood with arms folded, scowling yet again.

Only now did Laura come to open the front door.

'Mrs Chadwick?' the officer asked.

'Yes. Please call me Ms, though. I never married.'

'You called for urgent help, I believe?' The officer was studying both Susan and Nina as she spoke.

'Yes, and I do still need help. This is my late nephew's wife, Susan Jones, and she won't leave me alone. She keeps trying to move in and she's pushed her way into the house several times. The mere sight of her makes me feel nervous and threatened. And what's more, she's taken some of my favourite ornaments and I want them back.'

'That's not true.'

Susan took a step back, turning away as if to leave and the officer said sharply, 'Stay there, please, madam.' She then looked at Nina. 'Who is this other lady, Ms Chadwick?'

'Nina Thomas. She's a friend of mine, a good friend, who's come round to visit me.'

'She can't be a friend. I've never seen her before!' the Jones woman exclaimed.

'Do you live here, then?' the police officer asked Susan, looking puzzled.

'Not yet. But my aunt has asked me to move in and look after her. It shows how absent-minded she's become.'

Laura stared at her in patent astonishment, then turned back to the police officer. 'I did not ask her to move in! I'd never do that.'

'She's getting very forgetful,' Susan said, with a poor attempt at a sad expression.

'I'm not! I don't even like her only she keeps coming round and pushing her way in. It makes me so nervous I've started keeping the doors and windows locked.'

The officer studied Laura's face and the way she was still barring the entrance, and what she saw must have passed some sort of test, because she turned and said, 'The lady has asked you to leave, Ms Jones.'

Susan glared at them all, hesitated then turned to go.

'Wait!' Laura said. 'Could you please tell her to bring back my ornaments?'

'See how forgetful she is!' Susan exclaimed. 'She said they were presents when she *gave* them to me!'

'I did not give them to you! You took them sneakily. And they're quite valuable as well as having sentimental value.'

'Perhaps you'd bring them back, madam, since you've admitted to having them? I'll call here again tomorrow afternoon and check that you've done that. Could you make a complete list for me, Ms Chadwick, then we'll tick them off together?'

'Yes, I will. I know exactly which ones are missing.'

Susan glared at them all again and strode off along the street, getting into a small car. She didn't drive away, however, but sat watching them.

'She's been sitting there a lot of the time recently watching the house,' Laura said. 'I daren't even go out into my garden these days.'

'I'm afraid I can't do anything about her staying in the street as long as she doesn't break any parking rules, Ms Chadwick.'

The officer was about to walk back to her car but stopped when another vehicle drew up and parked in the drive of the house. A woman of about Nina's age got out and hurried across to the group at the front door. 'Are you Ms Chadwick?'

'Yes.'

'I'm Pauline Gray. You phoned for help. Are you all right?'

'I am now, thanks to my friend Nina and this kind officer.'

The newcomer looked round, nodded at them and said, 'I'm a social worker employed by the local council to help older ratepayers experiencing difficulties of any sort.' She turned to stare at Nina before asking Laura, 'Is this the lady who's been pestering you?'

'Oh, no. That was Susan Jones. She's gone away from the house now, thanks to this officer, but she's still sitting in her car – that blue one over there – watching us.' She pointed to the car then explained the situation and the difficulties she was having.

Pauline scribbled down the names and the vehicle's make and registration number in a small notebook then turned back to Nina. 'How did you get involved, then? Older people can be very vulnerable and trusting so I find it best to check any new acquaintances openly.'

Laura spoke before Nina could. 'She's an old friend of mine who's just come back to live in the area. She's called Nina Thomas and she kindly helped me stop Susan forcing her way into my house earlier.'

'We thought she'd taken the hint,' Nina said grimly, 'but when I nipped across to my flat to change out of my running clothes she came back.'

Laura nodded. 'Yes. As soon as Nina had gone I saw Susan getting out of her car so I locked the door. Otherwise she'd just have walked in. She doesn't hesitate to do that. This time she kept thumping on the door and she looked so fierce I felt frightened. I was worried she was going to break the glass panel to get to the lock, so I called the helpline that we were told about at the talk.'

'That was the best thing to do.'

'There's another thing you should check, Ms Gray,' Nina said. 'Susan had made some coffee for Laura and it smelt rather strange to me, so I put it in a cupboard in the kitchen to show you. Perhaps you and the officer would both sniff it? I may be mistaken because I'm not a big coffee drinker, but better safe than sorry, eh?'

Laura sighed. 'Oh dear! I've lost most of my sense of smell as I've grown older, and Susan knew it. I wouldn't even have noticed that.'

The police officer said quietly, 'Can you get out the coffee, Ms Thomas? I'd definitely like to be involved in checking it.'

Nina led the way into the kitchen and got the mug out of the cupboard.

The officer took it and asked Laura, 'Is this your mug?'

'Yes.'

'Did you make the coffee in it?'

'No. Susan insisted on making some for me. She always does if she can manage to sneak her way in, but I pour most of her stuff down the sink because it tastes awful.'

All three of her visitors sniffed it a second time and frowned at one another.

'You're right, Ms Thomas. It does smell strange. I think I'll take it away and get it tested,' the police officer said thoughtfully. 'Do you have some clingfilm to put across the top, Ms Chadwick, and perhaps an old plastic container to stand the mug in? I don't want it spilling in the car on our way back to the station.'

Laura nodded and made the coffee safe to travel without spilling.

'If you're all right for now, I'll get on with my day.' The officer gave her a card then picked up the box containing the mug. 'Don't hesitate to call if you need further help, though, and let me know if Ms Jones doesn't bring your things back tomorrow morning. Oh, and I may need to get back to you if there's anything wrong with the coffee.'

When she'd gone, Laura turned to the social worker and said firmly, 'I need to see my lawyer ASAP and change my will. I should have done that when my nephew died a couple of months ago but I kept putting it off because last time I redid my will, it made me feel as if I were going to drop dead any minute. This one still leaves a large percentage of my possessions to him. How absolutely stupid of me not to have changed it before! But I was so worried by Susan's antics, it slipped my mind.'

'You should get a check-up from a doctor first to say you're compos mentis,' Pauline said bluntly.

Laura stared at her open-mouthed, then said, 'Nina was going to take me to see both my doctor and lawyer, weren't you, dear? But I'd not have thought of proving I was compos mentis *before* asking the lawyer to redo my will. I just assume that I still have my wits intact because I may be old but I'm not forgetful or anything like that.'

'Did you need to see the doctor for any other personal reason?' Pauline asked.

'Not particularly. I was going there mainly to ask whether the people at the medical centre have been talking to Susan about my health as she'd said they had. I know about my own problems but there's no reason for her to.'

'Ah. I see. Well, I'll take Ms Chadwick there if you don't mind, Ms Thomas,' the social worker said with a smile. 'Though I doubt we'll have any difficulty getting confirmation that she still has all her wits about her. I meet a lot of older people and I'm a pretty good judge of that.'

'Fine by me. I'll leave you to it. Let me know if you're not available for tea tomorrow, Laura, and we'll reschedule. I'm very flexible.' Nina looked at the social worker and added, 'I've just moved into a flat at the far end of the street.'

'Can you let me have your address and phone number, Ms Thomas?'

Nina pulled out one of the temporary handwritten business cards she was using till she left Australia and apologised for that. 'I'm only going to be here for two or three months. I'm in the middle of arranging to go and live in England for a while and have been sorting out the possessions I want to take with me. I got a sudden cash offer to buy my house if I moved out quickly, so I have put some of it into storage. I'm living temporarily in a flat my parents left to me and I'm trying to sell that too.' She handed a card to Laura as well. 'You'll need my new phone number. I'll look forward to catching up on everything when we have tea together.'

'So will I.'

The following afternoon, Nina enjoyed her neighbour's company for an hour or so.

She was glad to hear that the social worker had taken over the details of helping Laura sort out her new will, and had also found her a voluntary helper who'd take her shopping twice a week. Her companion was a lot more relaxed now she'd seen the doctor and then changed her will.

The two of them got on really well, so agreed to catch up once or twice a week and she walked the older woman home, just to be sure Susan wasn't still lurking.

The helper had also been briefed on the need to keep Susan Jones out of the house, though for some strange reason she was still coming and parking in the street.

Then two days later two police cars turned up suddenly, their flashing lights bringing Nina across to stare out of the window of her flat. One of them parked outside Laura's house and the other blocked Susan's car from leaving. Nina stayed to watch, wondering what on earth was going on.

One police officer spoke to the woman in the car. By his gestures, he was asking Susan to get out. When she shook her head, he pulled out some sort of tool and held it as if he was going to break the car window so she unlocked her vehicle, scowling and moving with exaggerated slowness.

It was just like a TV show. They even made Susan stand with her hands on the roof of her car while they checked her pockets, then they handcuffed her and took her to sit in the back seat of one police car.

When Nina looked at her friend's house, the door was open and a police officer was standing in the opening with Laura watching what was going on.

Good heavens, what had happened? She went back inside her kitchen to finish making her coffee, intending to go back to watching with it.

However, someone rang her doorbell. She saw through

the glass in the upper half of the door that a police officer was standing outside, so hurried to open it. There were in fact two of them standing there.

'Nina Thomas?'

'Yes.'

'All right if we come in and speak to you about your friend Laura?'

'Yes, of course.'

'She says you're the woman who suspected something was wrong with the coffee.'

'Yes, I am.'

'We wondered if you'd make a formal statement about that?'

'What did it contain?'

'We can't go into details but let's say there wasn't only coffee and it contained a substance that would be harmful long-term.'

'Well, I'm happy to do anything to help my friend. Do you want to take the statement now or do I need to come to the station?'

'We could do it now, if you don't mind. It won't need to be complicated and there are two of us to witness it.'

'Of course I don't mind.'

Only when both police cars had driven away did she give in to temptation and go along the street to see Laura to discuss the surprise arrest of her nephew's wife.

'They think she was trying to poison me,' Laura said with an involuntary shudder.

So Nina gave her a big hug and sat next to her holding her hand for a while till she'd calmed down.

She thought her neighbour was looking exhausted

and unhappy, so didn't stay long once she was looking calmer.

'If you need anything, any time, don't hesitate to ask me.'

'You're so kind. I'm sorry you're going to England so soon.'

'Well, it won't be until I've sold my flat, so not for a few weeks at least. I have too much to sort out. And we can keep in touch by phone and email afterwards.'

'That'd be lovely.'

Chapter Two

Weeks passed and Nina was fed up to the teeth about how long it was taking to sell her flat, and to get all the paperwork and official permissions completed for her to go and live permanently in England. She'd been told by her older son it was better to arrange that sort of thing from your present country. It was a good thing she had Laura to keep her company.

Nina might have been born in England, but her parents had emigrated to Australia when she was a baby and they hadn't kept any of the necessary documents to prove that. Indeed, they'd always been very secretive about where they had been born and lived and had even changed their names, so she'd had to investigate her own situation and get validated copies of every scrap of information needed. And even with her sons helping, it had all taken longer than expected.

But the delays had been made worse because her sons

had patches where they were incommunicado, either for a lock-up, shut-up workshop with their employers, from which they couldn't contact any outsiders, or an urgent project overseas for a week or two.

Shakers and movers, those two, or as she sometimes thought of it, they were 'shaken and moved' by their employers.

She'd been to England before, of course, but had simply used her Aussie passport for that because it was easier and she was only going for a couple of weeks. But that had been years ago, before her sons were born and the family had had to take cheaper holidays closer to home.

After Charles died, she'd not been able to afford overseas trips for a good while, or anything else much, either. He hadn't been brilliant with money, on the contrary. She'd taken a job as a personal assistant, and had proved so efficient at organising her employer's business life that she'd earned and saved more than her husband ever had. But she'd missed Charles greatly. He'd been such fun, a good friend as well as a beloved husband.

Perhaps that was why she'd moved so quickly into another relationship. And had to move out of it equally quickly.

Over six months had passed now since she'd first started organising the necessary changes to her life to join her sons Brandon and Kit in the UK. She couldn't believe it when at last she found herself in possession of the necessary documentation to settle permanently there.

She hoped that another benefit of moving to the UK was that her ex, who didn't have UK citizenship, wouldn't easily be able to follow her and continue his harassment.

The company she'd worked for had moved its office across the continent to Sydney, but she hadn't gone with them because she'd expected to arrange the move more quickly. During those intervening months she'd done some temping in office work to pass the time, but actually it was to be with people as much as to earn money, because the house had sold for far more than she'd expected. Though it never hurt to add to your savings.

So she'd spent quite a lot of time with Laura and, in the end, her biggest regret about the move was that she'd be leaving her friend behind. She'd also come to understand how much her visits meant to the older woman, who seemed to have gone noticeably downhill health-wise in that time.

Laura wasn't very good with technology and couldn't be bothered with what she called 'fiddling on the phone' but she was better at emailing and going online, so they agreed to 'chat' that way after Nina's move to the UK.

One evening her estate agent rang to say that he had a good cash offer on the flat, and that the whole sale could be finalised and possession given to the new owner in only a couple of weeks, since there was no mortgage to pay off. Within the hour, Nina had booked a one-way flight to Heathrow and emailed both sons with the news.

Laura was visibly saddened by her coming departure but said that she understood why Nina had to go to England. 'I know that you were meant to live there,' she said, although Nina couldn't understand why Laura was so certain that was case. Did she consider herself psychic or something? Surely not.

They had a final meal together and Nina promised – cross her heart! – to email every day. And she would. Only it wouldn't be the same as being there. They both knew that they might not see one another again in person because of Laura's deteriorating health – make that *definitely* wouldn't see one another, Nina amended mentally, feeling very sad.

After the meal, Laura hesitated, then said, 'I wonder if you'll look after some important family papers for me?'

'I'll be in the UK, remember.'

'It doesn't matter. I'll specify in my will what needs doing with them, and they'll be going to someone there.'

'Let's hope that'll not happen for a good while.'

Laura smiled sadly. 'We both know I'm getting worse.'

She stopped pretending. 'Can't the doctors help at all?'

'No. I'm getting a bit old now, eighty-three, just imagine it, so I haven't done too badly. Nature is still our boss. But I didn't want to leave these papers lying around here and I don't want to give them to my lawyer, either, because he's going to be retiring soon and they'll be taking on a new partner who'll handle my affairs. So will you look after them for me, dear?'

'Yes, of course. I'll take them with me in my hand luggage and keep them very safe once I'm there, I promise.'

Laura pointed across the room. 'The documents are in that big file on top of the bookcase. They're my original family documents from the past couple of centuries. Such beautiful manuscripts, even if they are faded. Are you sure you don't mind? They won't use up too much space in your luggage? I can pay for any extra costs.'

Nina picked up the folder and smiled. 'These weigh

nothing compared to all the sentimental stuff I'll be taking with me. I'll be paying for excess luggage as well as sending a couple of tea chests full of bits and pieces so your folder won't make any difference at all. And anyway, I'm happy to help you in any way I can.'

'Good. When the inevitable happens my lawyer will let you know what to do with the papers.'

At least the horrible niece was still in prison awaiting trial, because there was little doubt that she'd caused her husband's death. That meant Laura would have no safety worries, just the usual ongoing concern about how to fill your days when you were confined to the house, mainly on your own due to the deaths of friends and lacking the energy to be very active even inside your own home.

Their final hug was a long, lingering one and they both had tears in their eyes as they drew apart.

Sadly, other changes had seriously marred Nina's plans. Her son Brandon's partner had left him a few months previously and she'd quickly found someone more ready to settle down and start a family than he had been.

As a consequence, he'd become restless, especially as the two of them still ran into one another regularly because they were part of the same crowd. It turned out that he'd started looking to move on to a new job without telling anyone, and had found himself one in California with excellent future prospects.

He apologised to his mother but moved over there almost immediately and before she was anywhere near to being able to leave for the UK. 'At least you'll still be getting away from Ratface,' he'd said.

'I'm not doing this to get away from Sandor.'

'But it'll be another advantage of the move to the UK, won't it?'

So much for them persuading me that the family should be living nearer to one another! she thought angrily. *They aren't mentioning that at all now.*

Brandon's apologies hadn't rung true. He'd been happy and excited about his new life and a mere few lines of apology to her showed where his priorities really lay. And yet he had been the one who'd first contacted her about moving so that they'd all be living in the same country.

Perhaps he'd been tempted to settle down with his partner and then changed his mind. He didn't seem to be tempted by anything but work and making money now, so that family idea hadn't lasted.

Well, at least Kit would still be around.

Then, two weeks before her big move, her younger son had phoned her. 'Ma, there's a problem. I've been offered a job in New York at double my current salary.'

'Oh, no! Sorry! I should have congratulated you, but what a time for it to happen.'

'Yeah. And the company wants me to start work within a couple of weeks. I'm not going to do that. I'll delay my departure by a few days beyond that so that I can at least help you settle in the UK.'

She spoke her thoughts aloud. 'I'm not sure I want to come now.'

'But you've sold your Australian house and the flat and you'll still need to get away from Ratface. And I won't be gone for ever, I promise you. Probably two years at most for this job.'

'You can never be sure of that sort of thing, as you and Brandon have just proved. And there will be other job offers over there, I'm certain.'

'Well, I'm certain that I prefer the UK to America, Ma, and that's where I intend to settle long term. In the meantime, I thought you might like to move into my flat. I don't want to sell it and if you pay enough rent to cover the mortgage, it'll be much cheaper for you than other commercial rents would be, and I know it'll be looked after. I don't want or need to make a profit out of you.'

'Hmm.' She didn't know what to say or think.

'And the flat is fully furnished so you'll not have to worry about buying furniture and stuff until you're ready to settle permanently somewhere of your own.'

She sighed. 'I suppose taking your flat will help me transition more easily, though London isn't my preferred place of residence, not permanently.'

'It does have some advantages. There's a lot to see and do in the capital.'

'Yes. I suppose so.'

So she went on the flight she'd arranged.

Kit met her at the airport, giving her a big hug and then holding her at arm's length. 'I'm truly sorry about this, Ma.'

She didn't try to pretend. 'So am I. With neither you nor Brandon here, I doubt it's been worth all the upheaval and I'll probably go back to Australia again. At least I have a few friends left there.'

'It's unfortunate, I know, but this is a dream job and it'll not only be interesting, it'll set me up for a highly lucrative future and I'll probably transition to starting a business consultancy of my own. Don't you fancy having a billionaire son one day, Ma?'

'No. Just two sons within reach.' *And maybe even grandchildren too*, she thought, but she never let herself say that. There had certainly been no real signs of either son settling into matrimony.

'Well, for the record, Ma, I didn't apply for this job and I won't be applying for any others. They headhunted me. And I really do intend to settle permanently in the UK in a few years' time. It feels like home and always has done, even though I was born in Australia.'

That's what you say now, she thought but kept it to herself. You couldn't tell other people how to live their lives.

'At least you've got away from Ratface,' he said, as Brandon had done.

That was not why she'd moved. Sandor had been a bit annoying but not desperately bad, only she didn't say so.

After a few moments he waved one hand at the world outside the car window. 'I've always been happy in England. Remember how much I liked it when I came here for that school trip all those years ago. Strange, that, because Dad wasn't so keen on coming and always managed to avoid it.'

She could only shrug. She'd done the move now, so the least she could do was give it a try. Anyway, you didn't hang yourself round your sons' necks like a millstone, or anyone else's for that matter.

Kit helped to carry her luggage into the lift and then into his flat, which was a two-bedroom place on the fourth floor, with one large living and cooking area, and an ensuite for each bedroom. It was clearly not designed for families. There were apparently two other similar flats on this floor and it was the same on each floor, with two larger flats on the sixth floor.

His place was comfortably furnished in a minimalist style, not at all to her taste but the chairs were reasonably comfortable so she'd put up with their appearance for a while.

But even going into the six-storey building with its series of homes had made Nina feel a sense of pressure at having so many people 'living all of a heap', to use her grandma's way of describing multi-storey buildings.

She had never been a big city girl, much preferring the open spaces and greenery of the countryside. Living down under had suited her nicely when Charles was alive, even if the grass hadn't always been literally green but bleached beige in the hot, dry summers of Western Australia. At least it never snowed in Perth.

'I'll stay here for a while,' she told Kit, 'but I doubt I'll want to settle in London for more than a month or two. If I do decide to stay permanently here, it'll be somewhere in the country, a village preferably.'

'Oh.' He stood frowning then said, 'Well, I'd better find an estate agent tomorrow, someone who can manage the renting out of this place once you move away.' He gave her a guilty look and added, 'I have to leave the day after tomorrow, I'm afraid. That was all the postponement I could negotiate. Will you be all right?'

Pride kept what she hoped was a convincing smile on her face as she lied to him. 'Yes, of course I will. I'm a grown-up and I've been completely on my own for a few years now. I may one day need an end-of-life carer, but that won't be for a good few years yet, if ever, I hope.'

'I don't like to even think about you growing that old and needing assistance,' he said softly. 'You've always been a strong woman, physically as well as mentally.'

'*Merci du compliment.*' She dropped him a mock curtsey and managed to keep the smile on her face – well, she hoped she'd managed some sort of grimace that looked convincingly cheerful.

She didn't know where she wanted to live permanently now, not even in which of the two countries. But definitely not in London or any other big city, wherever she wound up. That was a start, wasn't it? She'd manage to find somewhere acceptable, surely?

She probably had relatives here and there in the UK but her parents hadn't kept in touch with them, so she'd not know who they were, let alone where to start looking for them. And anyway, they'd not be close relatives.

She might hire someone with relevant expertise to find them for her later on, though, out of sheer curiosity. Or she might not bother because they might be as inward-looking and quiet as her parents – talk about joined at the hip and not much into socialising with other people. She'd never met anyone as focused on themselves as her parents, but at least they'd been happy living together like that. You couldn't ask for more than happiness in what you were doing, could you?

For a day or two after Kit left for New York, it was touch and go whether Nina cancelled everything and went back to live in Australia straight away; she felt so very alone in what was, to her, a foreign country. She occasionally met another resident in the lift, but those interactions didn't go beyond a nod or a brief exchange of comments about the weather.

Then, as the jetlag ebbed away, she grew angry at herself for moping around and thought, *To hell with everything.* She'd be stupid not to give the UK a decent try-out, and anyway, if she stuffed things up there would only be herself to know about it, wouldn't there? She was in her early fifties, which wasn't exactly antique for a human being, and she had some money saved, after selling her house and flat and previously inheriting a pleasant sum from her parents, who had only made it to seventy-five. If she managed her finances carefully, she wouldn't need to look for a job for years, perhaps never.

She decided to travel round the UK and visit a few of the more interesting historical and scenic places she'd not managed to see while on holiday here previously. If she found some region she liked, she could rent some furnished accommodation there for a while and try the area out for lifestyle and friendliness of locals.

There! That was a plan, wasn't it? It showed she was coping – well, more or less.

If she wasn't tempted to live anywhere in England, she could always go back to Australia later, so it would be a no-lose situation from now on. She'd make sure of that by not rushing into anything.

A distinct factor in her final decision to stay had been her ex-partner. He couldn't easily spy on her, and he wasn't likely to move to England to continue his harassment. Well, it had already been fading and he'd probably found someone else. He was really looking for a wife-cum-mother to look after him, the lazy oik.

Sandor had been charming at first but not for long as he'd gradually begun to act as if he were her owner, not her partner. He'd started bossing her around, telling her what to wear or not to wear and becoming unpleasant when she didn't do what he wanted.

Although the time they had spent together was mainly in her house, after the first week or two he'd made no contribution to the housework, made no effort at tidying, leaving his discarded things strewn around the house, and expected the provision and preparation of meals to be entirely her responsibility. So she'd begun cooking meals for one and leaving his dirty dishes and clothes lying around wherever he'd dropped them, still unwashed. She didn't like doing that, preferred to keep her home tidy, but you had to make a stand when someone tries to use you.

If he hadn't been such a good lover, she'd not have stayed with him even for those few difficult months. But their quarrels had often ended up in bed and he could be very persuasive there. Nothing, however, had changed his dinosaur views about a woman's role.

Boy, had she made a mistake with him!

But so had he with her, if he'd thought he could train her into his chauvinistic ways and turn her into a submissive wife. Ha! As if! When he refused for the umpteenth time to discuss his attitude towards women, let alone try to change, she'd simply chucked him out.

That evening she'd watched from the window as his

car screeched to a halt beside the pile of his possessions she'd dumped on the footpath outside. But he'd surprised her and turned really nasty, making threats and throwing a stone that cracked one of her windows. She had to call the police when he tried to batter his way back into her house another day.

The trouble was, she might have got Sandor out of her home but he occasionally popped up when she went out with friends.

Clearly he was still keeping an eye on what she was doing, though how he was managing to find out was beyond her. She'd had her home checked for spyware and it came out clean so someone in her circle must have been passing information to him.

Why he was doing that utterly baffled her. He surely couldn't think it was any way to win her back. Maybe he had an even more warped brain than she'd realised underneath that glossy surface charm.

He had never fooled her sons, had he? They'd called him 'Ratface' from the start and avoided him as much as possible.

So here she was, on her own not really wanting to go back to Australia but living in the sort of place where you didn't meet neighbours. And she didn't know anyone else in London.

Her feeling that the capital city wouldn't suit her as a place to live had only been reinforced by actually living there, and reinforced by one hundred million per cent as time passed, to quote an Aussie friend's small granddaughter.

Nina did her research online about where she might

like to live and was about to start visiting those parts of southern England when she received an email from Laura's social worker to say that her friend had passed away suddenly and peacefully in her bed the previous night.

That upset Nina for days so it was later than planned before she set off to look round the UK. She needed to put roots down emotionally, even if not permanently, so she was determined to find a place where she could enjoy living for a while. Above all, she was desperate to meet a few people who could become friends.

She started looking in Kent because it was close to London but on her second day away, while she was still staying at a hotel in Canterbury, she received another email from the social worker in Australia, asking her to contact Laura's lawyer directly about a bequest her friend had left her.

That upset Nina all over again, and it was three days before she could do this anyway because another tedious, lonely weekend had intervened. She didn't need a memento of any sort to remember her lovely friend by, but she guessed it was probably just instructions about what to do with the file of family papers, so she'd have to deal with whatever it turned out to be.

And though the social worker had attached a video of the funeral, Nina didn't even attempt to watch it. She'd rather remember Laura alive and chuckling over something gently humorous. Far rather.

She got the times of day in the two countries wrong when she tried to phone the lawyer's office in Australia on the

Monday and it wasn't open yet. Annoyed with herself for being so careless, she left a message.

When her phone rang later, she recognised the lawyer's number so braced herself to talk about Laura.

'Nina Thomas here,' she announced and waited.

'Ah, Ms Thomas. Thank you for contacting us. John Baldock here from Baldock, Lancing and Jenkerson in Perth. I took over as your friend Laura's lawyer.'

'Pleased to meet you.' If you could call this meeting.

'I was wondering if we could meet electronically on some program with visuals? This is a little complicated to explain and you'll probably have quite a few questions. I'm afraid I'm rather old-fashioned about preferring to see a person's face when I'm discussing or explaining something.'

She was a bit surprised, having expected just a brief message about what the item was and getting it to her, but said, 'Very well.' They exchanged details and then re-connected with a visual link.

A plump, balding man offered her a bland professional smile from the computer screen and said, 'Ah, that's much better. So, let's begin. You will, I'm sure, be happy to know that Ms Chadwick has left you a substantial bequest. She didn't think you'd have been expecting one and I can tell from your expression that she was right.'

'Yes, she was. I definitely didn't expect anything. Is whatever it is too big to send to me here in the UK? Because I'm not coming back to Australia for a while.' She was incurably honest enough to add, 'Well, probably not.'

He laughed gently, his eyes disappearing into two

curved folds of flesh like a jovial cartoon character. 'Yes, it's far too big to send by post. She's actually left you everything she owned.'

There was dead silence because he was waiting for a comment and Nina was trying to gather her scattered wits together. She managed only a feeble response in a scratchy voice: '*I'm the sole heir?*'

'Yes. And I think you'll find it an extremely generous bequest.'

'Oh. Right. What does it consist of exactly?'

'A whole portfolio of items. There are some investments and money in a bank account but the main bequest is two properties: her home in Australia and one in Wiltshire, England.'

Nina gasped. '*No!* I don't believe it. Why on earth did she do that? I hadn't known her for long, even though I quickly grew fond of her.'

'To be frank, when she made this will a few weeks ago, I queried what she was doing and she told me she didn't have any close relatives left or even close friends because most of hers had been even older than herself and had died of various age-related problems over the past few years. She said you'd been particularly kind to her at a difficult time in her life.'

He paused and when Nina still didn't speak, he added, 'So it's all yours.'

'I don't know what to say. I've seen her house in Australia but I haven't seen the property in Wiltshire and she never talked about it. What is it like?' If it was bigger than a tiny cottage, she could perhaps go and live there, at least for a while. That county was renowned for its beauty and on her list of possible places to settle.

'Apparently it's rather run down though still of historical interest and is a multiple-occupancy place. But she believed the group of dwellings would be well worth renovating. And anyway, there is also a legal obligation attached to it, something connected with a charity, and that is co-managed by a small government department. She feels she can rely on you to continue to co-operate with them and help deal with their charity efficiently.'

'So there is nowhere on this property that I could live?'

'Oh, yes. She kept the house her cousin had used there and hoped to use it herself. Sadly, she never got to do that owing to ill health but you may like to live there.'

'I'll certainly do my best to continue helping this charity. What sort of effort does it require?' She stared at him, frowning and waiting but he seemed to be having difficulty thinking what to say to her next.

'She apparently gave you some of the paperwork associated with the property before you left Australia. She told me she had decided to leave everything to you even then. I presume you still have those papers?'

'Yes. I brought them with me, as she asked, but I haven't looked at them. I thought I was just supposed to pass them on to the heir.'

'I think you'll need to read them now, because the charitable aspects are fairly complicated. In fact, I've discussed the situation with my colleagues and we feel the best thing we can do is give the task of helping you to handle this legacy to a legal group we work with regularly in England and they'll contact the government department to find someone to help you sort things out.'

'Oh. Right. Yes, that sounds a good way to go.'

'They'll liaise with both you and the government department but the person originally handling it there has moved on so they'll need to find someone else to help you carry out the associated duties.'

'Goodness, isn't that rather drastic? Is it really so complicated that I can't work my way through it on my own, with occasional legal help perhaps?'

'I'm afraid it's too complicated because of the government involvement. But do bear in mind that this is a very worthwhile charity and we'll be handing your side of things over to a highly reputable legal firm, so you can trust anyone they recommend to help you, and trust them implicitly, believe me. It turned out they already knew someone suitable and contacted him immediately, but he was overseas and has to wind things up there before returning to England.'

She didn't comment beyond a little grunt to show that she was paying attention but she was surprised at all this fuss.

'The chap in question is called Sean Reynolds, by the way. He'll be tasked with taking you through the necessary steps to sort out your inheritance and then helping you to get started on whatever needs doing after that.'

She still thought this was excessive. 'His fees on top of renovations to a historical property would be rather expensive, I should think. I won't be out of pocket, will I?' It would be no use inheriting something that might cost more than she could afford to pay out.

'Um, such payments are already allowed for in the

bequest because it has a separate joint bank account set up to pay any costs of running things. Like others in her family, Laura was a very shrewd lady financially and you will definitely not be out of pocket. There are several factors to be considered when you start on the necessary work.'

She was startled. 'That does sound complicated.'

'I fear so. But at least the bequest side of things will be dealt with under Australian law, so you won't be subject to the UK's inheritance tax. That will save you having half the value of what you inherit taken away before you even start.'

'Oh. Right. I don't know much about that sort of thing.'

'Um, will you continue to be involved in handling the duties involved in working with the charity or shall you wish simply to sell what you inherit and hand the charity work over to someone else? That would be an alternative course of action. And actually, I'd advise you to think about it very carefully before you do anything and to look into it all more deeply.'

'One thing I'm certain of is that I'd *like* to do as Laura wished about this inheritance. She was a delightful woman and I'm grateful to her for the bequest. I'd also welcome an interesting and worthwhile project to occupy my time till my sons come back to settle in the UK so maybe helping with this charity will be a good thing to do.'

'I see. I wish you well, then. If you give me your permanent address over there, we'll get this Sean Reynolds to contact you. It's apparently a very complex set-up, you see, and the government part is confidential too, so even we don't know all the details. I'm sure they wouldn't offer you help if they didn't expect you to need it.'

That seemed strange to her but she supposed you got all sorts of situations when you were dealing with people's wills and historical properties set up as charities. Well, you did in some of the novels she'd read, if that was anything to go by.

She gave him the address of Kit's flat as her home. She'd have to go back there till she heard from this man who'd been so highly recommended. Luckily she'd left most of her own possessions in the flat and not yet asked the real estate guy Kit had chosen to rent it out again. There were some items she'd shipped to the UK that she cared about, paintings, a few small pieces of antique furniture, and it wasn't all that much more expensive to keep paying her son's mortgage than it would have been to find secure storage. And besides, she'd also decided it'd be good to have a base to return to from her various travels until she'd decided where she wanted to live long-term.

'Can I ask what it is exactly that Laura wants me to do for this charity?'

'I can't tell you the details because she herself only recently inherited this estate in Wiltshire, which is a property called Lavender Lane, and she hasn't been well enough to go and see it, let alone get involved in any of the necessary work. I gather parts of it have been closed down temporarily as a consequence.'

Nina was startled by that. 'Who did Laura inherit it from? Did the person not pass on the relevant information to her?'

'It was bequeathed to her last year by an elderly male cousin of hers called Murray Ashworth, who had been ill for over a year. And his long-term caretaker at this property died soon after he did. From what I can gather it consists of a group of dwellings that need some attention and renovations, and which the government department makes use of from time to time to lodge employees who aren't well. I'm afraid we don't have full details as to how many they can cater for or how bad a condition such people are in, or even who selects them, let alone how exactly the properties and patients are serviced.'

'But that sound impossible. How could it have been left like that?'

'I gather that it was nobody's fault, just blind chance.'

He paused as she lost touch with her wits again for a few moments, not even knowing what sort of other question to ask when she had so little to go on. 'I find it hard to believe that someone has left me one house, let alone a group of dwellings,' she admitted.

He smiled like a benign old Buddha. 'Believe it! That at least I know to be true. You now own a group of units.'

'But how can you not know anything else about them? You'd think there would be systems set up, paperwork and so on.'

'I think it's because several key figures died one after the other. And because there is a confidentiality agreement between the owner and the government about how they're used when they're up and running. No one else knew all the details.'

He sighed and added, 'We have been told that the units are rather run down and in need of attention. The government and the charity share the costs of upkeep and renovation apparently so you'll have to sort that out. Since you'll have the use of the big house, you'll be in the best place to sort that out after you move there, I should think.'

'Well, that's something, I suppose. When she inherited from her cousin, did Laura have to negotiate a new contract with the government or just allow the old one to continue?'

'The old contract simply stays in place, apparently, and doesn't need changing. But use of Lavender Lane has been suspended for nearly two years because of various people's health issues and deaths. So that's the reason you'll need help. This chap was talking about retiring but they persuaded him to stay on to help you. He's very highly thought of.'

The lawyer paused for a moment then continued his rather patchy explanation. 'Laura felt it was a very worthwhile charity because apart from anything else some of the buildings are historically interesting though fortunately not heritage listed.'

'I shall be particularly interested in that. Do you have a photo?'

'I'm afraid not.'

She couldn't hold back. 'Good heavens! What a mess! How can you not have even a rough idea of what this place looks like?'

'We were not the primary lawyers.' He shrugged and gave her another of those polite meaningless smiles. She tried to smile back at him but couldn't manage it. She'd been wanting a project, something worthwhile to do with her time, but she'd prefer to know more about what she was facing before she dived into one. Well, Laura had tossed her in so she supposed she had no choice but to accept responsibility for it.

'Now, I gather Sean Reynolds is happy to undertake this job, so we'll get the UK lawyers to sort out the financial details and maybe you should both go down to Wiltshire as the first step and find out exactly what is involved.'

Well, that at least made sense in all this chaos.

'Reynolds has sent a message to say he'll phone you to organise all that. He's in some remote location at the moment, rather out of touch with modern communication methods.'

When the call ended she sat there for a while, feeling shocked to the core. A substantial legacy like this was the last thing she'd have expected from Laura, the very last. The size of it astonished her. She'd never expected to be rich. And she'd never expected to be heading a substantial charity, either. What if she messed things up?

Her friend Laura had given the appearance of someone who had to be careful with her money, which was strange when she was actually quite well off, no, *very well off* would be a more accurate description. She hadn't been pretentious in the slightest and Nina couldn't imagine her living extravagantly even if she hadn't been in poor health. Any more than she would herself.

Money couldn't buy you good health, could it? Or give you a family to leave your possessions to. That was sad because a woman as kind and interesting as Laura had deserved loving children or grandchildren to spend her last days with and leave her possessions to.

But life didn't always give you what you deserved, did it? Let alone what you wanted. Look at how her sons had left her!

Nina began to smile as it slowly sank in that she didn't have to go house or location hunting now and would probably never have to work for other people again. She'd had to put up with some highly inefficient managers at times and had loathed having to do their bidding.

And to add to the positive aspects, this bequest sounded as if it would give her something interesting and worthwhile to do for a long time to come, several years probably from the sounds of it. How wonderful!

If it was worthwhile? Or interesting? Hmm. When would she find out? And what did the government's involvement actually consist of?

There seemed to be nothing but unanswered questions confronting her at the moment. Thoughts kept zigzagging round her mind and she couldn't settle to anything.

There was something else she needed in her life, too, and nothing to do with this legacy: the move to England had taken her away from her Australian friends, because although you could stay in touch online she didn't find it the same as being with someone. Surely she'd be able to make some new friends once she'd settled in Wiltshire? She usually managed to get on well with the people around her.

She wasn't looking for another husband or partner, though. She'd been there, done that and lost her beloved husband. And she hadn't won a gold medal for success in her recent attempts to tiptoe into a new romantic relationship. On the contrary, she'd made a right old mess of things, rushing in without taking care.

It was so sad that Charles had died young. He hadn't deserved to get such an aggressive form of cancer. Did anyone?

He'd not only been a lovely man and a good husband, but he'd have relished doing the renovations with her.

She was tired of being alone, which was why she'd moved to England. So she was determined to make new friends.

Chapter Three

It was days before Sean Reynolds contacted Nina and by then she was feeling distinctly miffed about the delay. Why was it taking so long? She was sick of hanging around in the elegant sterility of her son's flat.

She went online as she waited to hear from him and spent quite a lot of time researching how to set about doing renovations to historic properties, a topic she found fascinating.

When she wanted to rest her eyes from using the screen, she started going through the papers Laura had given her. These too she found interesting. They were early documents concerning ownership of a house, a place not big enough to be considered a manor house but still bigger than most people's dwellings, and some attached former servants' accommodation.

Was this what she'd inherited? How exciting if it was. Some of the documents went back a couple of hundred years, and a few of them showed floor plans of the house with the number of rooms increasing over the years.

She also skimmed through long lists of the latest rules and regulations from various official organisations, which were not nearly as interesting but would still have to be understood if they were to get anything done to bring the properties up to scratch.

Apparently certain groups within the various organisations had to approve what was projected for heritage properties that were 'listed', then make sure that what had actually been done was correct, even down to using the correct mortar between bricks, and applying it in the correct style.

That must be why the Australian lawyer had said it was good that Laura's properties were not heritage listed. She'd never deliberately damage valuable artefacts, but she would want to proceed at more than a snail's pace if something needed doing and not have to wait around for approvals.

One thing annoyed her particularly: why hadn't anyone told her the exact address and location of her inheritance? As the days passed, she was impatient to have more information.

If she'd known the address, she could have gone to see the properties the documents referred to, would have loved to do that and could perfectly well have driven there on her own in her hired car.

The only other thing she could think of to do online over the weekend that might be helpful was study images of Wiltshire. It was certainly a beautiful county, mainly rural and, as her friend's grandfather apparently used to say when he was taken out for drives in the countryside, it had 'a lot of land not built on yet'.

That saying had become a joke among her friends when she was young and they would chorus it fondly at appropriate moments when driving round the West Australian countryside. In contrast to England, only a tiny percentage of land in the outback was actually built on, due to the desert-like nature of many of the vast inland expanses.

When she received a phone call on the Monday morning from the legal firm of Pinworthy, Atherton and Fosterby, she thought, *At last!* and hoped she hadn't said it aloud.

The secretary there put a man called Sean Reynolds on the line and she was immediately struck by his lovely deep voice. She'd always been a sucker for voices like that. If she had to spend time with him, it'd be good to have a pleasant voice to listen to.

'Nina! Glad to meet you. What an interesting inheritance you have.'

'Yes. I didn't expect Laura to leave me anything, let alone to be so generous, but I shall be happy to do as she wished and renovate any cottage that needs it.'

'Or whatever they turn out to be,' he corrected gently. 'We can't tell exactly what sort of buildings the bequest consists of yet.'

'I suppose not. But I'm hoping we'll soon find out. I'm really looking forward to seeing Lavender Lane. Don't the English lawyers know anything about it at all?'

'No, but that's not surprising, since they've only recently been handed the commission to deal with it by their Australian colleagues – who are equally ignorant about the details of most places in the UK.'

'So you're not a lawyer then?'

'Well, I qualified as a lawyer originally but I've moved in other directions so I haven't been practising law for a good while. I'm not employed by Pinworthy et al but by the government.'

'Oh. I see.'

'I've actually been out of the country working on a project in a remote location, so have only just got back. I'm sorry to keep you waiting to go and see your inheritance but I had a few details to tie up before I could start to help you. At least, I hope I'm going to help you. I'll certainly do my best.'

He sounded to be hesitating then said, 'I'm still researching the background to your inheritance and will be able to tell you more once I'm sure of the facts. What I am sure of is that it'd be better not to talk about the details on the phone. You never know who could be listening in on a public phone connection like this one.'

'You surprise me. Why should that matter?'

'Well, lawyers' phones can perhaps be targeted more often than others so let's contact one another online instead. I know a very secure site from which we can link up with one another safely. I'll send you a link to click on, then we'll continue our discussion of our plans there, if you don't mind.'

'If you think such precautions are necessary.' She didn't, but then what did she know about this sort of thing? She'd never worked for a government department, let alone one in the UK.

When they were connected again, he smiled at her and said quietly, 'Humour me on security precautions from now on, please. It's quite simple: the more money and property you possess, the more likely you are to be targeted by criminals.'

She stared at him in shock. 'I never even considered that side of things.'

'I'm paid to think of them.'

'All right. Point taken. Now, do you know anything at all about Lavender Lane? The lawyers haven't even given me its address.'

'I don't think the address would have meant much to you anyway. It's on the outskirts of Essington St Mary, which is a small town in an isolated valley in Wiltshire. The Lavender Lane property is outside the main town so is even more isolated.'

'Oh.' She'd rather be living closer to amenities and other people but you couldn't look a gift horse in the mouth, could you?

She was having trouble holding back her impatience with all this cautiousness. Up to now, this inheritance seemed to have provided her with nothing but a whole series of problems as well as potential benefits, and she had a feeling more were going to pop up. Nothing about it seemed at all straightforward. What was she going to find there?

She studied Sean's face as they chatted. He looked to be about her age and was rather good looking, not overwhelmingly but in a nice way, with brown hair just turning grey at the temples but mostly still of a lovely chestnut colour. You could tell a lot about people from their smiles and his was warm and looked to be genuine.

'Let's get our personal situations absolutely clear,

shall we, Nina?'

He waited, a questioning look on his face now.

'Yes, let's.'

The smile returned. 'I'm not working on any other projects at the moment so I shall be giving my full attention to helping you sort out your inheritance. I'm afraid it sounds to be quite complicated in its ramifications because of the government connection. Will my services be all right with you or have you taken a dislike to me on sight? It has been known.'

He grinned as he said that, clearly not expecting a negative answer from her, and not getting one. Heavens, he was actually a very attractive man, so she'd better watch out!

'Of course I haven't taken a dislike to you!' she said crisply. 'If you're able to devote yourself to this project, does that mean that you're not married?'

'Definitely not. I've had a busy working life, moving here and there in the world and have somehow never found anyone I wanted to settle down with.'

'So no children?'

'Not that I know of. What about you? No man hanging around?'

'I was very happily married but my husband died a few years ago. I met another guy after a while but he turned out to be a louse, so I didn't stay with him long. I have two grown-up sons.'

'Good to know. Anything else you want to ask me about?'

'Not at the moment. The lawyers seem to think some sort of help is necessary and there's money been set aside already to pay you, so I'm happy to go along with it for the time being. And I don't mind you having a sense of humour in case you think I haven't noticed the humour sliding into your comments at times. In fact, I prefer it. I have been known to see the ridiculous side of life myself every now and then.'

He gave her a slight bow. 'Good. To get back to our business situation, I must confess that I'm doing this for the interest as much as anything. I was due to take some leave and was wondering about taking early retirement, but I really enjoy new experiences and I prefer worthwhile jobs, so I was tempted into joining you at Lavender Lane.'

'I was happy at the thought of doing something worthwhile.'

'So there we are, both happy about the situation.'

'How do we start, then?'

'We start in Wiltshire, of course. Are you free to travel there tomorrow to look at this property?'

'Not just free but eager. In fact, I'm absolutely dying to see it.'

He chuckled gently. 'Good. So am I. If you can catch a train out of London to Swindon tomorrow morning, you can meet me at the station and we'll drive you on from there.'

'Might it not be easier for me to drive to Wiltshire and meet you at Lavender Lane? I've already got a hire car.' Which was sitting in the car park under the flats for much of the time doing very little because she mostly used public transport in London. And she hadn't been going out on her own at night, not even to the theatre. She'd attended one or two matinées instead, felt safer then as she was going to be on her own during such outings.

'You'll see more if you allow me to drive you. You'll surely want to look at the nearby countryside as well as the inheritance? I've been to Wiltshire before.'

'Mmm.' But she didn't like the thought of being in his power for travelling around.

'And on our way back I reckon we may need to chat about what we find there and what needs to be done next. After all, I've been hired partly to help you deal with what we find.'

'Oh. I see. And yes, of course we'll need to discuss what we find.'

Chapter Four

Nina frowned at the image on the screen as his words sank in. 'Why do you say partly? What else are you expected to do besides help me with the inheritance?'

'Act as bodyguard and guide, and represent the government's interests in the charity.'

That puzzled her and she must have shown it. 'Bodyguard. But – why ever would I need one?'

Sean was looking at her as if wondering whether to answer that question, so she repeated it. 'Why would I need a bodyguard?'

'I'll explain in a minute. Just to give you the background to my taking over the driving, since I've visited that area before I'm happy to do that and let you get to know the surrounding countryside. I've been staying temporarily in Reading to the east of Swindon with an old acquaintance, so the most direct route to your property will take me near Swindon, which is why I suggested meeting your train there then travelling on to your property together.'

She held up her hands in a surrender gesture. 'Very well. You've convinced me. The train to Swindon it is.'

'It'll be a lot safer for you to do it that way, too. Could be cheaper too. Never say I don't care about being careful with money.'

'Very well. Whatever. Though I can't understand why you're so concerned about safety.'

He was starting at her solemnly again, as if working out how much to tell her, so she couldn't resist saying, 'Now explain about the bodyguard part of it. All of the details, since it clearly concerns me. Don't you feel you're being a little over-careful about this?'

'No. I'm definitely not.' He gave her a very serious look. 'I'm being extra-careful because we know the situation could be dangerous and because the legal firm has already had an imposter turn up at their rooms in Reading. She even produced ID with your name on it but it had her photo, not yours. It'd have looked legit if we hadn't already known what you looked like. She wanted to be given the details of the property, which she claimed to have been told she'd inherited from her aunt Laura. But unlike you, she insisted she would prefer to go and see it on her own.'

'*What?*' Nina was shocked and couldn't speak for a moment, this was so unexpected.

'It surprised everyone. Of course the lawyers contacted the police immediately, but she had disappeared by the time they arrived. The details they were able to give the police were yours, not hers. So not much use. However, they have handed over their CCTV footage, so at least the police should have a picture of her to work with.'

'Wow. I hope they catch her quickly – she sounds like a very unpleasant and determined woman. I'll take greater care to check the IDs of everyone I have to deal with from now on.'

'We both will.'

She shook her head in bafflement. 'I'm surprised by that, I must admit. How could anyone have found out about the inheritance and why would they think they could get away with breaking into it?'

He didn't say anything, just frowned, so she persisted. 'Who could it be? Susan Jones, the woman who tried to poison Laura? No, she is still in prison, isn't she? Perhaps she wasn't convicted, or escaped? Anyway, even if she is free, surely she didn't expect to get away with that pretence of being the heir? What did she expect to steal? You can't pick up a piece of land and carry it away, can you?'

'Definitely not. I doubt there's anything valuable at the property, except for the land it stands on. No, what she was after must have been to look at the place. Could be a property developer trying to suss things out before attempting to push you into a sale. Or . . . something else.'

'How were they so sure she was an imposter?'

'John Baldock had already sent the lawyers a photo of you so they were aware from the start that they were dealing with an imposter when she turned up and they kept her talking while they called in the police. But she sneaked out before they arrived, after having said she had to go to the toilet urgently. She didn't return.'

'Good heavens!'

'The police are searching for her but are leaving it to me to protect you from now on. And, just to be honest with you about where we stand, I've also double checked you as well to make quite sure that you are indeed the legitimate heir. So, considering everything, that incident is another reason for us to travel together in order for me to keep watch on your safety.'

This seemed to be her time for encountering criminals, she thought, first that horrible weirdo woman trying to kill Laura and now this stranger trying to get hold of the inheritance her friend had left her.

She told him about that. 'Laura seems to be the link between both these incidents.'

He nodded thoughtfully. 'Yes, indeed. We'll both bear that in mind and be ultra-careful what we do and especially share all our information. All right?'

'I'll definitely be careful, Sean, but I must admit I've had no experience of this sort of thing before so if I forget to share something you'll have to forgive me.'

'Well, ask me if you're puzzled about anything. Now, let's get back to our plans for tomorrow. If you catch a reasonably early train from London, that'll give us most of the day to check out your inheritance.' He frowned for a moment then added, 'And it might be a good idea to bring a change of clothing with you in case we need to stay for more than one day.'

'All right. I'll do that. I'm surprised at how little is known about this Lavender Lane, even by those who're handling it. That does seem – well, rather strange, Sean.'

She watched him nod in agreement then she realised that she still didn't know the exact address of her inheritance and asked him.

'It wouldn't mean anything to you because Lavender Lane

doesn't give much information about itself on the internet and there are no details about it provided in Ms Chadwick's will, either, except the information that your legacy consists of all the buildings on the property at Lavender Lane.'

'That's a strange way to put it, don't you think?'

He pulled a wry face. 'Yes. That could mean three or thirty-three cottages for all we know. I gather Laura was quite ill by the time she inherited so unfortunately, she was never able to go and see the place for herself and that may be why she was so vague.'

'She was rather frail when I had the pleasure of spending time with her and getting to know her. Sadly, it was only for a few weeks towards the very end of her life, and she was fading visibly, I could tell. But I truly enjoyed her company.'

'Your friendship must have meant a lot to her and perhaps that was why she left everything to you. Old people can get desperately lonely, you know.'

'Yes. People say that, but no one does much about it, do they, except for putting on amateur concerts or providing morning teas for groups of oldies? You can imagine how that chimes with extremely intelligent older people like Laura.' She chuckled. 'She was particularly scathing about a couple of extremely amateur concerts she'd been dragooned into attending.'

'I don't blame her.'

'But I wasn't aiming for her to leave me anything, believe me. In fact, I hadn't the slightest idea she owned more than the house she was living in, which she said had been her family home.'

'Stop worrying. I believed you the first time when you

said you didn't set out to con her out of a legacy. Has anyone ever told you that you have a very honest face?'

Nina was about to say yes, because she knew how easily she betrayed her real feelings when dealing with people, but he was speaking again.

'I never met her but I gather that she was charming.'

'She was, yes. Very. And her conversation was very wide ranging. I truly enjoyed her company. Believe me, our friendship wasn't based on pity.'

He seemed to understand her need for a few moments of silence after speaking about her friend, so waited a few moments to speak again.

'Well, if there's nothing else I'll let you get on with booking your place on a train tomorrow morning. If you let me know which one, I'll pick you up at the station entrance.'

'I'll catch the first one I can. I'm an early riser anyway.'

'Me too.'

Only after they ended the call did she realise that he still hadn't given her the actual address of her inheritance. Had he been deliberately avoiding doing that? For some reason, she'd bet he had. How annoying.

She looked up train times and chose a fast train leaving Paddington station at six in the morning, which would get her to Swindon, its first stop, by about seven. She booked a seat on it then sent Sean a text, to which he replied immediately and very briefly.

I'll be there to meet you.

She'd definitely pack an overnight bag. She wanted

to give herself as long as she could to look round her inheritance and take photos in case the houses were indeed interesting historically.

And she was also hoping she'd find one that she liked among those she'd inherited, so that she could make a proper home for herself again. Even if the larger house, whose plans she had seen among the old documents, was still habitable, it'd probably be too big for one person, but perhaps one of the other homes might be just right.

She was a settling-down sort of person, she knew. Not purely a homebody but getting on that way, needing a real home as a basis for her life, even without a partner, if she were to be genuinely happy.

Perhaps, if the cottages were tiny, she might put two of them together to make a home of the right size. Fancy having the choice! She'd never expected to be in that fortunate position.

The future looked wonderfully promising, but there were bound to be problems. Life rarely gave you the moon on a silver platter without also asking you to pay a price for it. That was one of her mother's old sayings when things seemed too good to be true.

Her mother had not been an optimist about life.

Nina didn't mind getting up while it was still dark the next morning. She took a taxi to Paddington, and then enjoyed the short train journey to Swindon. It was a journey through a world where most people still seemed to be in bed, judging by the drawn curtains at upper windows, easy to see in the chill dawn light as they rattled steadily past row upon row of small terraced houses set neatly along the sides of the railway. She'd not like to live in one of those, she thought.

When the train arrived in Swindon she followed the other passengers to the station entrance where she immediately recognised the face of the tall guy waiting to one side. He smiled at the sight of her and raised one hand in greeting.

He'd taken the suitcase she'd been carrying out of her hand before she realised it, leaving her with the small backpack she preferred to a handbag.

Instinctively she tried to grab the suitcase back. 'Thanks but I can manage.'

He chuckled. 'Aw, allow me to make a good first impression by playing the gentleman.'

She smiled back, relaxing and liking him even more than she'd expected to now that she'd met him in the flesh. It was that smile again. It seemed utterly genuine and she could usually tell. But did she dare believe that? After all, she'd only just met him in person. 'Very well, Sean. Just this once. But make the most of it. I'm usually fiercely independent.'

'Yes, ma'am.' He tugged an imaginary forelock. 'I fell lucky for once and got a parking spot just round the corner. This way.'

When they had driven out of Swindon and left behind the worst of the main roads crowded with early morning traffic, most of it going in the other direction, he asked, 'Would you like to stop for a coffee and what an American friend calls a "comfort break"?'

'Not at the moment, thanks. I grabbed a quick breakfast before I left home and it was a corridor train. But if you want to stop to eat?'

'No, I'm fine. Like you, I fuelled my body before I left home. But we'll have an early lunch if we can, eh?'

'Yes, that'd be good.'

They'd left the built-up areas completely now and she concentrated on the scenery. To her relief, he let her study the countryside in peace. That was another point in his favour: he didn't try to fill every minute with trivial chit-chat. It could be hard to keep the talk going with someone you'd only just met.

'Wiltshire is as lovely as it looked online!' she said after a while.

'Let's hope your inheritance is in a pretty village. I don't know this part of the county as well as some others, except for driving round parts quite near to your property once or twice, and that wasn't recently. I've just come back to the UK after working overseas for several years, you see.'

'In interesting places?'

His smiled faded instantly. 'No, not really.'

She could see that some memory upset him, so didn't pursue that as a topic.

It took them over an hour to get to Essington St Mary, even though the roads were far less crowded for this part of the journey. After they'd turned off the main highway onto a narrow country road, they saw hardly any other cars or heavy goods vehicles.

'I'd better start using the satnav from now on,' Sean said. 'I was told that this valley is a small place with its only major internal road running up from the town centre to a private estate at the top end. Its lower entrance is apparently framed by larch trees, which is how the road got its name.'

'Where does the road lead after that? Is there another village nearby?'

'It apparently comes to a dead end at the top, so there's no through traffic at all, just a hikers' track through the woods. I think the town or somewhere nearby sounds to be a nice, peaceful place to live.'

'Tell me about it!' She rolled her eyes. 'I like it already and I haven't even seen it. I've been staying in my son's flat in London since I moved to England from Australia, but the crowds and general busyness of life round there don't appeal to me at all. Where exactly is this Lavender Lane with regard to the town, though?'

'On the outskirts somewhere. We'll have to let the satnav lead us there because I've never been to Essington St Mary before, remember.'

'Sorry. I wasn't thinking.'

'No wonder. You must be feeling very excited about seeing your inheritance.'

She nodded, beaming at him and liking the kind understanding of her feelings that shone in his face – well, she thought it did. If it wasn't genuine, he was one of the best actors she'd ever met – far better than her ex-partner had been for the brief time they'd been together.

'I am rather excited,' she admitted.

'Who wouldn't be in your position? I felt excited when they offered me the job of liaising with you and helping sort out the charitable work they're doing there.'

He slowed right down as they passed through the town centre, not just for traffic safety but so that they could study it.

'Pretty little place, isn't it?' she said.

'Very.'

After that they followed instructions issued by the elegant, cultured voice of the satnav. Nina had made him laugh by immediately christening it 'Felicity' the first time he'd used it and the name had stuck.

There was something about shared laughter that could draw strangers closer very quickly, she thought, still smiling.

Following Felicity's crisply delivered instructions, they turned right off the main road a few hundred yards up the gentle slope, then wound their way through a twisting series of residential streets containing houses from different eras in a variety of architectural styles, none of them large or imposing.

'Today's town planners would hate this, wouldn't they?' he said.

'Yes, but I love it. And I like the houses too. This mixture of styles looks so much nicer than a soulless modern estate with only two or three house designs, don't you think? Planners seem as if they're trying to regiment people even when they're asleep.'

'Good way to describe it. They do indeed.'

They passed an ornate sign at one turnoff on the left indicating the entrance to a local park called Magnolia Gardens.

'What a lovely name for a park!' he said as he drove on.

'Isn't it? I wonder if there really are magnolia trees in it. I love to see them in bloom.'

'We'll take a look when we have a few spare moments and feel like a stroll. They're beautiful trees even when they're not in bloom.'

A few minutes later he slowed right down as the satnav told them they were approaching Lavender Lane. He slowed to a halt to look at a sturdy house on the left, which must have been having some repair work done, because in front of it there were bits and pieces of the sort of small debris builders leave behind even when they clear up the big stuff.

The house looked old and neat, about the size of a four-bedroom modern house, but much prettier, with ornate window frames and trims.

He started moving again but only slowly, letting the car roll past the house and when the satnav announced almost immediately that they had arrived, he come to a halt only a few yards further on. They were now in front of a pair of high wooden gates set back from the road.

'Aha!' He pointed. One of the gates bore a sign saying *Lavender Lane* in faded dark grey letters. It certainly wasn't there to attract attention. The gates were shabby and the ground in front of them wasn't paved but looked compressed as if it had been used for many years of parking and that had discouraged grass from growing on it.

The gates were fastened together half-heartedly by a large, rusty padlock. Where they were attached to the gateposts they were overhung by untidy shrubs and they didn't look as if they had been opened for years. However, there was a small gate to the right of the big one, which didn't appear to have a lock on it. Presumably that was to let in people on foot.

He turned the car into the rather unwelcoming space and switched off the engine. 'Nice to have a break from the noise. However quiet an engine is, it's still *there*. Let's get out and try to have a better look at the place.'

They had to stand on tiptoe to look over the main
gates. A short, single-width driveway led up a gentle slope,
stopping in front of some smallish buildings set back
among overgrown bushes. Here and there were drooping
trees of the sort that never grow really tall and often bear
beautiful blossoms in spring, and there was a whole line of
untidy shrubs.

'Correct me if I'm wrong,' he said, 'but aren't those
lavender bushes?'

'Yes. I think they are.'

The drive came to a dead end at the top of the slope just
below a much larger house, which stood looking downhill
at the smaller buildings. It was fronted by a small garden
containing an elegant collection of tall weeds.

'We'll have to get the car into that place first. Let's go
back to it and see whether we can find the right keys to
open the gates in that huge bunch I was given.'

But before they could do that, a woman came out of
the house they'd passed next door and yelled, 'Hoy!' then
strode along the edge of the road towards them, not looking
at all friendly.

Chapter Five

The woman was well built and about sixty, Nina guessed, and she didn't look at all pleased to see them stopping there.

'This is private property. You can't have business at this house because there's no one in residence, so why are you stopping here?'

'I'm the new owner,' Nina said.

'Name?'

'Nina Thomas.'

The woman stilled, staring at her, then said, 'And about time, too. These houses need looking after.'

'I haven't even seen them properly yet.'

'You've come to the wrong place anyway.'

'What do you mean? The sign says Lavender Lane.' She pointed.

'Yes, but the parking spaces for cars are at the rear of the house. These spaces are mainly used by people delivering goods to the cottages. That's when there are people in residence there, which there aren't now.'

Sean looked round. 'Which way do we go to get to the main parking area, then?'

'If you'll give me a ride, I'll show you. There's something else I want to show you, then I can walk back home. It's not far if I come down the front way.'

'How about you tell us your name too?' Nina said.

'Elizabeth Jenkins.'

'Do you live in that house?'

She grinned at them. 'I certainly do. I'm the sixth generation of my family to do so.'

'Good heavens!' Nina stared at her enviously. 'My parents moved to Australia and I have hardly any relatives. And even there my own family moved around a lot, so I don't know my distant relatives at all.'

'I know just about everyone in this part of town and I'm also the current president of the local gardening and horticulture group, which I'll tell you about later. Is that respectable enough to be allowed to get into your car?'

Sean smiled at her. 'Sounds highly respectable to me. Can you get into the back of the car now and tell me how to reach this parking area?'

She did that, taking them back to the other side of her house and then up a narrow road to turn right up a slope and right again at the top, then turning in at the rear of the house they'd seen from the street.

'They call this "the big house", but the whole group is called Lavender Lane,' Elizabeth explained. 'It's a lovely house, don't you think?'

'It's beautiful.' Nina smiled at it. If she really had inherited all this, something she still found hard to believe, she knew where she'd like to live from now on, even if the house was too big for one person.

Sean stopped the car close to the rear of the house and switched off the engine.

'Let's walk round to the front of the house and go in through the front door,' Nina suggested.

'Do you have the keys?' the woman asked.

'We have a bundle of keys.' He reached sideways to lift the lid of the storage compartment between the two front seats, pulling out a fat, jangling bunch of them. 'The lawyer we've been dealing with gave me these, but unfortunately they don't have any labels, so we'll have to try them one by one till we find which one it is that opens which door.'

'For the front door it'll be one of those fancy wrought-iron ones,' Elizabeth said. 'The others are too small and modern for these ancient locks.' She touched one, smiling at it as if it were an old friend. 'I have one similar to this for the front door of my house. I think our two houses must have been built around the same period in history.'

'They're certainly impressive. Which key do you fancy trying first, Nina?'

There were several big, ornate keys, but she was strongly drawn to one of them and pointed it out, liking the symbolism of his suggestion that as the owner she try to find one first.

He wriggled it off the huge key ring and handed it to her with a slight bow, then stepped to one side, so that Nina could insert the key into the front door lock. Elizabeth and Sean stopped slightly behind her and they both waited for her to act. She took a deep breath then inserted the key in the brass-rimmed hole, surprised when it went in easily and turned smoothly with only the faintest of clicking sounds.

The other two edged a little closer and stared at it then at her, looking surprised.

'Wow, bullseye! I was sure it'd be the very last one you tried that turned in that lock, not the first,' he admitted.

'Well, you should certainly feel welcome here with that piece of luck to start you off,' Elizabeth said.

'It didn't feel like luck. I just *knew* that was the key. But it did feel a bit weird because when I used it I had a feeling of familiarity, as if I'd turned that same key many times before.'

'Is this where we play spooky music?' he teased.

'It did feel rather spooky, Sean, and that's not something I usually experience. In fact, I'm normally rather cynical about that sort of thing.'

'Then you really must be the owner by birth,' Elizabeth said. 'This has happened before, I gather from neighbourhood gossip.'

She could only shake her head in bafflement, then try to pull herself together and get on with things. 'I'm not the owner by birth, though I am the legal heir.'

She didn't move to go inside yet and couldn't understand that. She didn't normally dither about.

'Aren't we going in?' Sean asked. 'We can't stand here all day or we'll get nothing done.'

Elizabeth smiled at her. 'Identifying the true heir is a big step forward, my dear. And I'm sure that's why you chose the right key.'

'But I told you—' She broke off. Clearly her new neighbour was determined that she was the blood heir. Well, she wasn't going to waste time persuading her differently at the moment. She was still getting used to the idea that these houses were hers now.

Sean asked quietly, 'Does everything feel more real? Aren't you going to go inside?'

'In a moment. I'm still trying to feel like the owner.'

They stared at one another again in that way they couldn't seem to help doing, as if each was trying to get to know and understand the very soul of the other person. Then both of them jerked back into normal mode and turned to their companion.

Sean spoke first. 'Sorry for ignoring you, Elizabeth. Do you want to come inside with us?'

She stepped back, shaking her head. 'Not today. I need to talk to you about the lavender bushes at some point, though. I'm more interested in them.'

'Oh?'

'They're a bit special and we need to check them, and we may need to replace some because they don't have a long life. But I think Nina needs to settle into the ownership of Lavender Lane before she focuses on anything else, and she doesn't need me butting into this special moment, so the lavender can wait a day or two longer.'

'I don't know much about English plants and gardening,' Nina confessed. 'I'm from Australia.'

'And I'm a townie from way back,' Sean admitted.

'Then I'll contain my enthusiasm, stroll back home and let you look round your domain in peace. It's nice to meet you and I can come back in a day or two to discuss the gardens. In the meantime, don't hesitate to nip round and ask me if there's something specific you need to know about the area. You'll have a lot to learn as you settle in here, I'm sure, and I'm happy to help you any time.'

When they were alone, Nina didn't attempt to go inside but stood looking at the group of buildings. 'I don't know what to say or do next, Sean. It feels so strange to think that this house and these cottages all belong to me. How can I possibly own all this?' She gestured around her.

'You do own it, though. The will was unequivocal about that.'

She shook her head as if bewildered. 'I know that mentally but they don't *feel* as if they're mine. And for some reason, I'm reluctant to go inside.'

'Maybe they will feel as if they're yours after you've been into them all and got to know them.' He gestured down the gentle slope. 'Meanwhile, let's walk slowly down the lane and look at the outsides of the cottages as we go, then study the big house from a distance before we come back and brave the inside.'

'I'm being silly.'

'No, you're not. This place is going to be a huge responsibility. You can take all the time you like walking into it.'

'I like your suggestion. It's lovely and sunny. Real spring weather. Perhaps my brain needs warming up literally before it confronts the reality of this place.'

She was still looking rather anxious so he shoved the bunch of keys into his pocket and held out his hand, joking, 'Want to hold my hand for comfort?'

To his surprise she didn't hesitate to take it. 'Yes, please. If you're sure you don't mind. Your hand feels so nice and warm, it seems to prevent me feeling that I've lost touch with reality.'

'Happy to oblige.' Very happy, actually, because it was ages since he'd met such an attractive woman, though of course he didn't say that aloud. He was out of practice at chatting anyone up and doubted he'd ever been particularly good at it. But he did like Nina. It surprised him how much.

Enjoying the feel of her warm soft hand in his, he set off. He half expected her to pull the hand away after a few steps, but she didn't. Good.

He had the strangest feeling that this was how things were meant to be, and he didn't normally believe in such premonitions.

Damn! She wasn't the only one to feel strange today.

Chapter Six

Nina glanced sideways at Sean as they walked down the gentle slope. Their steps matched nicely and his hand felt comfortable in hers. She couldn't remember the last time she'd been so quickly attracted to a man.

She realised she was staring at him again, so forced her attention away and made herself concentrate on the cottages, which were set out in two trios. Elizabeth had been right: the gardens did need attention. And if those scruffy-looking shrubs were the lavender the group of houses was named after, they looked as if they needed someone not only to tend them but to love them.

They stopped for a good look at the front of each cottage but didn't attempt to go inside any of them.

'So this is Lavender Lane,' she said quietly as they stood at the bottom of the small path between the trios of building. 'Six cottages and one big house. It's pretty here, isn't it? Or it could be if everything were brought up to scratch and the gardens weeded and filled with flowers.'

'Yes. Very pretty.' But he was looking at her as much as the cottages.

When she realised that, she flushed slightly but still didn't pull her hand away. They had come back to the top of the path again and were standing just outside the small garden in front of the big house.

'This place could be stunning if it were properly cared for. Look at that pretty ornamental brickwork round the windows.' But she still didn't go into the garden and into the house, only made a sweeping gesture to include the whole of the lane and cottages. 'I can't think what this place would have been used for. Do you know, Sean?'

'I do know the general background, but I thought the authorities had briefed you about that and described the broad picture at least.'

'Well, they didn't. They've hardly told me anything beyond the fact that I've inherited this place and that you'll work as my partner on behalf of the government to set it all up again, whatever "it" is.'

'That's what comes of dividing jobs between organisations,' he said. 'The bureaucrats must have thought the lawyers had explained the situation to you and vice versa. But in fairness to them, this was all done in a rush. I think you inheriting it has come as a surprise to them.'

She frowned. 'Why? Surely someone had to inherit.'

'I gather they'd expected it to revert to the government as a gift after Murray died because he told them he was going to do that at one stage. And then they found he'd left it to his distant cousin so they waited for her to do something with it. Only Laura fell ill and died within less than a year, leaving it to you. I get the impression they aren't quite sure what to do about that. It's been an unusual set-up for the last few decades anyway, started in the Cold War after World War Two by an extremely patriotic member of the Chadwick family to provide somewhere private and out of the way for security personnel who are in urgent need of rest and recovery.'

He paused for a moment, waiting till she took that in and nodded to him to continue.

'One major recommendation was apparently to make a compulsory purchase from you and put things on what they called a more organised footing. The people at the top of this area, however, felt that the present arrangements had worked well in the past *because* things had been done fairly casually, so decided not to change that, since there was still a need for the services it could provide.'

'The arrangements are still very vague.'

'Yes, but also very cost effective, another reason Lavender Lane has been allowed to continue to function.'

'All I knew was that I'd inherited a group of properties from a friend.' She stared at him as something else occurred to her. 'Were these disagreements the reason why it took several days for you to join me?'

He shrugged. 'No. I was summoned back to the UK from a climbing holiday to be briefed and take over.' He smiled. 'And I was rather miffed at first, I must admit, because it was my first proper holiday in ages. But I'm quite happy about it now because the possibilities are starting to look both interesting and worthwhile. There's a generous financial bonus attached to the task as well, which will swell my retirement funds nicely.'

She gave him another puzzled look. 'They didn't even hint at what to expect so please go on and tell me more details, Sean. What exactly is this place used for? You said something about convalescence, but not of whom and how the people who come here are selected, let alone cared for.'

'Well, there's one big difference between this and other convalescence homes: it's a place where people who've been working under cover for the government in all sorts of weird places can come and rest, safe from the public gaze.'

'Doesn't anyone in the nearby town wonder why they're here?'

'The local folk have been told that it's a convalescent home for government officials and in a sense that's true. But as you now know, it's more – to put it crudely, it's a safe recovery place for ex-spies and their like. So while it is generally known as a convalescent home, its precise function is a closely guarded secret.'

Nina looked at him in surprise. 'So that's why it isn't run like a normal government department?'

'Yes, in fact it really is owned privately and has been for decades by a series of patriotic people, of whom you are the latest. Which may put you at risk as well.'

She gaped at him. 'I'm in danger here?'

'You may be. You may not. I shall do my best to keep you safe, I promise.'

'This whole scenario is starting to sound like something from *Monty Python's Flying Circus*.'

'That could be why it's worked so well. However, you won't lose out financially, whatever happens in the future. If the government wants to take it over completely, they'll have to buy it from you – and a place like this is quite a valuable chunk of land.'

'No wonder I couldn't find much about it on the internet. And no wonder the lawyers were worried when a stranger had tried to find out where this place was and gain access to it. It could only have been Susan Jones. Have you heard what happened to her, by the way?'

'She was apparently recognised by an off-duty policeman in Reading and taken into custody. So she will be dealt with by the authorities in the usual way and I doubt that she will bother us again. I'm afraid you've been thrown in at the deep end, Nina, and I hadn't realised how little you'd been told. You can always offer to sell it to the government immediately if it feels like too much to take on.'

'I'll have to think about that!' she said. 'It seems as if I've gone straight from a life that was too quiet to one that may be too active in some senses. I do care about my country, though. And I have you to help me.'

'My pleasure.'

They smiled at one another. Her pleasure too, she thought.

'I may as well finish the tale. It's more pleasant standing out here in the open air as we go over things. Because of the complexities of ownership, the place had been shut down so the SWD haven't been able to send anyone to recover their health here for a couple of years.'

'Why didn't they just close it down permanently?'

'The SWD have found it too useful in the past. They'd prefer to get it up and running but with someone they can trust in charge.'

'What does SWD stand for?'

'Oh, sorry. One gets so used to abbreviations and jargon: Special Welfare Department.'

'Which could mean anything.'

'Exactly why the name was chosen.'

'So we now need to get things running again.'

'Yes. But with myself as your partner, if I suit.' He gave her another of his quirky little flourishes of the hand to indicate both the place and himself.

'Thank goodness I'm not on my own. Um, what exactly does the SWD *do*, Sean?'

'As little as necessary. Actually, they've done some good work here over the years and saved quite a few lives. They've done that in a quiet way that wouldn't have been possible for a bureaucracy.'

'How were they found?'

'They've all been related to one another, though Laura Chadwick was only a distant cousin of Murray Ashworth and her branch of the family had settled in Australia a while ago.'

'Like my family,' she said thoughtfully.

'I gather that she and Murray had worked together in the secret service at one stage.'

'Good heavens! Laura had? Really?'

'Yes. How exactly are you related to her? I had to get ready to join you in a hurry and didn't have time to find the connection.'

It was her turn to frown as she suddenly wondered whether there might actually be some sort of connection. Oh, it was so infuriating to have been kept from that knowledge. It'd be a very distant connection, if so. Her parents had been very ordinary if secretive folk, not even going overseas on holidays or socialising much, just living quietly and happily together.

Or had they been escaping from a burden they didn't want to take on? She certainly couldn't imagine them getting involved in anything like the sort of covert activities Sean had been describing.

'We've had difficulty finding how your family fits,' he said quietly. 'As far as my contacts could work out in their first rapid search, your parents suddenly turned up in Australia out of the blue. They didn't maintain any links with the UK, or at least we don't think they did.'

'I thought I was just a casual friend as far as Laura was concerned.'

He frowned at her. 'Are you utterly certain about that?'

'Um – not 100 per cent, no. I don't actually know anything about my ancestry because my parents always refused to tell me anything about their family background.'

'They certainly hid it well.'

'They must have destroyed all their British documents when they first came to Australia because I never found signs of any. When I was in my teens I confronted them and insisted I had a right to know about my family background, but they refused to tell me anything whatsoever, said it was for my own good. I had never seen them that angry before and they threatened to cut off my pocket money for six months if I ever pestered them about it again.'

'How strange.'

'They never threatened what they weren't prepared to do, so I didn't ask again, but I continued to wonder about it and feel resentful till I got married. Then I pushed it to the back of my mind. I was very happy with Charles and loved knowing his family and having our own sons to raise.'

'Did Laura ever hint at anything?'

'Never. I had the privilege of being her friend during her final illness but I thought that had come about by chance, because I stepped in to help a stranger. However, now I'm wondering if the fact that my parents' flat was close to Laura's house was a coincidence – or did they actually know and even work with each other?'

'It's a possibility. There are wheels within wheels in this game. But if you're not related it'll be the first time in the history of Lavender Lane that it hasn't been passed to a family member, however distant, so that suggests that you were. In any case, the people I answer to will continue looking, I'm sure. Should you mind if they found something out?'

She shrugged. 'Not at all. In fact, I'd love them to find something.'

He was still frowning and giving her sideways glances. 'To tell the truth, I've seen photos of Laura and I reckon you could be related to her. When she was younger, she had dark curly hair and a high forehead like yours. And there's something about your eyes, too.'

'It'd be nice to belong somewhere and be related to someone apart from my sons.'

'Neither of them is married?'

She rolled her eyes. 'No sign of it. Their generation doesn't seem to be in a hurry to settle down as much as mine was.'

He snapped his fingers. 'I've just remembered something I was told. There's apparently a whole shelf of personal diaries in the big house.'

'Oh, I shall enjoy reading them. How far do they go back?'

'A couple of hundred years, with gaps. Not everyone keeps a diary. I gather they're amazing. And maybe when you read them you'll be proud of what quietly patriotic people have done to help their government over the decades. It's not all about fighting wars, and thank goodness for that. Um, I'd like to read them too, if you'll allow it.'

'Of course I will.'

He glanced up at the sky. 'Now, pleasant as it is to stand chatting in the sunshine getting to know one another, we'd better get on with it.' Even as he spoke, some clouds drifted across the sky and covered the sun as if to underline what he was saying.

'Is it going to rain?' she wondered aloud.

'I don't think so.' When she didn't move, he took her hand again and gave it a little tug. 'Come on. It's more than time we looked round inside the big house. Are you ready to face it now?'

'I suppose so.' But she paused on the threshold and turned to look down the short slope, saying softly, 'It feels lovely here, don't you think?'

'Yes. It's surprised me how peaceful it is. You can't hear any traffic noises at all. This seems to be a very quiet street.' He pushed the door open and stepped to one side. 'You should lead the way in, but please be cautious about where you tread. We don't know how dilapidated it might be. Some of this house must be over two hundred years old. It's probably the oldest property on the site, one of the oldest in this part of the valley.'

'And you know that how? Have you seen some records that I haven't?'

'No. I've had a fascination for architectural history ever since I was a lad, so I can often tell simply by looking at a building roughly when it was built. But if the floor doesn't feel safe, back away again slowly, treading gently and making no sudden movements.'

'Are you serious?'

'Yes, I am, actually.'

'I'll do that if necessary then, but I hope it won't be.' Actually, she was almost certain it wouldn't – she didn't know why.

Chapter Seven

Nina took a deep breath. 'OK, here goes.' There was a big old-fashioned doorknob below the keyhole made of multi-faceted glass that looked so pretty she couldn't resist running her forefinger round it before turning it and pushing the door slowly open. A dusty smell greeted them as they looked inside.

At that moment the sun peeped out again from the clouds and its beams shone slantwise towards them across the hall from the window part-way up the staircase. The sunbeams were full of floating particles that sparkled slightly, presumably caused by the dust they'd disturbed when opening the door.

Well, even if it was only dust, it looked pretty in this light, Nina thought.

For some reason she found herself speaking in a hushed voice. 'Better leave the front door open, Sean. It feels so stuffy I don't think anyone can have been in here for quite a while.'

'I agree.'

'You stay there and I'll move further in.' She couldn't resist teasing him. 'If I suddenly scream and vanish from sight, the floor will have collapsed under me and you'll have to be my Galahad and pull me out of the abyss.'

'Don't even joke about that!' he said sharply.

Nina blew him a mocking kiss and stepped inside. She moved part-way across the hall and the floor felt firm beneath her. She paused there to turn slowly round on the spot and study her surroundings. It was a pleasant space, neither large nor small, just right, somehow. There were windows on either side of the front door and above it as well, which had thin, patterned strips of coloured glass round the edges to match those on the big window over the stairs across from it.

But best of all, there was a distinct feeling of welcome and if she was being silly to think that, Nina didn't care. It really did feel welcoming to her.

She wasn't surprised when Sean came across to stand beside her and she welcomed the arm he put gently round her shoulders. In fact, his close presence seemed to add the finishing touch to her own pleasure in this moment. When she turned to look at him, he was studying her rather than their surroundings, staring as if he hadn't seen her properly before.

As they moved forward, he kept his arm round her, then they paused to look back across the hall and he murmured, 'This is a not only a pretty entrance but you're right. It does feel cosy and welcoming.'

'You can sense that too?'

'Oh, yes.' He removed his arm from round her

shoulders but took hold of her hand again instead.

That felt nearly as nice. What was there about this man that made him so attractive? More than that, she felt as comfortable with him as if she'd known him for years.

'Let's do a quick tour first, to get the overall picture,' he suggested.

'Good idea.'

They moved into the other rooms one by one, finding them equally appealing, not in a showy way but quietly elegant. The furniture might be dusty and old-fashioned but its quality showed even in that condition.

'Why did no one put covers over these pieces?' she wondered aloud.

'There was probably only the old caretaker left to do that after Murray Ashworth died and as the old man's wife had died recently as well, there must have been too much for him to keep up with. When he died too at the end of that year they closed the place up till the heir, in this case Laura, could take over. Only she was never able to come here.'

'I hadn't expected her to own such a large, lovely old house, let alone leave it to me.'

'It's a rare privilege and thank goodness no one's messed around with the original historical details.'

They'd seen from outside that it was three storeys high and there were iron grilles about two yards long in front of the ground-floor windows, showing the presence of cellars, but they hadn't realised that the house stretched further back than they'd expected, forming an L shape with the tail end at the left.

'I was told there were servants' quarters at the rear,' he said. 'That part looks slightly newer.'

Most of the rear garden was now given over to parking spaces, but she caught sight of a couple of clumps of rhubarb in one corner. 'It was probably once a kitchen garden. If that's ripe, I'll bake you a rhubarb crumble.'

'I didn't know you were so domesticated.'

'When it suits me. I love fresh rhubarb.'

It was silly to focus on something as unimportant as that, but everything about the place seemed to suit her taste, even the details. It'd make a lovely home once the facilities had been modernised and renovated, she felt sure.

They went back indoors and walked round the ground floor again, this time studying the rooms much more carefully, standing in doorways scanning each area and not moving on until both of them had seen enough.

One room was like a library with all the walls lined with shelves absolutely crammed with books of all shapes and sizes. 'Look at all those,' she said in a near whisper. 'It makes me want to sit down by a cosy fire and read.'

'That's one of my winter pleasures, too. But I bet that bay window would be nice for a reading nook in the summer.'

When they stopped again in the kitchen, she spoke without thinking. 'We could use this as our casual living area.'

'*Our area?* What about the servants?' he teased. 'Won't they need it?'

She rolled her eyes, pretending to be shocked. 'You're a spoilt brat if you expect servants.'

'Am I? It's more as though the house deserves them. And if this place begins catering for people who're convalescing again, we will definitely need more permanent domestic help.'

'We'll get a good cleaner or two, and I can cook sometimes but there will probably be takeaways in the town itself.'

'I like cooking too,' he said. 'Though I haven't always had the time to do it properly, in the ways my gran taught me.'

'You're a male treasure, then!'

'That's sexist, Nina.'

'Oops. Sorry. I can cook but I'd not exactly call it a hobby. I did teach my sons to cook, but some of their friends mocked them for that, even in this day and age.'

'More fools them. Every adult ought to be able to prepare healthy food and generally look after themselves. Come on. Let's finish our tour. We're going to need to stay overnight somewhere, aren't we? Do you think there will be a spare bedroom or two here?'

She laughed. 'There might be. But what about sheets and food? I think we'll need a B&B, at least for tonight, and we ought not to leave it too late to find one.'

Steps from the hall led down to large cellars and upstairs were six bedrooms but only one very old-fashioned bathroom. Nina pulled a face at the sight of it. 'I shall want a modern bathroom and a proper shower putting in. In fact, we'll also need to put in another couple of bathrooms and ensuites, if we're going to have people staying.'

Sean looked at her sharply. 'You keep saying "we" as

if we're both going to live here permanently. Have you decided that already?'

She stopped dead and gaped at him. 'I didn't work it out. The idea just settled in my mind and felt right. And . . . and I'm not taking it back. I like being with you.' She looked at him uncertainly, wasn't used to taking the lead in a relationship with a man.

His smile said he wasn't upset by that. 'Are you always this impulsive?'

'Heavens, no! But I was already looking for somewhere to live in England and this place has just dropped into my lap, so to speak. And – and you sort of did, too. After all, you said you were supposed to be looking after me, so you'll need to stay here as well, won't you? For a while at least.'

She hesitated then risked saying, 'At least I hope you will. So that we can, you know, see how we get on.'

There was another of those pauses, then he said quietly, 'I'd like to do that. I'd like it very much indeed. It's unexpected but not unwelcome.'

A cosy warmth seemed to wrap itself round them as if the house itself approved of what they were saying, then he said, 'I'd suggest we move into the house temporarily at first and manage with the amenities as they are, so that we can see exactly what we'll need if we go on living here together.'

'Will the authorities who employ you let you stay on here? Won't they have other projects for you?'

'They'll let me do anything that's needed to get this place up and running again. And also, I'm nearing early retirement and if they don't allow me to do what I want then I'll simply resign. You OK with that?'

'Yes.' The attraction had flared between them from the very start, she admitted to herself even if she didn't say it aloud. It was the last thing she'd expected, given how bad things had been with the guy she'd hooked up with for a short time.

What did the French call this sort of sudden reaction between two people? *Un coup de foudre.* Which was very apt. Lightning could strike suddenly. It had been almost the same for her with Charles. Perhaps it hadn't happened quite as quickly, but it had only taken a few days. He would have liked Sean, she was sure, and her sons would like him too. That was important to her.

They hadn't liked her ex, had been icily polite with him.

She realised Sean had said something. 'Sorry. My mind was wandering. Say that again.'

'I said that as you're the nominated heir to all this, Nina, and they haven't told you many details, you'll need to find out what will be expected of you if you live here. Or of us both, perhaps.'

'Expected of me – who by?'

He shrugged. 'The authorities, whoever they are at the time. And I daresay fate will poke its nose in as well. These houses aren't just sitting here basking in the sun. They've been preserved by a series of owners for a very real and worthwhile purpose. And I should tell you that I was sent to accompany you for a similar purpose but I'm not making up my attraction to you. That's genuine though totally unexpected. My job here is to protect you and help get the place going again, which will provide somewhere for some rather special government officials to rest, recuperate and hide, if necessary.'

'The need for some of them to hide puzzles me. It sounds like cloak-and-dagger stuff. In this day and age, for goodness' sake! Surely the need for that sort of thing is past now in the more civilised parts of the world? The Cold War ended decades ago, after all.'

'I don't think subterfuge and keeping an eye on other countries will ever be totally past and governments will always have to keep watch in secret ways as well as by open governance. So I'm presuming a certain sort of sneaky bureaucracy will always be around to manage that hidden agenda.'

'Do you know something that I don't about this place, Sean?'

'Yes, though not as much as I wish I did.' He hesitated before adding, 'But I'd genuinely like to move in with you here at a personal level, not simply because I've been hired to keep an eye on things and make sure you stay safe.' He plonked a quick kiss on her cheek. 'I like you enough already to *want* you to stay very safe indeed.' There was a pregnant pause, then, 'Look, we still need to finish exploring this place and then work out what our next step should be today.'

He didn't offer her any more details and in the end she was unable to keep the annoyance from her voice. 'And that's all you're going to tell me for the moment, is it, while I trot along meekly and do as I'm told?'

He winked and said, 'Surely not *meekly*?'

She had trouble not smiling at that, annoyed as she was. She was definitely not meek. It was a relief when he changed the subject back to the practicalities of their present situation.

'There's going to be a lot for us to sort out here, Nina.'

He waited and when she said nothing else, just kept staring, he prompted, 'What made you suddenly look at me as if something else had surprised you?'

'Because it had. I realised that I'd not only simply *assumed* that you'd be moving in here with me but felt quite certain that it'd be the right thing to do.'

'I'm glad you feel that because I do too. And it's saved me the trouble of persuading you to let me stay for a while.'

'There's a lot that feels strange in this situation, isn't there?' she said thoughtfully, letting go of his hand to gesticulate. 'It almost makes me believe in ghosts and woo-woo generally, because what we're doing seems to be so instinctive. *Meant to be* is a phrase I normally despise.'

'Now, woo-woo is a step too far for me. I do not believe in ghosts or that a thing can be *meant to be* in that sense. And surely you don't, either?'

'I've never quite been sure one way or the other about ghosts. But I have to confess to a strong feeling that danger is lurking ready to pounce on us at the moment. No proof, just a feeling. And what's more, I have sensed danger sometimes before, Sean, and that feeling has never been wrong. I'm getting it strongly now, though perhaps the danger isn't imminent but it's coming for us.'

He nodded. 'I feel a bit the same: the house itself doesn't feel dangerous, but something makes me feel *wary* – yes, that's the best word for it at the moment. I don't know why, though.'

He pulled a wry face. 'Some of my family sense things and I never know whether to believe them or not because I don't get that sort of feeling.'

'Interesting that both of us have that in our backgrounds. Most people laugh or mock me when I tell them about it.'

'I'd never mock you for believing something sincerely, even if I disagreed totally with it. Mockery can be a very nasty tool. But we'll let that discussion drop for today, shall we? Though I would like to see how we go at a personal level. I'd like that very much.' He shook his head in surprise. 'I'm shocked at how quickly that's happened.'

'Me too.'

When he held out his hand, she took it once more without hesitation. 'How about we go and look at the external area, how all the other houses, or cottages or whatever you want to call them, fit together? They're much smaller than this one, which seems to be the only big house on the site. I don't think we should even start going round their interiors today, unless we want to arrive at a B&B covered in dust and cobwebs.'

He yawned suddenly. 'I'm tired. It's been a long day. How about we go and find somewhere to stay for the night?'

'And somewhere to eat a hearty meal. I'm famished.'

'You're a woman after my own heart. And when we come back tomorrow morning, we'll look round all the cottages.'

He took her hand and they strolled back to the car together.

What a momentous day! Nina thought. *No way am I going back to Australia now!*

And it wasn't just about her inheritance; it was Sean, the possibilities with him, the feeling that her life was going to blossom in all sorts of ways.

Chapter Eight

Ilsa Platt walked from the free parking area just outside the town centre to the dress shop where she worked, which was on a small side street near the central shopping area.

She'd been worried about the owner for a few weeks. Ms Hayton hadn't looked well, and she'd disappeared a few times for an hour or two. The first time she'd said simply, 'I have a dental appointment.' But after that, she'd simply said, 'I'm nipping out for an hour or two.'

Ilsa knew something was wrong, seriously wrong, just knew it. Ms Hayton didn't usually get bad moods and was a decent boss to work with. But bad things happened. No one could keep them out of their life completely. Ilsa was living proof of that.

Her heart sank every time she arrived at work and saw that unhappy look on the older woman's face. She and Megs, the other shop assistant, kept wondering what was wrong and discussing the rumours that were beginning to circulate. Was the shop really about to be sold as people were saying?

If so, how would it affect her? Would these new owners close the shop down completely and turn it into something else, or if they kept it open as a ladies' dress shop would they sack her and Megs and bring in their own people? Who might be buying it, anyway? No one from Essington St Mary, that was certain. Someone would have known more about them if they'd been local. Ilsa and Megs might not have been born in the valley but they met enough members of the public to be aware of a major rumour like that.

It couldn't have happened at a worse time for Ilsa. She had very little money saved because she could barely manage to pay rent as well as feed herself and buy petrol for her rattletrap old car on the miserable amount she had been earning lately. Well, she'd been working only three or four days a week for the past year, depending on how business was going, and unfortunately sales had been going increasingly badly, so as the year passed it had become more often three.

It would be easier for Megs than her if the two of them lost their jobs. She was living with her boyfriend so had someone to help her out financially if necessary.

Ilsa had worked full-time when she started here three years ago, and had been renting a nice little bedsitter. Then business at the shop had gradually slowed down, partly because it stocked old-fashioned clothes for older women, and she'd been given the choice of reducing her hours or finding another job.

The trouble was, there were very few other jobs going

and she liked living here in this quiet little town, didn't want to move back to a busier place, so she'd moved to cheaper accommodation instead and adopted a much more frugal lifestyle. It cost nothing except a bit of wear on your shoes to go for a walk and nothing whatsoever to borrow books from the library. She felt sure business would pick up again eventually. Upturns and downturns usually came in cycles, didn't they?

But as the downturn continued at the shop, she grew increasingly pessimistic about her prospects.

Her employer, Ms Hayton, was in her mid-seventies and until recently she had seemed in good health, but she'd lost a lot of weight recently and, well, she just looked unwell.

The following Monday, Ms Hayton made a beckoning gesture when they arrived and called, 'Don't open up yet, girls! I need to speak to you both first.'

Ilsa and Megs exchanged worried glances as they hung their outdoor things on the hooks in the tiny space that was both cloakroom and kitchen, but didn't speak their fears aloud.

When they went into the office, Ms Hayton said, 'No need to bring another chair, Ilsa. This won't take long enough to be worth you two sitting down.'

She took a deep breath, sighed and gave them a sad look. 'I've got cancer and that's nudged me into selling the shop.'

Two gasps greeted this.

'They think they can cure it but I need to start treatment straight away. The new owners are going to take over from tomorrow onwards and I shan't be here, because I'm going into hospital.' She took a deep, shaky breath and added,

'So today will be my last day of work and I'll spend most of it clearing my things out of the building.'

'Your regular customers will miss you,' Ilsa ventured.

'Yes, and I'll miss them. But there you are. Things happen. Let's get back to you two girls.'

She always called them girls, but though Megs was only twenty-two, Ilsa was getting on for thirty now. She wasn't a girl by anyone's standards and given the start she'd had in life, she had never felt young and carefree like Megs.

'These new people will employ you two till the end of this week so that you can show them where everything is and get ready for a sale of unwanted goods. On Saturday, which will be your final day, they'll pay you an extra week's wages in lieu of notice and any accrued holiday pay. I don't hold out any hope of them continuing to employ you, because they're going to run it with their daughter, who is about your age, Megs. So if you can find another job anywhere else you should grab it with both hands, whatever it is.'

There was dead silence, then Megs asked, 'What about references?'

'I'll give you some really good ones on shop stationery today before I leave.' She gave the two young women a wry smile. 'You can write them yourselves and put exactly what you want in them. You can type them up neatly, Ilsa, then print them out and I'll sign them. After that the two of you can make as many copies as you see fit on the shop's photocopier.'

'Thank you,' they chorused.

'Don't hesitate to praise yourselves in these references, mind. You'll need to tell any future employer that you're very good value as employees. And actually you both are and I thank you for your unstinting help over the past few years. You've worked well for me and just as well with one another.'

She waited a moment or two then asked gently, 'No other questions?'

They shook their heads so she clapped her hands, said 'Chop! Chop!' and they went to work with the familiar words ringing in their ears for what would probably be the last time.

But Ilsa caught a glimpse of her employer sitting weeping in the office later in the day. She felt sad for Ms Hayton and worried sick about her own future. This was going to change her life, and not in a good way, she just knew it.

You'd think she'd be used to having her life upended, but you never got used to dealing with massive changes that you didn't want and, she had thought sometimes, that she didn't deserve.

The new owners were a very smartly dressed middle-aged man and woman, and they said their daughter would be joining them later in the week.

Mr Sharples didn't indulge in or encourage any small talk, and Mrs Sharples dribbled words now and then. Ilsa was instructed to go through the shop and storerooms above and behind it with Mr Sharples to answer questions and to leave attending to customers to Megs and Mrs Sharples, since it was a quiet time of day.

Ilsa and the new owner went through the shop and the building with the proverbial fine-tooth comb. He didn't miss a single detail as far as she could tell. He'd brought a box of light bulbs with him and put them in as they moved through the cellars. She was surprised at how far these stretched and how many outbuildings there were behind the shop. She and Megs had been forbidden to go further into these areas than absolutely necessary and since there hadn't been any light bulbs in most areas, they hadn't been tempted to go fumbling through the darkness.

She didn't find the Sharples couple at all friendly and wouldn't like to be served by them, that was certain.

She didn't volunteer any extra information to them, just worked as directed and counted off the days until she could stop working for these cold fish.

However, when Saturday came, the daughter still hadn't arrived and Mr Sharples asked her if she'd work another week for them, since Penelope had been delayed.

She agreed, of course. She'd looked for jobs in the paper but seen nothing even suitable to apply for advertised.

Chapter Nine

Ilsa didn't know whether to be sorry or glad when Penelope Sharples turned up on the following Saturday afternoon, looking sulky and as if she'd been partying till late the previous night.

Mr Sharples had Ilsa's wages and holiday money ready and, to give him his due, it was accurate to the penny. However, they did delay her departure by over an hour, unpaid, to allow their daughter to ask any questions.

Ilsa didn't dare refuse in case a potential employer asked them for a reference for her at some point in the future.

It was evening when Ilsa at last got away and went back to the room she rented, and she was exhausted. She just wanted to grab a quick snack, maybe a cheese sandwich, then go to bed and read a few pages of her library book.

However, her landlady came out of the front room and stopped her just inside the hall.

'I need a word.'

'Is something wrong?'

'I'm afraid so and I'm sorry to spring this on you, Ilsa, but I need your room back and I need you to move out tonight.'

'*What?*' The word seemed to echo down the narrow hall.

As they only had an informal agreement about her renting the room, Ilsa knew she had no legal recourse, and anyway she couldn't have afforded to hire a lawyer to protest on her behalf.

'But you can't just throw me out, Mrs Boales! What am I going to do tonight? It's probably too late to find another room. Can't you even give me a week's notice so that I can find somewhere else to go?'

'No. I'm sorry but my nephew who's been missing for three years turned up today in a terrible state. Brian's been living on the streets for months, poor lad. His mother is dead and his father won't have anything to do with him and has just remarried, so I've offered Brian a home. He's moving in with me tonight and I've got him booked in for counselling for alcoholism from Monday onwards.'

She avoided Ilsa's eyes as she added, 'But I shall have to keep an eye on him from the start. I've had to buy him new clothes. New everything, right down to the skin, his were so ragged and filthy!'

'Oh dear.' She wasn't worrying about the nephew when she said that, but about her own dilemma.

'I'm sorry to turn you away so abruptly, Ilsa, but family comes first. This is a very small two-bedroom place and there's simply nowhere else to fit you in. And anyway, the poor lad is ashamed of the state he's in, and he doesn't want to see anyone till he's sorted a few things out.'

She hesitated, then added with obvious reluctance, 'I'll let you off this week's rent as compensation so you'll be able to hire a room for a few nights till you can settle permanently somewhere. I'm sorry but I need you out straight away, within the hour if possible, I'm afraid.'

'But where can I go at this late hour?'

'Surely you have some friend who'll take you in for a day or two?'

'No, I don't have anyone. My two really good friends moved away a couple of months ago if you remember. They were going to work on a cruise ship and they'll be in the Bahamas now, so I can't even go and join them. And you know I don't have any close family.' Or any distant family, come to that, not as far as she knew, anyway.

'What about that lass you work with, Megs, isn't she called? Can't she let you sleep on her sofa?'

'She and her boyfriend share a tiny bedsitter because they're saving to buy a flat of their own. And I didn't tell you but I lost my job this week as well because Ms Hayton has sold the shop.' She'd had a vague hope that the Sharpleses' daughter might not turn up or might not even want to work there but it hadn't happened. 'I wasn't sure in advance, but today turned out to be my last day of work.'

'Oh dear. How inconvenient for you! I'm sorry for your problems, Ilsa, but I still have to put my nephew first because his parents are dead. Now, let me help you get started on the packing. I brought home some empty boxes from the supermarket to put your things in and I have a bag of rubbish bin liners for the left-over oddments. Not that you have a lot of stuff but you only have the one suitcase.'

Ilsa felt like a frozen woman and couldn't seem to get moving.

'I've put them in your bedroom so perhaps you'd start packing straight away? Brian is waiting in the living room to take over that room and he's exhausted, poor lad, desperate to go to bed. Luckily you don't keep any of your possessions down here, so he can stay quiet and watch TV while we pack.'

There was nothing Ilsa could do but make a start. It didn't take many boxes and bags to hold all her possessions but she made sure to clear every morsel of food from the pantry and fridge.

This seemed to be the pattern of her life. She'd been an orphan from the age of ten. She'd been taken into care by social services, and moved here and there until she turned eighteen, not because she was badly behaved but because foster families weren't always stable.

Over the years and because of the various moves she lost the few family possessions social services had kept for her. She hadn't realised how important they were until it was too late and of course none of the foster parents had ever wanted her to bring more clutter to their houses with her.

In her last two years in school she'd lived in a hostel and taken any part-time weekend job she could find to earn money. She'd joined the army as soon as she was allowed to and it had been as near to a home as she'd had since she lost her mother. In it, she'd learnt early on not to load herself with meaningless objects. Well, you had to move around, and at the drop of a hat sometimes.

When Ilsa had finished her second term of service, she'd

wanted a chance to try out civilian life as an adult for the first time since she'd left school. She hadn't enjoyed her so-called freedom as much as she'd expected and had been intending to re-enlist for a longer term. But first she'd gone on a skiing holiday, something she'd always wanted to try. The trouble was, she'd been badly injured when a clumsy idiot got out of control and mowed her down.

She'd slowly recovered her general health, and again been found a place in a hostel, but due to serious damage to the bones of one leg she could never now get fit enough to go back to active service again, even though she didn't limp, so hadn't been able to re-enlist.

Since she didn't enjoy studying and wasn't good at it either, she'd begun working in a shop because she preferred to move around as she worked. She'd have gone mad sitting still at a desk all day long. She'd got a bit low in spirits at times since then, couldn't help it, especially after the main friends she'd made here had left the area.

This wasn't really the sort of life she'd wanted to lead but she couldn't figure out what else to do. And it was harder to meet people than it had been because she was getting a bit old to go clubbing or do anything like that, even if she'd enjoyed it, which she had never really done. She preferred being outdoors and most of the guys you met there were too young for her these days, and too juvenile in their attitude to the world. And she didn't like getting drunk. Where was the pleasure in losing control of your body?

Tonight was the final straw. Her world had fallen to pieces big time and just under two hours after she'd left work, she found herself sitting in her car outside the house, watching the front door close and seeing the shadowy outline of a man behind the living room curtains, which were pulled tightly across the brightly lit room. Somehow the sight of them shutting her outside on her own made her feel even worse.

She felt so numb and shocked that it took her a while to pull herself together enough to drive away. She tried the only two B&Bs she knew of and they were full already. And she certainly wasn't going to pay the much more expensive costs of a hotel.

Instead she went up to the car park at the very top of the main street, which was where hikers left their vehicles when they went out on the popular woodland walks. The parking area was usually empty at this time of the evening, except for the odd pair of lovers, so maybe she could find a quiet spot and spend the night in her car there.

To her dismay, tonight there was a group of rough-looking men sitting in a cluster of outdoor chairs near a couple of vehicles at the far end. They were smoking and drinking beer, with more cans standing in coolers full of ice nearby. They turned to stare at her hungrily when they realised it was a woman on her own at the wheel.

When she stopped the car for a moment, one of them blew her a kiss, the one next to him called out a lewd invitation and others whistled or made insulting signs. Then one started walking towards her so she swung the car round and drove straight out of the car park again.

She didn't stop till further down Larch Tree Lane, in a quiet part of the long street, pulling over and sitting slumped behind the wheel wondering where to try next. It was near some elegant houses so she felt safer there and switched off the engine to save petrol while she had a think.

Where the hell could she go to spend the night safely? If she stayed here on the main street, she might manage to drop off to sleep for a while but she was sure that sooner or later some police officer would rap on her car window and tell her to move on.

You read about people not just sleeping but living in their cars, but she couldn't think how to organise her tiny, old-fashioned vehicle to make it even remotely comfortable for a person with long legs. She'd slung everything into it hastily and couldn't even try to improve how things were crammed in until it was daylight because you'd need to see clearly in order to rearrange the contents of a vehicle.

Here with her was everything she owned in the world. Every single thing.

And even if she could rearrange things well enough to have room to lie down, where was she going to park it each night so that she'd be safe? Could she really live in it all the time? She'd hate it, but might have no choice if she couldn't find another job.

She certainly couldn't do anything tonight and she didn't want to pay for a hotel, needed to keep as much money back as possible for food, petrol and emergencies till she could find another job. She'd not got as much money in the savings bank as usual because she'd had to pay for some major repairs to her car not long ago.

Everything seemed to be going wrong lately.

She doubted she'd have any choice but to apply for social security, which she absolutely loathed the thought of. They had an office in town but it'd be shut now, so she couldn't even make enquiries about it till Monday.

She wasn't at all sure what they did for you if you were homeless as well as out of work, but was certain there were no full-time jobs going in other shops in Essington at the moment, except for a few hours of casual work a week in a supermarket or bigger store. Well, she'd already been looking, hadn't she?

She shivered and the darkness seemed to press down on her. She wished there were a full moon brightening up the world instead of just that miserable little crescent.

She couldn't even afford to cruise the streets for long searching for a place to stop for the night because she would need to be ultra-careful with her petrol. And anyway, she knew the town already from her walks, knew it from top to bottom. No new and safe parking places would appear like magic however hard she searched.

Oh, hell! She might have to leave the valley if no other full-time work was available. She hated even to think of doing that. Essington St Mary was as near home as anywhere she'd lived since she was ten.

In the end there was only one place where she thought she might be able to park safely for the night, a place she'd explored sneakily on foot one quiet Sunday evening when she first came to work in the valley. She'd kept an eye on it ever since out of sheer nosiness and had wandered round the area on foot a few times. She knew it was unoccupied now, had been since the last owner died.

So Lavender Lane it was. Just for a night or two.

Ilsa decided to park her car behind the big house in the gated group of dwellings called Lavender Lane. She drove there straight away, desperate to find somewhere to lie down safely.

The parking area behind the big house was empty but had space for about twelve cars. She went to the furthest corner and reversed her vehicle as far under a tree as it would fit.

The back of the car was loaded with her possessions so there was no chance of her fitting in as well as them. She tried sitting in the front passenger seat, but even with her pillow she was too tall to get comfortable enough to sleep. After a while she got cramp and had to get out of the car quickly and move her body around.

In the end she was so weary she took her sleeping bag and pillow with her, as well as her backpack and went to find somewhere to sleep. The ground was damp from a previous shower and the moon was hidden behind dark clouds that were threatening more rain, so she couldn't sleep on the ground next to the car. She locked the car up, praying that no one would try to break into it and steal her belongings, then set off to find somewhere to sleep.

She didn't usually let herself cry because it didn't help solve any problem that she knew of but she was very close to tears as she trudged past the big house and down the narrow central lane between the six cottages to the middle cottage on her left, the one with the rosebush near the front door in the little garden area between the two rows of cottages.

She could cope with a hard floor but not with rain, and she needed to stretch out to sleep, always had done, she was too tall to fit into small sleeping spaces.

The cottages were all locked, of course, but they didn't have full security systems on them, let alone CCTV cameras – well, she didn't think they'd installed them since her last visit. There only seemed to be alarms covering the front and rear entrances, and there were substantial, old-fashioned locks on the very solid front and back doors to keep people out.

She walked round to the rear of the cottage she'd got into before and used her torch to study the kitchen window. She'd found that its lock was loose the first time she came here, when she was dying to get inside such an old building and have a good look round. She'd been right in her guess about the situation. There were no signs that the lock had been repaired.

Please let it still be open, she prayed as she jiggled it about in the same way she had done that other time. To her enormous relief, fiddling with the catch worked once again and opening the window didn't set off any alarms – well, none that she could hear.

She managed to climb in through the rather small window but left her sleeping bag and pillow hanging over the windowsill in case she had to make a quick getaway. The kitchen and front living room were empty of everything except the same few dusty pieces of old furniture as there had been last time she'd looked round.

She peered out of the front window and since there were no lights to be seen in any of the other houses and no sounds of people talking or doing anything else, she went back for the rest of her things. She pulled them inside and closed the kitchen window, letting the catch fall loosely into place again.

And still everything stayed quiet with no one coming to investigate. Thank goodness! Oh, thank goodness! For once, luck was on her side.

She went to check upstairs but didn't even attempt to lie down on either of the two narrow single beds because if she did that, the crumpled bed covers would show someone had been there, as would the lack of dust on them.

She didn't want to be seen sleeping downstairs, though, if anyone looked through the windows, so she spread out her sleeping bag in the long narrow storage room-cum-pantry with bare shelves, then closed the door on the world. She'd found a wedge lying on the floor near the front door and now put that firmly under the inside of the pantry door. It made her feel a lot safer because at least she couldn't be taken by surprise and there was only one tiny window high up on the outside wall so no one would be able to peep in at her, either.

She was so exhausted, she set the alarm on her watch and quickly let herself sink into sleep.

The next thing Ilsa knew, it was daylight. She couldn't at first think where she was and sat up with a jerk then realised abruptly, gasping in shock when she looked at her watch. She'd set it to wake her at seven o'clock in the morning, but she mustn't have done that properly because it was half past nine now.

Half past nine!

She'd been utterly exhausted by the time she got herself settled here but she doubted she could have slept through its irritating beeping.

Oh, heavens! She'd left her car outside in the parking area at the back of the big house. What if there were people out and about now?

She put the wedge back near the front door and climbed

out of the kitchen window again, taking the time to jiggle the lock back into place in case she had to come back here tonight.

She was ravenously hungry, thirsty too, but breakfast would have to wait. She needed to get away from here as quickly as she could. She'd be safer somewhere with other people around like a shopping centre.

She'd go to one and indulge in a takeaway coffee to wash down the stale bread she couldn't toast for breakfast as she'd planned to do yesterday.

And why she kept feeling like weeping, she didn't know. She never allowed herself to cry. Never. Well, almost never anyway. Whenever her life became difficult, she prided herself on coping.

If she had to leave the valley to get another job she'd be deeply sad, but she'd survive sadness, had done before.

Chapter Ten

Nina and Sean found a pub to provide them with an evening meal and enjoyed it hugely. They sat chatting quietly for a while afterwards and were never short of something to say.

They found they had similar views about many things including how the world could be improved. They both felt equally helpless to cure the seemingly incurable urge of an increasing number of people to committing violent acts, whether as an individual or a big group.

This was followed by a less than comfortable night at the nearby B&B, which seemed to have chosen its beds for durability rather than comfort.

'I'm not using the same place if we have to stay here another night,' he muttered as they met for breakfast. 'As well as being rock hard, that single bed is far too small for a man as tall as me to get a good night's sleep in. I'd have been comfier in the back of my car, far comfier, because I could have laid the back seats flat and stretched out at least.'

He caught her eye and smiled ruefully. 'Sorry to bang on about unimportant things. I'm a man who values his sleep. I hope you at least managed to sleep well.'

'I didn't and for a similar reason, an uncomfortable bed.'

When they'd finished bowls of cereal from the small breakfast bar, the landlady brought them the cooked breakfasts they'd ordered.

'At least the breakfast is good.' Sean dunked his toast into the runny egg yolk and took a big bite with relish.

Nina didn't answer, because she was also enjoying her meal.

'Nice to see a woman enjoy her food,' he said as they finished.

'I'm always ravenous in the mornings.'

They stopped on the way at a small supermarket to buy some basic food supplies, mainly substantial snacks and good supplies of coffee and tea to see them through the day and to leave behind in the big house for future use.

When they drove into the parking area at the back of the big house, however, Sean slammed on the brakes at the sight of a car parked under a tree in one corner with no sign of a driver in it or nearby.

They got out and went across to study it more closely.

'If it had broken down, the rescue service would have towed it to the nearest garage, surely?' he said. 'So it must have been left here on purpose.'

Nina studied its position, frowning. 'And the owner seems to have parked it as far out of sight as possible. Look at the way we have to hold back the lower branches of the tree to see into the back of it.'

They both studied the vehicle again, then Sean said, 'It looks as if it's got someone's entire collection of personal belongings in it, far more than just a night's worth like us. But where did the owner sleep last night?'

'I wonder if the person walked into town and found accommodation for the night? I'd have come back early if I'd done that, though.'

They both stood staring at the piles of contents in the back of the vehicle, then Nina said, 'This doesn't look to me like the belongings of someone who could afford a hotel room. Most of it has been stuffed into old grocery boxes or rubbish bin liners.'

'I agree. So where is the person?'

'It's a woman, I think, judging by some of the things left here.' She pointed to a jacket lying on the passenger seat, its embroidered panel winking in the sunlight with a few sequins. 'That isn't a man's garment.'

He grinned. 'Well, I'd definitely not be seen dead in it. I wonder . . .'

'What do you wonder?'

'Whether our mystery owner has broken into any of the cottages looking for somewhere to sleep. There were some light showers during the night. I think that's far more likely than trudging all the way into town to find a B&B, especially if she's a stranger to the area and doesn't know where to go anyway.'

'Or can't afford to pay for a B&B. Give me a minute to check something.'

Nina walked across to the top of the narrow lane that ran along the backs of the cottages and glanced down at the soft earth it was covered in, calling, 'Hey! There are some fairly recent footprints under the shelter of the foliage of this tree, ones that last night's rain didn't wipe out. Come and have a look but be careful where you tread.'

He came to join her, whipped out his camera and took a quick photo of the footprints, then they both studied them more closely.

'Hmm. With sneakers it's harder to tell whether it's a man or a woman,' he said.

She held her foot out close to the nearest full footprint. 'Similar size to mine so I think I'm right that this intruder is a woman.'

He held out his foot next to the print and it was indeed much bigger. 'I agree. But just in case it isn't a woman, let me do the job of taking a look round the cottages and checking for whether someone's broken in, unless you're particularly good at fighting, that is?'

She rolled her eyes. 'I know some basic self-defence tactics, which I've never had to use, and that's all. You're bigger than me so it makes sense that you go and check.' She clasped her hands together and said, 'My hero!' in a sing-song voice, which made him laugh.

'I won't be long. You keep an eye on our car. Here you are.'

He tossed her his car keys. 'Sound the horn if anyone turns up and I'll come running. If necessary you could bar the exit with our car. I don't want this person driving away before I've found out what the hell they think they're doing here, as well as how they found it. Visitors to the town don't normally know their way into the rear car park and the locals leave the place alone because they think this is just a convalescent home.'

He scowled at the elderly car. 'I don't like to see that lump of old tin left here. I hope the Lane hasn't become known as a place for vagrants to stop.'

'They could just be visiting someone at a nearby house.'

'I doubt it. Not if they parked the car like that, so close to the tree. Anyway, it's part of my present remit to guard these cottages – as well as to keep an eye on you. So I'm going to see if I can catch whoever it is.' He winked at her. 'Though you're a lot more fun to look after.'

He didn't wait for an answer but went off to check each of the three cottages at the far side. He found no signs that anyone had been messing around with them to break in, then, as he was about to move down the backs of the nearer row, he saw a woman climbing out of the kitchen window of the middle one.

He took a quick step back and stayed hidden behind the top cottage, peeping out through the foliage of a tall shrub and trying to keep quiet as well as out of sight. He waited there until she had nearly reached him, then moved out of hiding to block her way and ask, 'Sleep well in there, did you?'

He watched in satisfaction as she jumped in shock and then froze, looking at him in horror. *Serves her right.* Then he noticed that her clothes were crumpled and she had a deep-down weary look on her face that suggested she hadn't been sleeping soundly for a few days. It was a look you couldn't mistake. Her stomach growled as if she hadn't eaten, and in spite of his concern about what she was doing there, he couldn't help starting to feel sorry for her.

'I didn't do any damage, I promise you,' she said pleadingly. 'I'm homeless. That's my only crime. Even the window lock was already loose the first time I came here over a year ago and no one's mended it since, so I thought the cottages weren't being used.'

He continued to study her carefully, then said in a gentler voice, 'Come and tell my partner and me why you're homeless.'

'Can't you just – you know, let me go on my way? I promise I won't come here again.'

'My conscience won't let me. If we do, you'll still be homeless and it upsets me to see how deep-down tired you look. Come along.' He began walking the rest of the way up round the big house to the car park at the rear and with a weary sigh, she joined him. She didn't seem afraid of him. Well, she had no need to be, had she?

When she fell over, he thought at first that she'd tripped, only she didn't get up again or even move. He knelt to examine her and could tell immediately that she wasn't faking this faint, so called out for Nina, who came running round the corner of the big house to join him.

Together they carried the woman round to the parking area, by which time she had started to regain consciousness.

'Shh. Don't struggle. You fainted,' he said gently and held her upright against him while Nina opened up the back hatch of their car. They helped her to sit down on the edge of the boot and she leant against the side as if finding it difficult to stay upright.

'What's your name?' Nina asked.

'Ilsa.'

'Ilsa what?'

She hesitated then shrugged and said, 'Platt.'

'You're not well,' Sean said bluntly.

'I'm not ill. At least, I don't think I am, though I may be a bit run-down. I don't usually go round fainting, but I reckon I've forgotten to eat anything for a while. Hmm. Since breakfast yesterday, actually.'

She frowned, stared into space for a moment then nodded. 'Yes, I didn't even manage to take a lunch break yesterday. It's been frenetic this past week. I've lost my job and was handing over to the new owners.'

'How come you're homeless if you've only just stopped work?'

'To cap it all, when I got home last night my landlady asked me to leave at once.'

'Was there a specific reason for that?'

'Yes, but it wasn't because of anything I'd done wrong. It was because her nephew needed my bedroom. He's been sleeping rough and he's an alcoholic, so now that he's got in touch again she wanted him to move in with her straight away and attend rehabilitation sessions.'

'Didn't your rental contract specify the number of days' notice that had to be given?'

'I didn't have a contract. I needed a cheaper place to live last year when my hours of work were cut and my landlady didn't want the tax department to find out about her extra money. So we kept it informal.'

She sighed and volunteered the rest. 'I was only on short time at work and as you can see, my car is quite old. It needed repairs to keep it going and as a result I don't have much money saved at the moment.'

'Hard luck on it all happening at once.'

'Tell me about it. Anyway, I was too busy packing to think about food. Sorry. I don't want to hold you up but could you let me have a few more minutes to recover before I move on because I still feel a bit dizzy. I'll get out of your way as soon as I can stand up without the world spinning round me, and I won't come back to that house, I promise.'

'Or we could give you something to eat and drink, and see whether we can help you in other ways, Ilsa,' Nina said gently.

Sean nodded agreement. 'Take as long as you need to pull yourself together, then we'll all go into the big house. We've got some bread rolls and jam there, as well as biscuits and apples and I'll make us all mugs of coffee.'

'We'll stand you a proper meal later on as well,' Nina said.

'But I—' Ilsa looked from him to Nina and back. 'You aren't doing this so that you can keep me here while you call the police on me, are you?'

'Heavens, no! We're going to feed you and then help you, if we can.'

She must have believed them because she blinked her eyes furiously, then wiped them with the back of one sleeve as tears couldn't be held back. They continued to trickle down her cheeks and Nina shoved a clean tissue into her hand.

'I've been – you know, a bit upset about losing my job and then my home,' Ilsa muttered as she dabbed at her eyes.

Nina held out another tissue. 'Anyone would be in your situation. Don't you have any family or friends you can go and stay with?'

'No. I don't have any family at all, and my friends are working overseas and I don't want to go travelling. And now I need to find a job and a new place to live.'

Sean didn't comment but she looked so shaky he insisted she take his arm as they walked across from the car to the big house at the top of the drive. When they were inside, he helped her to sit down at the dusty kitchen table while Nina got the gas stove working, filled the old kettle they'd found and cleaned earlier, then put it on to boil.

By then Sean had opened the packet of biscuits and offered one to their guest.

Ilsa took it and hesitated. 'I'll get myself a drink of water first, if you don't mind. My throat's rather dry.'

He pressed her shoulder to keep her from standing up. 'I'll get you a glass. It'll have to be tap water, I'm afraid.'

'Thanks. It's all I ever drink. I don't have the money to waste on fancy water. As long as it's clean and wet, it'll be fine.'

Sean kept an eye on her but she did nothing except gulp down some water then take a small bite of her biscuit. She leant back in her chair, closing her eyes as she chewed and slowly swallowed the rest bite by bite. She accepted a cup of coffee and ate two more biscuits, probably not realising that she was sighing from time to time.

She looked as if the world had not been treating her well for a while, poor thing. When she'd finished, she put her empty mug down and looked from one to the other, not saying anything, simply waiting for them to speak.

But Sean spoke to Nina first. 'Seems to me that we've just found a way of getting help to clear up the places for our new convalescent homes.'

'That's exactly what I was thinking.' She turned to Ilsa. 'We've been told that these cottages were intended to be

used as convalescent homes where government employees
could come and stay for longer than usual at no cost, in
fact as long as was necessary to recover properly. You look
as if you have a similar need for a refuge.'

'I suppose I do, but unfortunately I'm not a government
employee.'

'And we're not experts at the job of running this centre,
so perhaps we could all work together to get things ready?
You seem to be in need of a job.'

'I am. And I'm not fussy what I do to earn money as
long as it's honest.'

'Oh, it definitely is. We plan to spruce up the cottages
before we put them to use again, but if you don't mind
living in the servants' quarters attached to this house,
which are like a small bedsitter, we could give you the
job of helping us run them afterwards and then you could
stay there.'

'Helping you to do what exactly? I'm not the strongest
person you could hire if you're needing help with DIY
work. I broke my leg quite badly on a ski slope a couple of
years ago and have to be careful how I go if I need to carry
something heavy.'

Sean and Nina exchanged glances of approval at her
honesty, then she said, 'I don't think you'd find it too
onerous to help clean the cottages then open and close
them for a variety of tradespeople to do any little jobs
necessary, Ilsa. We need to renovate the place, you see.
What do you think?'

'I could easily do that. In fact . . .' She hesitated, then
said, 'I enjoy organising things.'

'Good. That'll fit in well. We neither of us enjoy

fiddling-around-type jobs. When each tradesperson has finished a job, you'd need to check that they've done what we wanted and done it properly. And at the same time, perhaps you could clean the cottage interiors and the rest of the big house. In other words, act as a sort of caretaker-cum-cleaner. If you don't mind that sort of work, that is.'

Ilsa's utter astonishment at this showed. 'I can't believe you're offering me a job when you've never met me before today. How do you know I'm trustworthy?'

'Well, we'll be coming and going for a while, so though we won't always be around to keep an eye on the people working here ourselves, we'll still be able to work with you regularly. And apart from the fact that you have an honest-looking face, if you're short of money, I doubt you'll run away from a chance to earn some once you're started and found you can cope, as we expect.'

She looked at them with hope brightening her face so visibly that Sean smiled at her. 'We'd have to find someone to do that job and you've just dropped into our hands like a ripe plum.'

'But you don't know anything about me. Though I do have references from the shop.'

'I'm sure you're going to tell us the basics about your background but I always go by what people seem like, rather than words on paper,' Sean said. 'Written references can be forged, but few people can conceal all their feelings and attitudes if they chat to you for a while.'

Nina took over. 'We'd pay you a wage and, of course, your accommodation would be free, but it won't be the most fun job and you'll be rather tied to this place, plus you'll be working seven days a week to start off with, except for occasional short trips into town for food and other bits and pieces we might need. You'd have to fit your own shopping in with the work going on as well.'

'I'd not cheat you,' Ilsa said fervently. 'I promise you that.'

'I believe you,' Sean said gently.

Nina gave her another of those lovely encouraging smiles. 'We both do.'

'We're setting up an internet connection and will open an account for you to order things online as well as to use for your own needs as long as you don't use too much.' Nina's voice took on a teasing tone. 'And of course we'll notice if you try to nick off with the contents of the houses.'

Ilsa didn't smile at the mild joke, just stared at them as if she was finding it hard to believe what she was hearing.

'Interested?' Sean prompted.

She nodded vigorously. 'Oh, yes. Very interested indeed. I've stayed in Essington, struggling on part-time wages because I love this little town and I prefer to live quietly here rather than in a big, busy city.'

'Did you grow up here?'

'No. I grew up in foster homes but the last couple were here.'

'Oh, I see.'

'I don't like big towns nearly as much.'

'Because you don't want to face the sharp, crowded rat race?'

'Yes. And – I'd better tell you: I've been a bit depressed rather than suffering from a physical illness, partly the result of the accident that stopped me doing what I wanted.'

'Can I ask what that was?'

She told them about her time in the army and her attempt to try life outside it as well as details of the accident.

'What about your family?' Nina asked gently. 'Did you never go back to visit any of them?'

'I don't have any family left, at least none that I know of. When I recovered, I had to find something to do that was less demanding physically and I found the valley and what used to be Hayton's dress shop.'

She was suddenly overcome by a huge yawn. 'May I save telling you any other details till I'm not so weary? I slept for a long time last night, but it still doesn't seem to have been enough and I hope I'm making sense at the moment.'

'Yes, of course you can tell us more later. I should have noticed how exhausted you were.'

'Thank you.' She waited, eyeing them hopefully. 'I promise I won't let you down if you still want to employ me.'

Sean smiled. 'I'm sure you won't. I'm rather good at judging character and you seem like an honest soul to me.'

That kind remark brought more tears to her eyes and elicited a husky 'Thank you.'

They let her sit for a few more moments pulling herself together, then Nina said, 'Let me show you the servants' quarters. The flatlet is in the part of the house at the side of the car park, so that we can put up a sign outside it telling people who've come to do jobs here to sign up with you on arrival. And you can tell them where to go.'

'What are these quarters like?'

'A very small flat with all amenities.'

'I don't mind as long as it's safe.'

'I think you'll feel quite safe there. What did you do to feel secure last night?'

She gave them a reluctant smile. 'I slept inside the pantry and wedged the door shut from inside. But the floor was rather hard.'

'How very enterprising!' Sean couldn't help chuckling. 'I wish I could have seen it. Mustn't have been much room to wriggle about.'

'There wasn't but if anyone had come to the house they wouldn't have seen me, which was the main point, because there was only a tiny high window in there with bars on.'

Nina held her laughter back for a short time, then it escaped her. 'Slept in the pantry! Oh, my!'

Sean couldn't help joining in and in the end Ilsa had to laugh with them and admit, 'I'm hoping for a softer mattress tonight, I must admit, and room to wriggle about.'

'You shall have it.'

Chapter Eleven

While Nina was putting lunch together, Sean phoned the lawyers who were his first point of contact about managing the finances for this project. He wanted to report on the general conditions at Lavender Lane, and of course he described the woman he and Nina had just employed.

'Getting the place clean and tidy sounds a good first step to re-starting the main work at the property,' James Pinworthy said. 'But we'll check out this Ilsa Platt, just to be sure she's all right. If she was in the army that should be quite easy to do.'

'I don't think you'll find any nasty secrets in her background. She has a very open, honest face.'

'Glad to hear it and probably she's fine. You've a reputation as an extremely good judge of character, Sean. But with a project like this it pays to be extra-careful so we'll check anyway. How is the new heir doing?'

'Very well. Nina reminds me of what you'd told me about Laura, not so much in looks, judging by the photos, though there is a faint resemblance, but in her caring attitude towards other people and the world in general. I really like her.' More than merely liked but he didn't want to admit it publicly yet.

'That's a glowing analysis from you for someone you've known for such a short time.'

'Well, sometimes you just know that a person has a decent soul, don't you?'

'*You* do, more than anyone else we've dealt with over the years. You're almost psychic about that sort of thing.'

Sean could feel himself stiffening. He didn't like people to attribute psychic traits to him. It was careful observation that told you what people were like, he always said. He didn't bother to protest, though he was quite sure they'd find nothing wrong about Ilsa, however much they investigated her. Well, if she didn't have any family, she couldn't have any dodgy relatives, could she?

'Oh, and Max said he needed to speak to you, so I gave him your new phone number.'

Sean had only just ended this call when his phone sounded again and Max's ID came up. He smiled and clicked to accept the call. You didn't keep Max waiting.

'Are you free to talk privately?' a deep voice boomed.

'Yes. Always nice to hear from you.'

'Hmm. Maybe. We have a problem here and need to find somewhere to hide one of our operatives while he convalesces, to keep him safe. How long do you think it'll be before you can get a cottage up and running? Make that a couple of cottages while you're at it, so we have a spare. There are a few things still to settle about the project he was working on.'

'How long it'll take to get ready depends how much money we have to throw at the situation.'

'Unlimited. Just charge the usual accounts to pay the people you hire.'

Sean was startled. Max was famous among the people he dealt with for being ultra-careful with public money. 'It's that serious? What's happened?'

'One of our undercover guys was spotted and only just escaped. It'll be best if he stays out of sight for a few months, and anyway, he was badly injured and will need time to recover properly.'

'A cottage can be ready for occupying within a couple of hours if it's that urgent. It won't be fancy but the living area and one bedroom will be dust-free and comfortable enough, and the sanitary facilities seem to be adequate, if not all that modern. There is a shower and a bath, which will probably both be needed for his therapy.'

'Thank goodness! A few peaceful weeks will probably work wonders for this chap. But unless there are other people staying in the Lane, he'll stand out like a sore thumb.'

'I've found some notes about locals who'll come in and play the part of convalescents in such situations. We'll make sure he gets a good long rest. When will he be arriving?'

'After dark tonight. We've been told of a doctor who lives in the village near you and has been happy to visit our guests in the past. He knows how to keep his mouth shut about what he sees. And I know about the trio of oldies you're talking about. They long retired from active service with us but they like to use the Lavender Lane cottages for little social gatherings. They'll be glad to see it up and running again.' He chuckled. 'They've missed having it as an occasional escape from their families.'

'I didn't realise you had such resources here in the valley as well as the buildings at Lavender Lane.'

'Yes. An old-fashioned town like this is perfect for our needs. The residents are still very much into people power as well as the digital stuff, and at times people are what you need most.'

'Is this guy you're sending us badly injured?'

'He was rather seriously damaged but he's already had a stay in a big hospital and the extra attention it could provide and is well on the way to recovery. He's a tough chap but though he'll live to fight another day, it won't be in a front-line position again. He's done enough for his country now. But we could probably do with someone to look after him and do his household chores for a week or two. He had to have quite a lot of stitches and still hasn't got to do anything too active.'

'Yes, of course. In fact, we've just hired a caretaker-cum-cleaner, who'll be able to do some of the work, and Nina and I will be happy to help out as well, if necessary.'

'I hope this caretaker is the sort of person you can rely on in an emergency.'

'She's ex-army, so ought to be all right, but head office are still checking her out. Nina and I will be around for a while too and we'll be able to make sure that everything's running smoothly before we start leaving Ilsa on her own for longer periods.'

'Sounds good. Anything else?'

'Yes. I shall need to tell Nina more about the general picture if she's to get fully involved from now on. She is, after all, the owner and custodian, and would have to find out eventually, though apparently we don't usually do that so soon after taking over. Will it be all right if I explain more about the situation to her?'

'You're that sure of her already?'

He laughed softly. 'I'd better be. I'm seriously attracted to her.'

'*You?* I thought you didn't do romance.'

'I thought so too. Seems I was wrong. Though it's early days yet. I'm not rushing in feet first, so to speak, but am enjoying the journey into getting to know her and hoping it'll lead to permanency.'

'Well, for what it's worth, I can highly recommend a good marriage from my own experience. That's the reason I was transferred to backroom work. They think families interfere with some aspects of active service and they're probably right, so they make such changes automatically. Be warned. You'll have to do the same if anything comes of this attraction.'

'I was considering retiring anyway – well, as much as the service allows us to retire.'

'They won't want someone with your skills to retire fully yet. You're too good at sorting out problems.'

Sean chuckled. 'Thanks for the compliment. You only dish them out when you want to keep someone on side.'

'Are you still on side?'

'Of course I am. I don't stop being a patriot just because I retire.'

'Good. I'm bringing this guy to join you myself and will get in touch again when we're about half an hour from Essington St Mary. You can put the percolator on.'

'We haven't got one here yet.'

'Good heavens! You're right about one thing, then. Our friend will be roughing it.'

Max's addiction to fancy coffees was well known. 'Does this guy you're bringing have a name?'

'He hasn't decided on one yet. Call him 007 till he does.'

Sean whistled softly in surprise as he put his phone down. That temporary name did have its amusing side but also a sad side too because it meant that their guest would probably never be able to use his own given name again, a major step not normally needed when you left the service. The poor chap didn't have any close family or he'd not have been sent into difficult situations, but if he had found anyone, the relationship would be over now.

Well, you knew what you might have to face when you joined this rather special wing of the security services.

All in all, he was glad he was leaving dangerous work and still surprised at his own reaction to Nina. He'd never been as deeply or quickly attracted to any woman in his whole life and was already hoping she felt the same and that they'd be able to stay together. There was something so frank and open about many Australians that he'd always liked.

He shrugged mentally. He'd work out the details of how they could organise their lives together when things were more certain of their feelings – or at least, when she was. He was pretty certain of how he felt about her and had been thinking of leaving active service anyway. He'd been lucky to stay safe, unlike this 007 chap.

In the meantime he had to bring Nina up to speed and tell her what was going to happen tonight. And she needed to know about the occasional other uses of her inheritance.

He smiled as he thought of one use that he liked the sound of. The three oldies were apparently a delight to interact with and would be happy to start coming here again, from what he'd heard.

He went to join Nina, his spirits lifting at the mere sight of her in the kitchen, humming quietly to herself as she worked.

Nina looked up as Sean came into the kitchen. 'The food's nearly ready. I was just going to pretty it up a bit.'

'Leave that. We'll gobble it down quickly whatever it looks like, because I have something important to tell you and then we'll need to get busy.'

'Not bad news?'

'No. Well, I don't consider it bad exactly, just a bit sensitive.' In between bites he explained about the injured agent who was being brought to them that night, and the three oldies who'd also be joining them, then waited for her to respond.

She sat frowning at him, the sort of frown you get when you're thinking carefully about something important, he felt. Then she looked down at her hands for a few moments and when she looked up again it was to stare directly at him. 'I had no idea things like this were happening still. I thought the set-up here was an anachronism.'

'No. It definitely isn't. This sort of stuff is still going on all over the world, with governments and political groups plotting, planning and acting sneakily – or viciously in some cases.'

'Goodies and baddies, we used to call such people when we were playing games as children. Only this isn't playing – it's horribly, deadly serious, isn't it?'

'Yes. And if you don't want to take part in it, now is the time to speak out and perhaps sell Lavender Lane to someone who is happy to do that. I must admit I'd prefer to think of our lot as "goodies", not the other sort.'

He waited to give her time to think, then went on gently, 'I'd wanted to give you more time to settle in here before getting things going again, but fate has stepped in and has pre-empted any breathing space. There's a person who needs to move here as a matter of urgency to stay safe and then move on into a new life.'

'It's surprised me how serious it all is, and that I'm involved in such a thing is, well, mind-boggling.'

'Yes. It is extremely serious.'

She looked round the kitchen and then went to stand by the window and stare out. When she turned round, she said, 'It's my country too that may need protecting. And my inheritance that can help do that. But you'll have to tutor me because I'm not at all used to this cloak-and-dagger stuff.'

He smiled and walked towards her, pulling her into his arms and simply cradling her against him. 'I'm glad you took that decision because I really want to get to know you better.'

'I'm glad you're here to help me, very glad, and I'd really like to get to know you better too.'

They stood quietly for a moment or two, then she asked, 'How long have you been doing work of this sort for?'

'A couple of decades, give or take.'

'Were you ever injured on active service?'

'Yes. But I was lucky. I only had a minor problem to recover from.' He hesitated, then said, 'You may not be related to Laura but you're following in her footsteps and you'll need to make the same sort of agreement with this government department.'

'All right.'

He stared at her, then smiled. 'Is it as simple as that for you to agree?'

'Yes. Because it means I won't lose this very beautiful home and I'll be doing a job that matters. Two wins.'

'You're not worried about the danger?'

She looked a bit surprised. 'It's not extreme, is it?'

'Not usually in places like this, no. For me this is probably going to be a retirement job. If you can stand to have me around, that is?' He gave her a questioning look and saw her whole face soften into a lovely smile. It reinforced the fact that he really had fallen in love with her. That had happened so quickly because it felt utterly right, for the first time in his life. You just – knew.

'I can definitely stand to have you around, Sean.'

'Good. We'll . . . take it easy, though, getting to know one another, I mean.'

She didn't pretend not to understand what he was referring to by this. 'Yes. I'd prefer it that way. I rushed into a relationship last year in Australia and it was a big mistake. Very big. I don't think you will be, but I still don't want to rush in, even with you.'

'Nor do I. It's too important. Besides, we're going to have another focus to our lives for a while besides what we might want for ourselves.'

However, he did allow himself to pull her close and kiss her again, just gentle kisses, one on each soft cheek, but they felt very nice. Then he stood holding her and breathing in the faint perfume that was very much a part of her.

As he pulled away, he asked, 'Do I smell a hint of lavender?'

'Yes. Strange, isn't it? I keep sachets of lavender in my underwear drawers and have done for years and now I own a place called Lavender Lane with lavender plants growing in my garden.'

'I've always liked that perfume, as long as it isn't overdone.'

'No perfume is good when it's used too lavishly.'

'It's as if this place was waiting for you, Nina. I haven't really looked at the gardens but Elizabeth next door clearly has. It's good that there's lavender growing here. And let's hope she and her friends can help us protect it and make the whole garden area flourish.'

'Yes. I agree. Now, finish off your lunch, then we'll choose a cottage and start to get it ready for occupation by our guest.'

'I think we'll need several cottages if we bring in

help from the town, and need them quickly. How about asking Ilsa to call her friend Megs and see if she wants a casual job for a day or two?'

'Good idea. Ilsa is a good find, isn't she?'

'I think so. I like her.'

'So do I.'

Chapter Twelve

Just before midnight, a vehicle purred into the car park behind Lavender Lane, its engine just about noiseless. Its windows were almost as dark as the black bodywork and it didn't have lights on.

A burly man slipped out of the front passenger seat and went to stand in the shadows near the rear entrance to the big house, looking more than ready to deal with any problems that dared to confront them.

The only thing that happened was that Sean came quietly out of the house, nodded to Max and offered his arm to help the wounded man to limp inside and sit down. Max followed closely, and another man followed them from the car, carrying two large bundles.

'Peter here is a paramedic,' explained Max in a low voice once they were all safely inside.

'I'm happy to tell you that the patient has stood the journey remarkably well, considering,' added Peter.

Sean saw the annoyance on the injured man's face and the way he mouthed the word 'patient'. 'We've decided to call the people who come here "guests",' he said quietly.

The injured man nodded. 'Sounds a lot nicer than "patient" to me.'

The paramedic shrugged and set the bundles down, putting one on the floor and the other on a side table. He tapped this bundle. 'Medical supplies for changing the last of the dressings, as well as painkillers if needed. Our friend can be trusted to say what he needs with the latter because he's more likely to take too little than too many. Watch out for that.'

'I will.' He winked at the guest, who blew him a mocking kiss in return. They grinned at one another, already on the same wavelength.

'The other bundle contains miscellaneous clean clothes. His own things will be forwarded in a day or two, once we're sure he's likely to be safe staying here.'

'Sorry to be such a nuisance,' the guest said in a husky voice, leaning his head against the chair back in a way that betrayed a deep physical weariness he was attempting to conceal. However, he still had an alert look in his eyes as he studied his new surroundings.

'We're happy to help you in any way we can,' Sean said. 'Just so that you know who's here in the house and therefore safe to interact with, this is Nina, who owns the property, and there's another woman who'll be helping out with miscellaneous tasks around the place – Ilsa Platt – but she's in bed at the moment. She was seriously short of sleep so she helped get your room ready then went to catch up on her own needs. She'll be available to start helping us in any way needed from tomorrow morning onwards, I should think.'

'Our friend here should go straight to bed as well,' the paramedic said. 'And he ought to stay fairly inactive for a day or two, building up what he does in free movement gradually.'

The newcomer's expression said what he thought of that, and it wasn't positive.

'But he probably won't!' the paramedic added.

'So the doctor won't be coming to check him tonight?' Sean asked.

'No. I think it's sleep that will do most to help your guest now, normal sleep and the time needed for his wounds to heal fully and his muscles to build up again. But don't hesitate to call the doctor if you need him, Mr Reynolds.'

'All right.' Sean turned back to their guest. 'We've made up a bed for you in the library here for the first night or two, 007, then after that you can move into your cottage. Also, it won't attract the neighbours' attention if anyone checks up on you at intervals during the night to start off with.'

'I'd be perfectly all right on my own tonight,' the man said in a tone of voice that was more like a low growl. 'And it'd be a lot quieter if people don't keep checking up on me so that I could maybe get some solid sleep for a change.'

'We'd rather make sure you're all right before we do anything else,' Nina said. 'Now, would you like a mug of cocoa before you go to sleep? We're about to have one.'

He'd clearly been about to protest again but his face brightened at this offer. 'You know what? I'd absolutely love some cocoa. That's the first thing I've really fancied in days and the doctor told me I should keep up my fluid intake. Goodness, I haven't had cocoa for years. It was one of my childhood favourites. Are you sure it's not too much trouble?'

'I'm happy to make a mug of it for you, now and at any other time. I'm a bit of a cocoa addict myself so I'll be joining in. Anyone else want one?'

Sean nodded but Max shook his head, moved towards the door and made it clear that he and Peter had a long return journey ahead and they would need to get on their way.

After a very brief farewell, Nina went across to the kitchen while Sean took the newcomer into the library.

When she took their guest a mug of hot chocolate, she said, 'I've put a spoonful of sugar in it, but if you prefer more I can get you some.'

She watched him sniff it, smile then cradle it in his hands. She guessed he was enjoying the comforting warmth as well as the drink itself so decided to make him a hot water bottle, which would probably also feel comforting. The kettle had recently boiled, so she went to fill one immediately to put into the sleeping bag on the couch being used as his temporary bed.

She came back with it in time to see him finish drinking the cocoa in a big, happy gulp. She wasn't surprised that he didn't accept an offer of help to move across to the sofa. As he slid down under the covers, she held out the hot water bottle to him. 'This might feel good too.'

He took it from her. 'Are you a mind reader? Thank you so much. Like the cocoa, it reminds me of my childhood.'

She didn't comment when he added in a very low voice, 'And of happier days physically.'

She pointed to a small handbell on the low table beside the bed. 'If you need something, anything at all, don't hesitate to ring that. It'll be our pleasure to help you in any way we can. Sean and I will only be in the next room. We'll be sleeping there tonight to be within call. Luckily there are a couple of recliner chairs so we'll be perfectly comfortable.'

'Thank you. You're so kind. I doubt I'll be disturbing you, though.' He gave her a wry smile. 'I will admit to being rather tired.'

'Have you decided on a new name yet? It feels strange calling you 007.'

A roll of the eyes said what he thought of that choice. 'No, not yet. It isn't every day you get to choose a name and I never did like the one my parents gave me. Even they always shortened it.' He gave her a wry smile. 'I'm taking my time with the new one because I want it to last. I'll let you know what to call me tomorrow. I think I need to go online in the morning and look up names, if you have a computer handy. I want to find a common name that won't stand out like a sore thumb as different and yet one that I like the thought of living with.'

'I'm sure I saw a book of baby names in here when I was looking for something to read yesterday. Just a minute.' She walked across and found it on the second shelf she searched. 'There. You can look through it tomorrow morning.'

'Thank you. You seem to fulfil my needs before I even realise I've got them.'

She smiled. 'Well, then, here's my next prediction. I think what you need most at the moment is sleep.'

'Yes. But I hope there's no reason for you to keep waking me up every hour here as they did in the hospital?'

'No reason at all. But we'll maybe peep in at you once or twice from the doorway to check that you're still breathing softly and sweetly.'

He grinned then closed his eyes and his breathing began to slow down almost immediately, so she'd clearly guessed correctly what he needed most.

She lingered by the door to watch him sigh into sleep. He was obviously on painkillers still, which was probably what was slowing him down, but even so his personality shone through. He was incisive in the way he spoke and yet charming with it.

Why wasn't she attracted to him, then, the way she had been immediately to Sean? How strange human beings were about such things!

She'd better catch Ilsa first thing tomorrow and tell her what their other guest was like and might need. In the meantime, she was feeling rather sleepy again herself.

That made two new people staying here now, she thought as she blew a kiss to Sean, who was lying on the next chair, then snuggled down. Her friend Laura would probably have said her own convenient arrival was 'meant to be' to facilitate this reopening of the facility but Nina didn't believe that Fate with a capital F, as it sounded when spoken of by some people, had that sort of power over what happened to individuals.

She hadn't planned to live like this but the idea of helping people who'd been hurt serving their country pleased her and she already loved this old house.

In other words, she was *choosing* to take this path in life, not letting Fate impose it on her.

'You did well to think of offering him hot chocolate,' Sean told her as they snuggled down. 'I enjoyed it too.'

'Yes. He's settled into sleep already but I'm glad we'll be sleeping next door so that we'll be easily available if he needs help with anything.'

'And to keep him safe, if necessary. Don't forget there is an element of danger about this sort of encounter.'

'Well, to set your mind at rest, I'm not a helpless wimp. I've taken self-defence classes.'

'And have you had to use the tactics you learnt?'

'No. But I haven't forgotten what to do.'

'Well, we're probably not going to be in a lot of danger here because they've been extremely careful how they brought him to us. And it's my bet that he'll sleep right through the night.'

Indeed, their guest slept so soundly that when first Nina and then later Sean crept in to check that he was OK, the covers were so neat there was no sign that he'd even stirred.

The two of them didn't sleep nearly as well and even chatted from time to time.

At one point, Sean said, 'I'm not surprised he's sleeping so soundly. My memories of my one and only stay in hospital include the sheer frustration of being woken up every hour or so for them to check my pulse or something else I didn't care about because all I wanted to do was sleep. He'll relish the peace of this place, I'm sure.'

She wriggled into a more comfortable position. 'So do

I. Now, let's try to get some sleep. I've left a note on the kitchen surface, in case Ilsa wakes up before we do and comes across from the servants' quarters to make a cup of tea.'

She yawned and tried to stay alert and plan carefully because there was going to be so much to do. 'We'll set Ilsa to work on the cottages tomorrow and then—'

'You can sort all that out tomorrow. Go to sleep now while you can, woman.'

She closed her eyes. They'd have to have another very serious talk tomorrow because they both needed to be on the same page about the situation and their role here, but he was right to stop her talking to him. They both needed to get some sleep so that they'd cope with whatever they encountered the following day.

She yawned and snuggled down more comfortably.

Chapter Thirteen

The sound of Ilsa coming into the kitchen the following morning made Nina jerk awake so she didn't let herself go back to sleep as she would have liked but got up and went next door to explain about their new guest. It was a good thing she had done because Ilsa hadn't even noticed the scruffy piece of paper with the message scribbled on it in pencil, which was lying right next to the sink now. It must have been blown along the surface when the door opened and shut.

Ilsa listened and nodded, then got out some teabags. 'Want a cup?'

Nina hesitated. She still felt so sleepy. Sean had joined them and was standing in the doorway looking bone weary.

Ilsa made a little tutting sound. 'Why don't you two get a few more hours of proper sleep? I did a first aid course in the army so you can trust this guy to my care for a while.'

Sean yawned hugely. 'You sure?'

'Of course I am.' She gave him a mock salute.

He returned it with a smile. 'Then I accept. It was a very disturbed night and I would welcome some more rest.' He tugged Nina towards the stairs. 'You need it too. Come on. *Carpe diem*. Or *carpe* Ilsa's offer, at least.'

She hesitated then started moving, tossing over her shoulder, 'We won't get undressed so don't hesitate to come and wake us up again if there are any problems. We'll be in the two bedrooms to the right at the top of the stairs.'

She reached for Sean's hand, feeling a little shy about taking the initiative with that but wanting to touch him. He smiled sideways at her and gave her hand a gentle squeeze.

Ilsa had followed them to the doorway and noticed this interaction. She was keeping an eye on her new acquaintances, as she always did with new people, getting to know their ways so that she could fit in. As she watched them go upstairs, she smiled. Newly in love, she'd guess. She did a lot of people watching because knowing who was around and what they were doing helped keep you safe.

As the two disappeared from sight at the top of the stairs, she went back to check on the injured man and stood in the doorway of the library trying not to make a noise as she watched in case he was asleep. But he wasn't, though he didn't seem fully awake either.

He was moving about in the bed as if trying to sit up and she heard him curse under his breath when he had difficulty doing that. It was probably painful even trying from the angle at which he was lying. He looked to have wriggled too far down in the narrow sofa and the blanket was twisted across and then under him, so she went over to help pull it away.

He jumped in surprise when he first caught sight of her, looking so wary that she stood still and let him study her, then said quietly, 'Nina and Sean are both catching up on their sleep and I'm keeping an eye on you for them. My name's Ilsa. Let me help you to sit up properly.'

'Thanks. I thought I could manage it on my own, but I was tangled up in that stupid cover and didn't want to knock my few remaining stitches.'

'Very sensible.'

'I'm not stupid about my injuries, but I usually heal quickly and I'm trying to get back to moving around normally now.'

'They're just being careful with you at first, which is reasonable, don't you think? Humour them a little and move about slowly and carefully at first, then they'll worry less.'

'Yeah. I suppose so.'

She helped him ease up into a sitting position, sorted out the cover then put a pillow behind him for support.

He leant against it, looking more comfortable already. 'Ah, that's better. Thank you.' Then he sat forward again and added, 'Or it will be when I get back. Look, I desperately need to use the facilities.'

'There's a small cloakroom down here.'

And there was a tiny shower room in her new quarters, thank goodness, but she'd rather not share that with him or anyone else. It was so lovely to have a place of her own again.

'Where exactly?'

'Through that door. But I don't think you should risk walking around alone till you're moving more easily and know the premises.'

He glared at her. 'I'm damned well going on my own. I'm *not* a helpless invalid any longer.'

Goodness, he was touchy. She didn't let herself respond to his sharp tone but said quietly, 'I'm only trying to help.'

'Well, I'll ask for help if I need it.'

'Very well. Point noted. But you still look rather wobbly to me.'

'I won't be if I take it slowly. I need to practise walking around normally again to get rid of the instability.'

She wasn't giving in. 'And until you can walk steadily, I'll continue to stay nearby and keep an eye on you, whether you like it or not.'

There was silence then he studied her, head on one side. 'What's your name again? I'm afraid I can't remember it.'

'Ilsa.'

'Oh, yes!'

'I'm new here too.'

'What's your job?'

'I only arrived here yesterday, so it's a bit vague what I'll be doing. Anything they need me to do, as far as I'm concerned, they've been so kind. And what they need from me at the moment is to keep an eye on you while they catch up on some much-needed sleep. Your arrival here gave them a very disturbed night.'

'I shan't need that sort of help for long. What will you be doing here then?'

She shrugged. 'Who knows? The bottom line is I'm

going to live in the old servants' quarters and act as a caretaker-cum-general factotum helping them modernise the house and the cottages.'

'Well, that sounds better than the job the people who've been looking after me recently were talking about giving me when I get better. I told them straight I wouldn't put up with being kept in a stuffy old office staring at computers all day. No way.'

The poor man seemed to be fizzing with annoyance at the whole world. It was understandable if he was usually an active sort. She watched carefully, however, as he took a step forward, let go of the chair back and nodded as if he was pleased with how that felt.

He gave her a triumphant look. 'There you are, Ilsa. I feel less dizzy now, so I'm going to start moving across to the cloakroom *on my own*.'

He did that, walking slowly and trying to hide it when he wavered a little with what she guessed were moments of dizziness if he turned his head too abruptly. She managed not to rush to help him when he had to grab the edge of a small table to steady himself before taking another slow step or two.

He scowled at her after that incident as if daring her to comment but all she said was, 'Just continue to take it slowly, eh?'

As she finished speaking, he set off again, but moved too suddenly and wobbled more than before. She was so close she automatically put an arm round his shoulders to steady him. He stiffened and tried to pull away from her but she didn't let him. She was nearly as tall as he was so they were just about eye to eye, staring at one another.

'Thanks, Ilsa. But as I said, I'd very much prefer to manage on my own.'

'Don't be so prickly! We all need help at times.' She saw him breathe deeply to control his annoyance and wondered what to do for the best. She didn't want him falling, whatever it took to make him be sensible about this.

She felt him relax a little relax and they smiled at one another. 'I do appreciate your attempts to assist me but I've had more help forced on me than I've wanted in the past week or two, so I'd be truly grateful if you'd just leave me to get across the hall under my own steam. It should all be smooth going and—' He stared ahead, muttered something that sounded like a curse and said, 'Oh, damn! I might need a bit of help here, after all. That rug I have to walk across is badly wrinkled and one corner's caught against the leg of that little hall table. I'm not stupid enough to risk tripping on it, so if you could straighten it and then walk next to me, I'll put my hand on your shoulder as we cross.'

She didn't comment on him admitting he needed her help but went ahead to straighten the rug then came back and walked slowly across the hall beside him, feeling the warmth of his hand on her shoulder. It seemed to be enough to keep him steady, thank goodness.

It felt nice having him touch her. She didn't often get so close to other human beings.

After they stopped at the door of the tiny cloakroom, she moved away from him to open it.

'You're not coming in with me,' he said sharply.

'Of course not. You're a big boy now and anyway there isn't room for two of us inside, so I doubt there would be room enough for you to fall if you tried. But I am going to wait here for you just in case anything goes wrong, and then when you've finished I'll escort you back. Please don't lock the door. I promise faithfully not to come in unless you shout for help.'

'Isn't going to happen.'

'However, just in case—'

'Oh, all right. I won't lock it.' He moved slowly into the cloakroom and closed the door, trailing a muttered, 'Thanks!'

Wow, he was so touchy! She smiled. She could see his point of view and sympathise, still remembered how she'd hated having to be helped when she'd broken her leg. Besides, no normal person liked to be dependent on others for actions like using the toilet facilities.

And to make matters worse, he appeared to be in pain whenever he moved, even though he tried hard to hide that. Constant pain was enough to make anyone grumpy.

It was a few minutes before he opened the cloakroom door, but she could hear occasional faint sounds of movement, a toilet flushing and water running. And there were no sudden clatters or thumps of a body falling, thank goodness.

She passed the time by studying the hall and stairs. This was such a lovely period house. *Imagine growing up in a place like this.* It'd sure beat the orphanages and foster homes that she'd been shifted in and out of, not through any misbehaviour of her own, just a creaking, overloaded system making adjustments as best it could to house more and more children.

She spun round as she heard the cloakroom door open, studying his face, but he looked fine, thank goodness, and much more relaxed. 'Did you enjoy your peace and quiet?'

'Very much, thank you.' His voice sounded a lot calmer. 'I'm grateful to you for letting me take my time.'

'You're welcome. We all like a little privacy at such moments.' She could feel the tension between them ease a bit but when they got back to the library she could see that even this brief period of activity had tired him physically. He did look happier, though, and to her relief he seemed less dizzy now and mostly managed to move around steadily and he even sat down without her help.

He made no attempt to lie down again, however, and since she was hungry and thirsty herself, she wondered when he'd last had anything to eat or drink. 'Want some breakfast?'

'Not yet, thanks for the offer, but I'm rather thirsty so I could do with a drink of water if you don't mind.'

She fetched him one and said firmly, 'I'm going to stand next to you as you drink and take it from you when you've had enough, so don't tell me to move away. You don't want to spill what's left all over your covers, do you?'

'No, I don't. Fair enough. *If* there's anything left.'

He finished it all and grinned triumphantly as he held the empty glass out to her. 'That's better!' He gave her a calculating look as she took it from him and she guessed correctly what he was going to ask.

'A cup of tea or coffee would be wonderful now, if you don't mind making me one. Milk, no sugar. I'm not hungry yet, though. In another half hour I may be. That's my usual pattern for breakfast, anyway, coffee then eating something a little later.'

'Fine. I'll remember. Please don't try to get up and move

around while I'm making the coffee, though.'

'As I said before, I'm not stupid. I'll even admit to being physically tired now but I've started the next phase of my rehabilitation, walking on my own, so I feel good about that.'

She went into the kitchen, smiling at his stubbornness, and when she peeped into the other room while waiting for the kettle to boil, he was flicking through the book of baby names she'd placed on the side table. She saw him stop suddenly, mouth 'Aha!' then put the book down again. He must have found a name he liked. She turned back to attend to the kettle, wondering that was.

When she went back with a mug of instant coffee, he was staring into space, looking so alone and sad she asked gently as she gave him his mug, 'Want some company for a while? I've got a coffee waiting for me in the kitchen and there's no one else up yet. It seems silly for each of us to sit alone in adjoining rooms as if we can't stand the sight of one another. I could bring my coffee in here. Only if you want some company, though. And I promise faithfully not to talk your head off.'

'It'd be good to have some company and I'll even promise not to snap at you.' He gave her a rueful look.

She supposed it was as near to an apology as she'd get from him, so nodded and left the room.

When she went back, she took a packet of biscuits and two small plates on a scruffy little tray, together with her own coffee. 'Elegant service, my speciality!' she said as she used one knee to push the low table closer to him. She put the tray down on it, then flourished a bow. 'Milord is served.'

That made him smile, which she felt was a minor triumph.

He waited till she was sitting down to speak again. 'I've had too much thinking time and only myself to think about lately. How about you give me something else to focus on and tell me what brought you here to Lavender Lane and what you were doing before? You're clearly not needing to convalesce. I'm not just being nosy for no reason. I prefer to get to know the people I'm living and working with.'

'All right, but I've not been doing anything specially interesting. I was working in a shop, a ladies' dress shop, because that was the only job I could get round here, not because I'm fascinated by clothes, as you can probably tell at a glance.' She grimaced at the memory, then glanced at him, not sure whether to continue.

'Go on.'

'Before that I was in the army but when my time was up, I came out for a while. I felt I needed to try civilian life for the first time as an adult. I don't have any family, you see, so I felt very . . . isolated.'

'You would have done. What happened to your family?'

'I have no idea. I got shouted at for trying to find out when I was in foster care and told that things get lost and I should be glad to be alive with enough to eat and drink.'

'That was a rather unkind way to treat a child.'

'Yes. And sadly I found civilian life pretty lonely and decided after a few weeks that I preferred to re-enlist.'

He stared at her. 'If you really were in the army, why aren't you still in it, then? They usually find other jobs for people who get injured.'

'Sod's law. I'd booked a short winter holiday because

I'd always fancied having a go at skiing, so I went on that before I signed up again. I was involved in a skiing accident the very first day, caused by a careless fool who'd drunk too much.'

She drew in a breath, feeling the anguish all over again. 'I couldn't re-join after I'd recovered because I'd broken my left leg quite badly and could no longer pass the medical.' She stared down at the offending limb. 'It's now slightly weaker than the other, you see, and always will be.'

'You don't limp. I can imagine you in uniform. You look very upright and capable.'

She studied him, head on one side, grinning. 'Thanks. Well, I think that's a compliment but I'm not sure I dare believe you could offer one on purpose. I had you pegged as Mr Grumpy. Maybe the compliment slipped out by mistake.'

He gave her a genuine smile in return this time and clasped one hand to his chest. 'No, no! I said it on purpose.'

'I'll accept it with thanks, then.' She sketched a mock bow in return.

It seemed to dawn on him then that she'd been teasing all along and he relaxed visibly. 'OK. You got me going there. I owe you one.'

When he'd finished his coffee, he let her take his mug and then slid down in bed again. 'Thanks, Ilsa. For the company and for putting up with my grumpiness, as well as making me refreshments. The biscuits were enough food for the time being. I need to lie down, but I'm not quite ready for sleep yet, so please don't go because I'm enjoying your company. Unless there's something you have to do, of course, or you can't stand the sight of me any longer.'

'I'm fine to stay till the others get up if you want me to, because they asked me to keep an eye on you. Incidentally, you haven't told me your new name. Have you chosen one yet?'

'I think I have so you can be the first to know it. But only if you'll give me your honest opinion.'

'It must feel strange to have to choose one.'

'Yes. I'm going to be Ned. I always did like that name.'

'Short for Edward?'

'No. Just plain Ned. And how about Langley for a surname?'

'I like Ned very much and that surname sounds OK with it, but people will think it strange if it's not short for Edward.'

He frowned. 'Hmm. You're probably right. I don't want anything about it to seem strange or unusual, so short for Edward it'll have to be, then.'

'Shall you miss your own name?'

He shook his head. 'No. It was always too fancy for my taste. Other kids teased me mercilessly about it.'

'Kids can be like that. Some of the ones at school mocked me for having no family.'

'That must have hurt.'

'I could do nothing about it so I ignored their stupidity.' She shrugged and turned the conversation away from herself. 'I suppose you can't tell me anything about why you need to do all this?'

'No, sorry. I definitely can't. What got me injured is still top secret.'

She'd been keeping an eye on him and could tell that he was tiring rapidly now. 'Well, I've enjoyed our chat but

I think you should try to sleep again, Ned. You said you weren't feeling drowsy but you're starting to look tired again now so having another nap will probably help you get better faster in the long run.'

'I suppose you're right but I'm fed up of sleeping so much of my life away. Trouble is, the drowsiness sneaks up on you and grabs you, if you don't give in to it voluntarily, so sleep wins, however hard you try to stay awake. See you later.' He was already snuggling down.

She watched him for a few moments but he was soon fast asleep, so she went back into the kitchen and started to think about food. She was famished now. Scrambled eggs on toast, she decided. Quick and easy to make for one person, but nice and filling.

She started to get things out of the fridge and cupboards, keeping an ear open for movements in the next room.

She hadn't been expecting to help wounded people again. She had no formal medical qualifications, had just done a short army course because she didn't mind practical courses, only had trouble confronting pages of long words. Dyslexic, they called it. Mostly she managed to hide her problem.

After that she'd been a general assistant on the wards, organising the equipment needed and dealing with all the paperwork and other non-medical details. She'd found the work interesting and rewarding, though the patients she'd dealt with hadn't usually been as attractive as this guy.

She stared across at him. He wasn't good looking in what she thought of as a pretty-boy way, which had never attracted her, but something about him was definitely appealing. For a start, he had a lovely smile when he wasn't scowling. He was pale and tired at the moment, though, poor thing, and she wondered how long he'd been in hospital. Longer than average, she'd guess. He must have been badly injured.

She made a soft tutting noise, annoyed at herself. It was no business of hers whether he was good looking or not. She was working here as a caretaker, and was determined to hold on to the job. And he was here only temporarily, presumably till he'd recovered enough to get about more easily.

It must have been a very serious incident, though, and not just physically. Fancy having to change your name and not say a word about how it had all happened. She wondered if that'd have meant him leaving close family behind – a wife or children even? She hoped not. That'd hurt more than any physical injury, even if it had to be done to save their lives.

At some future stage the authorities would probably whisk him away from here as suddenly as he'd arrived, which was another very good reason for keeping her distance from him, attractive or not. And since she had to establish a new way of making a living for herself, she should avoid showing any interest in a guy till she was more settled in a new life.

She had no clear idea yet what the exact details of her job would be here at Lavender Lane but she could put up with being bored or whatever was necessary, as she had in the dress shop.

She hoped this job would last for a year or two at least because she hated to feel insecure financially and was very keen to save some money. That would be so much easier to do when accommodation was provided as it was here. Besides, she liked the people she was now working for, and they treated her like an equal. That made a big difference.

Just as she was about to light the gas and start cooking, she heard someone running down the stairs and Nina came into the kitchen, smiling at her.

'Feeling better now?'

'Yes, thanks to you taking over, Ilsa, and letting me rest. That was much appreciated. How is he?'

'A bit better, I think. He woke up for a while and has just gone back to sleep. Can I get you something to eat?'

'Yes, please. I'm ravenous. I'll have whatever you're having.'

She stayed to eat with Ilsa and they had another of those pleasant little chats. She was already hoping this job would last for a while.

Chapter Fourteen

Sean woke feeling refreshed and extremely hungry. He saw that the door of Nina's room was open and no one was lying in the mess of crumpled bedcovers so went straight down to the kitchen. A shower could wait till later.

He found Nina and Ilsa in the middle of eating scrambled eggs on toast with every sign of relish and the mere sight of the food on their plates made him feel ravenous.

'Any more eggs around?' he asked at once.

Nina smiled at him from the other side of the table. 'If you wait till I've finished this, I'll scramble you some, but if you want them more quickly, you'll have to do your own.'

'I can whip some up quickly,' Ilsa offered, starting to get up.

'You're in the middle of eating your own breakfast.

Stay where you are.'

'Well, there are some lovely fresh eggs in a box in the pantry.' She pointed towards a door at one side of the kitchen. 'In the meantime there's tea in the pot not long brewed. Pour yourself a mug while you're waiting. I used the big teapot so there should be plenty left still.'

'Good thinking. I will grab a drink but I'm absolutely desperate for food and am quite capable of scrambling eggs or even cooking a three-course meal for that matter.'

He was about to start work when their other guest came slowly in to join them and eased himself into a chair at the table.

They all gaped at Ned, sharing surprised looks because no one had expected him to be able to get up and move about on his own without help for another day or two.

He looked challengingly back at them from the chair. 'I need to start walking about. I had a little practice earlier, with Ilsa's help. This is my first go at doing it completely on my own. Little and often is the best way to go, don't you think?'

'As long as you don't overdo it,' Sean said. 'Are you hungry?'

'You know what? I think I am, for the first time in ages.'

Sean studied him and decided he wasn't going to faint on them. 'Then I'll make enough scrambled eggs for you and me both. I was just about to start cooking. Can I get you a mug of tea while you're waiting?'

'If it's not too much trouble.'

Sean poured them both a drink, then proceeded to prove that he could indeed cook and the two men were soon eating with every sign of relish.

'This is so good. It's a while since I've enjoyed any food.' The invalid beamed down at his completely empty plate. 'Thanks, Sean. That was great. Unfortunately I can't offer to help you clear up yet.'

'You're welcome. Have you had time to choose a name yet? No worries if you haven't but it makes it easier to include you in the conversations.'

'Yes, I have. What do you think of Ned? And Langley for a surname.'

They all murmured approval and Nina asked, 'No middle name?'

'Definitely not. Middle names are more trouble than they're worth and they give enemies a way of identifying you more easily.' He scowled into the distance as he said that, as if remembering something unpleasant.

When they'd finished breakfast, Sean helped clear up then studied the two women and took a unilateral decision to share the rest of the information about what they were involved in with Ilsa as well as Nina. He'd go over it from go to whoa just to make sure everything was clear. Ilsa didn't know anything more than the bare details officially but had, he was quite sure, worked a lot of the details on her own. Stupid she was not! It was one of the things he liked best about her.

And he felt their new employee deserved more than just a basic outline as he had been instructed. In fact, he was beginning to suspect that he'd fallen lucky to have her on his team because she too seemed very smart.

He studied her for a moment or two longer. He liked her steady, honest way of looking at the world and the bright intelligence in her eyes. He had a feeling she might come in very useful if there was trouble. A woman who'd been in the army should be able to look after herself better than most in difficult situations anyway.

He turned to Ned, who was looking rather tired now but hadn't yet shown any sign of wanting to go and lie down again. He didn't suggest Ned leave them either. The chap probably knew a lot of what was going to be revealed about this place after his own experiences, possibly even more than Sean himself did.

He took a deep breath and said, 'I think you all ought to know what's going on. If you feel you can contribute something else to the total picture, stop me and do that. As far as I'm concerned, we're all members of a team. First, I think we all understand that this work is very confidential indeed.'

Ilsa was the first to nod agreement.

He waited till they had all sat down in more comfort in the next room to say, 'I have a few things to tell you all about this place and to warn you about too. And this must stay in absolute confidence.'

He began by explaining the history of Lavender Lane, which had been used by the government as a sanctuary for many years, and prior to that the family living there had offered sanctuary to people in trouble as well. 'As far as the general public is concerned, this is a convalescent home and indeed it actually is mostly. But it can be more than that, if needs be. We're about to bring some pretend invalids here, some oldies who're happy to help. We've had to do that before actually.'

'How do you work out what lies you tell these people?'

'We use whatever story will fit the general situation at the time. In addition, we have historical records to refer to, showing what approaches have worked well before.' He smiled reminiscently. 'I once heard a very experienced older man say you can tell any lie you like and as long as you stick to it, there will be some people in the world who'll believe it. We seem to have been proving him right in our little corner of England for a good many years and saving the lives of some of our wounded heroes and heroines at the same time.'

He paused and let that sink in, then asked, 'How did they find you when you were out in the field, Ned? It can be useful to know what exactly has gone wrong.'

'Because of a weakness in the main system that a certain high-placed gentleman allegedly on our side insisted wasn't at all likely to affect the situation in the present circumstances. He declined to authorise the money needed to deal with it, on the grounds that it'd cost too much. He also accused me of being unrealistic when I mentioned it as a likely problem if it wasn't dealt with before I started and said he'd put other less expensive measures into place and I could trust in his experience.'

He looked angry as he added, 'When I got back, I suggested to the head of my department rather forcibly that precautions be reconsidered as a matter of urgency and he and his team backed me. I gather the gentleman in question has had a sudden desire to retire and the system has now been changed drastically.'

He continued to scowl as he added, 'No single person, however powerful, will be able to stop necessary steps being taken from now on.'

Ned glared down at his arm, which was still heavily bandaged, and muttered, almost as if talking to himself, 'I'm lucky to be alive, but I wish I could give him a taste of what it's like to be hunted and not know who to trust.'

Sean waited a minute or two for the furiously angry look to fade from his companion's face, then continued. 'We shall all have to be particularly watchful from now on till we're sure interest in this area has completely faded.'

'Are we watching for something or someone in particular?' Nina asked.

'Not exactly but we should always keep our eyes open for newcomers to the area who don't seem to fit in round here, people who don't join in socially perhaps or don't have recognisable sources of income. A few members of local families have been keeping watch on newcomers to the district on their own account for most of their lives, they care so much about their valley.'

'Do they know about how Lavender Lane is used?' Ned asked.

'One or two of them do and the descendants of these families have helped protect it for decades. When help has been needed they've stepped up to the mark and sometimes made a huge difference. You'll probably meet one or two of them at some stage because some of the oldies will be coming in here as convalescents.'

He paused to let that sink in, then waved one hand as if to indicate their immediate surroundings. 'We can summon up much tighter safety precautions here than normal if required. Developments in electronics have made that easier for our generation in some ways and harder in others. We're about to do a refit on all the systems here, another thing that a certain gentleman at head office slowed down implementation of.'

He turned to Nina. 'You're the first person for ages who isn't from one of the local families. But Laura was utterly convinced that you'd fit in well and I think you have done already.'

'Thank you for saying that, Sean. I'll try not to let you down.'

'I'm already quite sure you won't.' He paused for a moment, then changed the subject slightly. 'This is an interesting little town, a world of its own in some ways. How do you feel now about living here and owning a refuge like Lavender Lane, Nina?'

'Honoured.'

He nodded in what looked like satisfaction.

'My sons have shown me they have busy lives of their own so I know I can't rely on their company at this stage in their lives. I was feeling a bit lost as to what to do with myself before all this happened.' She waved one hand to indicate their surroundings.

She paused then said thoughtfully, 'It's not fashionable to say that you're patriotic but I am and I feel an affinity for Britain even though I've spent nearly all my life in Australia until now. The Commonwealth still means something to me, so I care about the work being done here at my new home. I may not be descended from the original family who owned this place, but I can still carry on their admirable traditions, can't I?'

He nodded and smiled approvingly at her, then turned to the other woman. 'And what about you, Ilsa? Does what goes on here put you off working with us?'

'On the contrary, it makes it sound far more interesting. I certainly didn't find working in a shop all that meaningful. I stayed there mainly because I love living in this valley and like everyone else, I need to earn a living. I'm beginning to think, no, I'm quite sure now, that I was clinically depressed for a time.' She gave Nina a very warm smile. 'Actually, I agree with you about one thing. I too like the thought that this new job has an underlying value to our country, something I was proud of about the work I did when I was in the army.'

'You must have been extremely upset when you couldn't re-enlist.'

'I was. Still am,' she added gruffly. 'I'm not one for a sedentary life, either.'

'One of my grandfather's sayings was: if someone locks a door in your face, find a window and climb in through that,' said Sean.

Ilsa grinned and added, 'I wish I could have met him. He sounds to have been a wise person.'

'Yeah. I was lucky to have had his guidance as a youngster. But think about the future this way now: you may be able to care about and contribute enough to what we're doing here to stay on at Lavender Lane in a more permanent capacity. When we find a capable person like you we tend to grab them, bring them into the team and look after them.'

The glowing look Ilsa gave him at that compliment, and her over-bright eyes didn't need words to say how much what he'd said meant to her.

It was Nina who asked, 'What do you mean by saying

you grab them?'

'We do whatever is needed to keep them happy to stay with us, so that we can have the benefit of their skills. Training can be made available if needed, and indeed it will be given priority if it can improve on skills useful to what we do in places like this.'

He didn't say it but there were one or two refuges tucked away in the countryside.

He waited, watching her carefully, then added, 'Or you could help us here for a while, Ilsa, do the work well, then we could give you references that would help you to get a job with a private security firm, for instance.'

She stared at him, open-mouthed. 'I hadn't even thought of that possibility. How stupid of me! Though I'd rather stay here. I'm quite sure of that already.'

'You've been in steady employment for most of your life, have faced big setbacks and still got here to join us without the help of a supportive family, so you can't be stupid in any way.'

She looked at him with tears now welling out of her eyes, trying and failing to blink them away. 'How kind you are, Sean, you and Nina both! You've been very tender with my feelings, too, even though you hardly know me.'

She frowned and stared into her memories for a few moments. 'I think part of the reason I've been narrow in my views is because of the limited experiences I had from when I went into care as a child. The people responsible for us focused on physical care, and I can't fault them for that, but not so much on the mental and emotional development of us children – at least that's how it worked in my time and I can understand that now when I look back.'

'You're quite a perceptive person,' Nina said.

'I've been driven inwards by my life. I didn't see much of the normal world locally, let alone life further afield. Nor did I get the chance to try a wider range of activities than were available at the schools I attended. You needed extra money to go on trips and to add extra lessons like special coaching in sports.'

She sighed and added, 'The activities on offer seemed to be so different each time I was moved to a new school, that I was mostly behind the others in coping with their world.'

'Must have been difficult,' Nina said quietly.

'It was.'

'We all do our best with what life hands out to us,' Sean said. '*Your* own best is all you can guarantee. No one can ever achieve the best possible outcomes in every single situation they meet, so one of the prime pieces of advice I'd give you, and others, is don't expect miracles of yourself, just do your very best. And actually you seem to me to have done pretty well so I shall look forward to working with you and extending your skills.'

Ilsa's voice was husky and she had to swallow hard before she spoke. 'Thank you, Sean.'

He nodded, understanding her feelings. No one should go through life without praise for effort as well for real achievements. Like some of the other people he'd met over the years, Ilsa seemed to him to resemble a thirsty plant that had not been offered enough water to produce its best blooms. And it always made him feel good to mentor people who were so avid to learn generally as well as to succeed here and there in the wider world.

He knew he wouldn't be allowed to work in the field again himself should he and Nina become formal partners or even get married, as he hoped might happen. And anyway, he'd been seriously considering retiring from too active a life before he got much older on the principle that he'd done a lot and should go while the going was good.

It occurred to him that he could work to prepare others for some aspects of the work that he was particularly good at and perhaps he could keep an eye on this place as part of his remit. With Nina. Both activities would be highly satisfying to him and to the organisation he was part of.

He realised they were all waiting for him to continue, so went on to discuss some aspects of the security systems here. The residential cottages would definitely need updating electronically as quickly as possible.

Nina sat staring into space and frowning, then after a while she took advantage of a pause in the conversation while they got themselves mugs of coffee to say, 'Whatever else we do, we need to buy a pile of groceries and have them delivered. There are no stores of any type of food here and not only do I have a distinctly healthy appetite, Sean, you have an even better one. We can't forget the practicalities of daily life.'

He looked at her ruefully. 'You're right.' Then he stared at the others. 'Anyone enjoy cooking regularly? Or even good at it?'

Nina shrugged. 'I enjoy cooking sometimes but not all the time. I'd never take a job as a cook.'

'I'm very average,' Ilsa said. 'I haven't had much practice at cooking for a group like a family.'

'I can cope if I have to,' Ned said.

Sean grinned. 'We'll check out takeaway places while we're out as well, then, though I'm a bit fussy about what some of them call food. I like to eat reasonably healthily.'

'I eat a lot of salads,' Ilsa said. 'Easy to put together and extremely healthy.'

'Barbecues aren't too difficult to manage once I'm better,' Ned offered.

Sean cut off the discussion about food. 'Well, we'll leave that for another time. Do you have any more questions or are we done here for the time being?'

'I don't have any questions,' Ilsa said. 'I need to check that the cottages are being properly cleaned.'

Ned sighed loudly. 'Unfortunately I'm feeling rather sleepy again.'

'I'll come and help you get settled, then,' Ilsa said at once. 'I bet you've left your bedcovers in a tangle again.'

Sean watched her stand with hands on hips and saw how Ned gave in to her quiet insistence and gradually let her take over. She was proving even more capable than he'd expected at dealing with people, not ordering Ned about but chivvying him gently and, from what Sean had seen so far, rather effectively as well.

The poor chap was looking tired but at the same time he was looking better in some ways, more relaxed perhaps to be out of a purely hospital environment. He certainly didn't have the white, washed-out look that sick people could sometimes show the world.

'Since we need food urgently, Nina and I will go into

town straight away. Will you two be all right here on your own?' Sean wasn't surprised when they responded with slightly surprised expressions and nods.

'Of course we will,' Ilsa said.

'I'll look after her,' Ned said with a grin.

Another good sign, that joking, Sean thought.

Once they were alone in the car, he waited to start it and asked Nina, 'What do you think of those two?'

'I think they're going to make good employees, or team members, or whatever you like to call them. And also they seem to get on quite well, so they might become genuinely good friends or even more.'

'Better friends than we're becoming?'

She flushed slightly. 'We agreed to take things slowly.'

He laid one hand on his heart and said, 'Am I not doing that?'

'No, not at this moment! You're pushing me.'

'I'm just teasing you and nudging you a little, that's all. And I'm enjoying doing it.'

The warm smile he gave her as he followed that by blowing her an elaborately flourishing kiss made her flush even though he didn't say anything else suggestive.

She took a deep breath and said, 'Stop that, Sean. I'm out of practice at flirting and we genuinely need to buy some food.'

'Be warned. I'm happy to form a friendship with you, but only as I wait to see whether a closer relationship will develop. And if I have any say in it, that will happen. I hope it's the same for you.'

'I'm a bit out of practice, but all right, I will admit

that I agree. But we shouldn't really think of ourselves so much while we're dealing with this problem.'

His smile faded. 'Unfortunately you're right. But afterwards?'

'Might be fun.' She imitated his action by blowing him a flourishing kiss like his own.

Chapter Fifteen

Sean drove into the town centre and used the satnav to find a car park near the supermarket. He looked at Nina. 'Where to first?'

'Let's walk round on foot and get to know the town centre a little better and after that we'll do our shopping at the supermarket, eh?'

'Fine by me. What do we need?'

'Everything. There was no food whatsoever in the house after it had stood empty for a couple of years, not even old tins of food, so someone must have cleared it all out. We bought some stuff yesterday to tide us over but that's just about used up now. We really do need to buy everything, not just fresh food but standard kitchen staples like flour and stock cubes. I vote to get the mammoth shopping job over and done with in one fell swoop and have nearly all of it delivered.'

'Good idea.'

Once they had nearly completed a circuit of the central shopping district, they slowed down in a more open area to stare round again.

'It's rather an old-fashioned little town, isn't it?' she commented. 'There's only really Larch Tree Lane that's big enough to call a main road and even that comes to a dead end at the top of the hill.'

'Some people might say being old-fashioned is part of its charm and I'd be one of them. I don't like most modern buildings and I loathe tower blocks. Most of them look like children's building blocks piled on top of one another, some of them higgledy-piggledy or in garish colours that make them look even worse.' He looked to one side and said, 'Ah! Isn't that little side street where Ilsa's former employer's dress shop is located?'

'Yes, that's it. Let's go and take a closer look.'

The street was only about fifty yards long, so they were soon standing in front of the shop with its two big windows.

'Hmm.' Nina studied the one marked *BIG SALE* and pulled a face. 'Well, they might be offering these clothes at low prices to get rid of them, but they'd still not tempt me. They're such horrid, old-fashioned styles and badly arranged too!'

She grimaced and studied the shop again. 'In fact, that window looks extremely amateur to me. They should have continued to employ one of the assistants for a while longer to arrange the sale items in the front window for them. Ilsa would have been an asset there, I'm sure.'

'But if they'd kept her on, we'd not have gained her services and she's already shown herself to be a really hard worker and an excellent organiser too. I definitely prefer to have her as our asset.'

She started walking again. 'OK. Let's get started. I bet as Ned gets better, he'll eat us out of house and home. He looks like the sort of guy who eats heartily and never puts on weight. And you're not a bad trencherman either.'

Sean stopped and pressed one hand to his chest. 'Me? I have the appetite of a bird.'

'Yes. A hungry vulture.'

He laughed, took her hand and they strolled back to the supermarket, where they bought not only enough food and supplies to fill two trolleys, but as an afterthought a dozen bottles of wine and a pack of beer, leaving most of their purchases to be delivered.

When they got into the car and he started driving home, he said quietly, 'I've enjoyed this time with just us.'

She smiled at him. 'I'm enjoying your company too.' And they were off again, chatting happily about shared interests, finding out about one another as they had been doing since their first meeting.

He'd never found anyone as easy to chat to.

Nina was reminded of her early days of courting her husband.

Could she be this lucky again and meet another soulmate? She did hope so.

After Sean and Nina had left to do the shopping, Ilsa tidied up the kitchen then went to stand in the doorway of the room next door to see how Ned was. He looked so fed up, she said, 'How about a short stroll round the garden, a very short stroll?'

He brightened up at once. 'I'd love that. I've missed being outside.'

However, a few minutes of pottering around was enough and he had to lean against the wall as a sudden surge of dizziness made his head spin.

She was standing next to him and of course she noticed. 'You're feeling woozy again, aren't you? You've been standing and moving about for too long. You need to rest again.'

He rubbed his aching forehead. 'You're right. I am feeling exhausted again now, though it was lovely to move around for a while.' He hesitated then asked, 'Can you help me back into the library? I don't want to fall over and yes, I admit that I need to rest for a while now.'

'Of course you do. You're not Superman. I think you've done brilliantly just now, considering how weak you still are. Put one arm across my shoulders.'

He did that, joking, 'We're just the right height to walk together.' Then he hesitated. 'There's an old couch in the dining end of the kitchen. I'll rest on that, if I won't be in your way. I don't like being left out of things.'

'Why does that not surprise me?'

He accepted her help to ease down into a sitting position and, once there, he let out a groan of relief and leant back, but refused to lie down. 'I hope I'm never, ever this weak again, because it's been the most frustrating time of my whole life.'

'It must be. You're getting better, though. I can see slight improvements even since yesterday.'

'You can? Really?'

'Yes. I'd not lie to you, Ned.'

'It was touch and go at one time whether I'd recover,' he told her suddenly.

'I'm glad you did.'

'So am I.' He was surprised that he'd confided in her, but she was so easy to chat to.

She gave him one of her lovely smiles. 'I'll get you a drink of milk, shall I?'

'*Milk?*' he asked scornfully.

'Yes. I'm a big believer in milk for building up strength – milk and red meat, I reckon.'

He was studying her face and said suddenly, 'You're an incredible woman, Ilsa.'

'*What?*' She gaped at him. 'You must be the only person who's ever thought so.'

'I'm sure I'm not because you are. Didn't anyone try hard to persuade you to sign up to re-join the army?'

'Um, yes. My commanding officer did. In fact, she made quite a big fuss.'

'I'm not surprised. She'd not have bothered with an inefficient soldier.' He let that sink in then added, 'And don't think I haven't noticed how quickly and efficiently you organise anything you have to deal with – even where the everyday crockery goes in the kitchen here. I think you must have an innate sense of logic about that sort of thing.'

She went bright red. 'Oh. Well. Glad you think so. Things seem to work better in patterns, which always seems obvious to me but other people often don't figure them out.'

He smiled at her and nodded. 'I rest my case.'

She went across to the back door, muttering, 'I'll just

have a quick look outside. I want to make absolutely certain they haven't returned.'

She opened the door and vanished from sight. Then there was silence broken only by faint noises as she looked round outside. After that she came back and went across to the fridge, then one of the cupboards.

She came back to him with a glass of milk and some chocolate biscuits. 'There you are. I raided their supplies till they bring some food back.'

He had a weakness for chocolate and couldn't resist picking up one of the biscuits from the plate she'd set temptingly close. 'You're playing on my weaknesses.' He grumbled but it didn't stop him from eating two biscuits and enjoying them hugely. His sense of taste seemed to be returning as well as his ability to move about more steadily.

Once he'd finished, she picked up the plate and glass and moved across to put them in the sink.

He sighed and slid down till he was lying nearly flat on the sofa again, feeling desperately sleepy all of a sudden.

Ilsa didn't continue chatting, just sat quietly and smiled as she watched him try not to doze off, then succumb suddenly to sleep. This sofa was smaller than the one in the library but he could just manage to lie down on it. She stayed there resting quietly, keeping an eye on him and waiting for the others to return. Let him have a nap. He'd pushed himself hard for a man who should be convalescing and being pampered.

And she was due a little rest, too. She sat in an old armchair and leant back, wondering if this house was often a target for thieves and burglars. She and the others would have to keep a better watch on it from now on.

It seemed a long time till Sean and Nina came home, and brought in a couple of bags of food.

'The rest is being delivered later,' Sean said. 'Someone put the kettle on. I'd like a big mug of tea, the biggest one you've got, not one of those fiddly cups they serve it in at cafés.'

That woke Ned, who jerked upright, staring round warily for a moment or two, not seeming to quite know where he was.

Ilsa saw the moment he realised but she put one finger to her lips when he would have spoken.

Chapter Sixteen

After a few more minutes' silence, he said in his quiet way, 'If no one has any other suggestions or thoughts, we could all have a lazy time for the rest of the day and catch up with the newspapers.'

They did just that or simply watched the latest news on a rather old-fashioned TV in the casual sitting area attached to the kitchen.

They ate an evening meal together but as they were finishing, Sean said, 'Put your crockery on the draining board, but come back to the table because we need to talk about something else now.'

He waited till they were all seated again to start. 'I've been reading about some of the ways they've approached keeping up the appearance of a simple convalescent home here and I think we can get this house set up to support that quite credibly without too much trouble.'

'Will it really do that, do you think, Sean?' Ilsa asked.

'It has done before. We've never tried to hide the fact that we have a convalescent home here, just concealed the special people for whom it's also been set up. Some of them need a longer convalescence and must hide here for a while. They're usually fairly safe because of the fact that others use Lavender Lane openly.'

He paused again, glad to see how carefully they were listening. 'We work on the principle that the more people who're here, the harder it is for anyone pursuing our special invalid to figure out whether we're doing anything other than looking after a few people who need to convalesce. Though, actually, I've got the beginning of a small idea that I might toss into the pot later for occasional use. I'll tell you more about this idea once I've worked out how best to implement it.'

He looked round and the others nodded slightly but no one seemed to want to make any comments at this stage, so he continued. 'Some of the people we bring in regularly are old friends and employees who live locally. They used to meet here every month for a drink or two and a social gathering away from their families. They've pretended in the past that their families are the ones who need a little respite since they care for them full-time for most of the year.'

'I know how to organise looking after ambulatory patients,' Ilsa said quietly. 'I did it for a while, dealt with the admin and practical equipment side of things I mean, not their medical treatment, obviously.'

'Good. That experience will be really useful here.'

There was silence as the others considered the situation, then Ned asked, 'Who are these special people

you're bringing in, Sean? And why do you trust them so
absolutely? I hope you don't mind my asking but I've
nearly been killed once and am still recovering from
the injuries I sustained then. Someone I'd trusted was
involved in betraying me and I definitely don't intend for
that to happen again if I can help it.'

'I haven't met these people personally yet,' Sean
admitted, 'but it was marked as proven in my briefing
notes that people from certain families in the town have
helped out several times during the past few decades and
proved their loyalty. When our side set up a convalescent
home that offered genuine respite care, and other secret
care, these people risked their lives on more than one
occasion to come here and act as patients.'

He waited for that to sink in before continuing.
'Unfortunately, that had to remain a secret and was
absolutely unofficial, so they couldn't be given the
medals they deserved. Various times locals have helped
in that way are mentioned in the diaries kept at the big
house, I gather.'

He looked at Ned. 'Since you're still not fully
recovered, you won't be available for action in setting
anything up, but perhaps you could read some of the
more recent diaries and see if we can learn anything
useful from them about how best to set about this? It'd
be a real help if you'd take that chore off my shoulders.
I'd not like to miss something helpful by being in a rush.'

He saw Ned brighten a little at being given a truly
useful task that was within his present reduced physical
capabilities, and gave him a quick smile before going
back to continue his original explanation to the group.

While doing that he couldn't miss the intent way Ilsa was watching Ned. She looked across and gave him a tiny nod as if to show approval. How had a woman as intelligent and sensitive as this one had her skills overlooked? Why was she not already working at a higher than basic level? He set that aside for later detailed consideration but would bear it in mind as he continued to work on his present task.

He ended by telling them, 'I'm going to slip out after it gets dark and visit the people I mentioned. I have their phone numbers so I've let them know I'll be coming tonight. I'd rather go there to meet them in person and see their reactions as I ask whether any of them are able to help us once more. I'll also ask them to explain exactly how they did things last time. No need for us to reinvent the wheel, is there?'

'No need at all,' Ilsa was the first to agree.

'This is a very complicated situation, isn't it?' Nina looked at her companions one by one and they were clearly in agreement, still looking thoughtful.

'It is at the moment but once we've got things in place, Lavender Lane should be relatively easy to run, and we'll be able to offer genuine convalescent shelter to locals as well as to occasional special people. At the present time, however, I want to alert all of you to the urgent need there is for us to conceal the fact that Ned is staying here as one of our special guests.' He smiled at Ned. 'Obviously, we need to look after you until you've recovered properly and I think there are enough of us to do that OK.'

'I'm sure you will. What happened to me in the field

was a very rare glitch. We don't often encounter traitors. How about I shave my beard off now? I grew it to look different while I was on this project and anyway, I found it too much trouble to shave every day then. I kept it for the same reasons when I was so ill.'

'I was going to suggest that.'

'I'll do it for him,' Ilsa volunteered. 'It still needs care taking in the area near the lower facial scar.'

'Yes, you do that. But nothing will happen to anyone who comes to recover here when I'm on watch, except over my dead body, whether it's you being targeted or anyone else, Ned.'

Sean looked very fierce as he let that sink in, then he relaxed a little and glanced at his watch. 'Right, then. If you've no more questions, I'll go and visit our local contacts next.'

He was gone so quickly, he left them sitting in frowning silence for a few moments as they mulled over the situation.

'I wish he hadn't left so quickly. I'd have liked to ask him a couple more questions,' Nina said.

Ilsa nodded agreement. 'So would I now that I've had time for the idea of the hidden use of this place to sink in. But since it's only eight o'clock I think I'll go and make a start on cleaning the first cottage. I'm not ready for bed yet.'

'No, don't even think of doing that,' Nina said quickly. 'None of us should do anything away from this house and especially not on our own at the moment. Cleaning would involve moving around the grounds in the dark as you go in and out of the empty house and cottages.'

'I'm quite good at taking care of myself,' Ilsa said quietly.

'No. You'd be too vulnerable. We'll be able to move around more freely once we've got other people we trust staying in some of the cottages. I think it's good that Sean has people he can bring in.'

She didn't know how she was so sure they should stay together, since she didn't have any experience of such dangerous situations. She decided she was going to follow her instincts, which didn't usually lead her astray.

Ilsa sighed. 'Yes. I suppose you're right. But I shan't be able to settle till Sean comes back safely.' She looked at the other woman. 'He'll tell us the details of what he arranges, won't he? I hate being kept in the dark about details till the last minute when I'm involved in something, especially when I might have to make arrangements for those very details.'

'I certainly hope he will because I too want to find out what to expect and I'll be happy to do my bit to help. And Laura must have thought I could cope or she'd not have left this place to me.' Nina looked round the kitchen area and added, 'I was so lucky to inherit. I fell in love with this place on sight.'

'Who wouldn't?' Ned said. 'It has such a welcoming feel to it.'

'I'm glad you think so.'

It was a moment or two before Nina said anything else. 'While we're waiting, you and I could finish cleaning out the other cupboards in here, Ilsa, especially the higher ones that are hard to reach. We'll need to remove two years of dust and possibly a few mice droppings or worse.' She grimaced at the thought of that.

'I'm happy to clean all those cupboards for you. I like to keep busy.'

'No, we'll both do it. I prefer to share both the pleasant and the unpleasant jobs. That's only fair.'

They both turned to study Ned, then Ilsa said firmly, 'You need to take another nap before you read those diaries, Ned. You're looking drowsy again.'

He scowled at them but she ignored that. 'Leave looking after him to me, Nina. I'll help him get ready for a rest.' She grinned. 'And at the moment, I'm the stronger one.'

'I'm not a child to be put down for naps!' he snapped.

'Then stop behaving like one. You know sleep will help you get better more quickly than anything else at this stage.'

'Well, I'm fed up to the teeth of sleeping. It feels as though I'm wasting my life.'

Her voice became soothing. 'I know. But you're convalescent now, not ill. And the good news is that your tetchiness proves to me that you're definitely getting better. Only, we need you to recover as quickly as possible, so please put up with the naps and give in when you need one. You're not drowsing off for long, are you?'

It was his turn to stare. 'How did you know I was feeling sleepy, Ilsa? I thought I'd hidden it.'

She looked at him in surprise. Now he'd mentioned it she too wondered how she'd felt so certain, why she seemed to be so attuned to his body and its needs. 'I

could just tell, somehow. Come on. Let's get you settled.'
She held out her arm.

After another scowl, he took it with obvious
reluctance. 'This is only to help me keep my balance,' he
said as they started moving. A minute later he stopped to
ask, 'You'll wake me if I'm still asleep when Sean comes
back? I'm part of this.'

'Yes, of course I will.'

'Promise.'

'I promise faithfully,' she said loudly and emphatically,
crossing her heart in a mock gesture. Then she chivvied him
into visiting the cloakroom before lying down again. She
even tucked him in and planted a quick kiss on his cheek,
saying with a teasing smile, 'Be a good boy for Mummy.'

He grabbed her wrist and said in a low growl of a
voice, 'Just wait till I've got my former energy back. You
won't know what's hit you, Ilsa Platt. And I definitely
won't be calling you Mummy!'

The look in his eyes sent a shiver down her spine,
though she tried to hide her reaction. But when she
rejoined the other woman in the kitchen, Nina grinned
at her. 'From the way he looks at you, he really likes
you.'

'Funny way of showing it, getting all grumpy on me.'

'What's more, I think you like him too.'

Ilsa shrugged and began to rattle pans rather loudly
about as she rearranged them in a cupboard next to the
cooker.

Nina didn't continue that conversation but she was still
smiling as she went across to start clearing out one of the
big cupboards. It was so nice to see the potential between

those two, something positive and normal brightening.

Like Ilsa, she was eager to see exactly what Sean had arranged and hear his new idea so found it difficult to settle down to work. She kept pausing in the cleaning to listen for his car coming back.

It seemed a long time till she heard it.

Chapter Seventeen

Sean had to use his satnav to find out how to get to where Arthur Keevil lived, so thank goodness for its help.

When he knocked on the door of what he and the satnav both agreed was the correct house it was opened by a woman of his own age, perhaps a little younger.

He introduced himself and mentioned the phone call, repeating that he needed to see Arthur Keevil.

'Oh yes. You phoned a short time ago. Gramps and Mum are in the sitting room.'

'I need to speak to your grandad privately. This is *rather important business.*' That was a sort of password mentioned in the notes and she clearly recognised it as such.

'Ah. Come in, then.' She held the door open, yelling, 'Gramps, it's for you. Shall I bring your visitor through? He says it's *rather important business.*'

'Yes, please, love.'

When Sean followed her into the sitting room, an old guy looked up from a big sofa he was sharing with a younger woman and studied him carefully before smiling and gesturing to a chair. 'Come in and sit down, lad. How can I help you? You didn't mention specifics on the phone.'

It was a long time since anyone had called him 'lad'. Sean gave him the required second phrase, glanced at the woman sitting next to him and said, 'Perhaps you and I should speak privately about this, Mr Keevil?'

'No need. My daughter is fully involved in all this sort of activity and, in fact, Jane will be taking over my role when I drop off my perch.'

His daughter made a tutting noise at this last phrase and shook her forefinger warningly at him, but he only grinned at her. '*Anno domini* comes to us all, love. Face it.'

'No, thank you. And I'd rather you didn't, either.'

So Sean explained to them both that he and Nina were in the process of making the convalescent facility fully operative again. 'So we need to make Lavender Lane look like a genuine convalescent home as quickly as possible, maybe put in a couple of so-called patients till we get some real ones. It's apparently been done before in order to protect someone. The thing is, the next special patient is due to arrive soon.'

The old man's triumphant smile at his daughter made him suddenly appear like a lively young lad to whom nature had given a wrinkled face and silver hair in error.

'I like to make myself useful,' he said cheerfully. 'And isn't that good timing, Jane lass? You might have tried to hide it from me but you and your two lasses really would like to go to your cousin's wedding and now we've found a place that'll look after my physical needs while you all do that.'

'I still don't like to leave you, Dad. If trouble's brewing I'd rather be within reach.'

'Get away with you! I'll be well looked after at the Lane.' He turned back to Sean. 'Will you be taking Ben Thorson to stay there as well?'

'I hope so. He's next on my list to ask and he used to be part of your monthly meet-up group, didn't he?'

'He did indeed. So there you are, my girl. I'll even have some pleasant company for the whole time I'm there. Did you say you were called Sean, lad?'

'Yes.'

'We were told someone with that name would be getting involved.' He chuckled at his visitor's look of surprise. 'Oh, we still keep an eye on our little valley and we have our own connections with the authorities.'

Knowing the calibre of the people involved, Sean wasn't surprised by this.

'Good. We all keep our eyes open, just like folk did in the old days. And things would be better if neighbours still looked after one another. Ben's great-grandson has a couple of his friends who keep watch with him sometimes. He's a very capable young chap, Norry is, and has some equally clever friends.' He chuckled. 'The two youngsters who're currently helping him are a lad and lass, who can look as if they're having a cuddle or two if they want to stop and observe something. I sometimes think they're not watching anything, just making an excuse for a bit of cuddling. And who's to blame them? You're only young once, aren't you?'

Jane gave Sean a very direct look. 'You'll keep a careful eye on Pop, then, while he's staying with you? And protect him in any way necessary?'

'With my life, if I have to. You have my word. Our country is already deeply indebted to you, Arthur.'

The old man flushed and waved one hand in a dismissive gesture. 'No need to waste any young lives on me, lad. I'm old enough to be at the tail end of my life whatever either of us does. However, this discussion has decided a little dilemma I've been having: whether to bring my little automatic friend with me this time as I did on my last special outing a few years ago. Can't be too careful, can we?'

'Dad! I thought you'd got rid of that gun years ago!' Jane glanced uncomfortably at Sean. 'It's not licensed. It's the one his father brought home from the Second World War.'

Arthur's voice was as calm as ever. 'No use a chap in my situation having a gun unless it's available to use when genuine danger threatens.'

Sean couldn't prevent a quick smile. 'I didn't hear you say that, and make sure you keep it hidden while you're with us so that I shan't actually *see* anything.'

The smile had vanished suddenly from Arthur's face. 'It'll stay hidden unless I need to use it, and my judgement will be as good as yours about whether that's necessary. I'm sure I'll still be a good shot. I think you're right to call me and Ben in. We'll be able to have one of our little gatherings again, and we'll all enjoy that.' He looked thoughtful for a moment then added, 'And it wouldn't hurt to invite Prue Gillings to have a little stay there with us, either. She's good to have around if there's trouble and if there isn't any, she's fun to be with.'

Sean looked at them both and saw that Jane was still looking at her father anxiously. 'Be reassured, Ms Keevil, that although none of us like guns, my colleagues and I will be equipped to protect your father and his friends in any way needed.'

'Or we'll protect you. So there you are, then, love.' Arthur smiled gently, looking perfectly comfortable and happy in spite of the seriousness of what they might or might not be facing. 'But we've had more success with simple solutions.'

'Now,' Arthur said complacently. 'When do you want me to move in and set up a smokescreen, lad?'

'I thought an ambulance might be sent tomorrow afternoon to bring you to Lavender Lane. We're still getting the place cleaned and ready for use again.'

'Good idea to send an ambulance. That way the whole town will know about me going there for a short stay and if we have any unwanted visitors, they won't need to poke around too much to find out.'

'I doubt there will be any. But we're taking precautions just in case.'

'Always best to be prepared. How about the doctor comes to see me an' Jane tomorrow morning then recommends I come for a short stay with you to give her a respite from caring for me.'

His cheerful expression faded for a moment as he muttered, 'Actually, it won't hurt for her to have a break and a bit of fun at that wedding. However hard you try to keep as fit and well as possible, old age can make you dependent on others in some ways, so my lass really does deserve a break.'

Jane reached out to squeeze his hand. 'I'm happy to look after you, Dad. You know I am. You're good company and I truly admire what you've done with your life.'

Sean gave the old man a moment or two to get over his upset feelings at needing help in his daily life.

When Arthur looked calmer, Sean said, 'We'll send the doctor to call before we bring you in. Good idea to say it's your daughter who needs a rest.'

Arthur took a few deep breaths and relaxed a little, then gave a sudden wry smile as he added, 'Whatever else, it'll be fun seeing the others. And since we're all restricted to one or at most two glasses of wine, you make sure you get some really good stuff in.'

Fun! And he really meant it. Sean looked at them, trying not to show how amazing he thought both Arthur and his daughter were. Who'd have believed that such ordinary-looking people as this man in his late eighties and a gentle-looking and rather dowdy woman in her sixties could be genuine heroes who had saved lives in their time and were still serving their country in minor ways?

'I'll go and call on Ben now, and then your friend Prue, if you'll kindly give me her address and phone her to let her know I'm coming.'

Armed with that information, he let the satnav guide him to another cottage a short distance away and held a similar conversation with Ben Thorson, who was even older than his friend Arthur and looked more frail physically. He might need to use a wheelchair for longer distances, but once they started chatting it was immediately clear that he was just as alert as ever mentally, with a quirky sense of humour that had Sean chuckling a few times.

Ben's great-grandson Norry joined them and the lad's affection for the old man was heart-warming to see, as was the fact that though he might be young, he clearly took after the old man, and came over as intelligent and caring about his fellow human beings. 'Wise beyond his years' was a phrase that came to mind and he seemed likely to be a future leader in this community. You could sometimes tell.

'When do you want me to bring Gramps across to the Lane?' Norry asked. 'And do you want me to do it openly or unobtrusively?'

'Arthur Keevil is coming here in a very visible ambulance, but I think it might be better if you brought Ben to move in quietly during the evening afterwards. You don't need to hide it but act as if his stay was expected. The cottages will be ready for occupation by then and a few people are bound to notice them both moving in. Unless you have any better ideas?'

Ben frowned and looked at Norry. 'What do you think, lad?'

'I think that'll work well. I can bring Gramps in my van. It's already adapted to take a wheelchair and people know that I sleep here at the house now in case I'm needed. I can let the word slip out afterwards that he's going into Lavender Lane for some proper care after a small health setback but he's fine now.'

Sean considered this. 'Good idea. Oh, and Arthur's suggested I contact Prue Gillings and ask her to join us at the Lane as well. Is that all right with you, Ben?'

'I shall enjoy her company. She always used to join us when these were regular outings and she's great fun to spend time with. She's also the best shot of the three of us.'

'Does that mean she'll be bringing a weapon too?'

'It never hurts to be prepared, does it? And if everything stays peaceful, as is likely, we'll have a very pleasant time together at your expense. We'd like to start doing that regularly again.'

Norry hesitated, then cleared his throat to get their attention and said, 'There's just one other detail I should mention. I'll need my friend Rahim to come along and help me with Gramps, if that's all right. There's not only the wheelchair but the luggage to be taken into the cottage. Gramps isn't much good at walking these days and you can trust Rahim. He's a good sort and helps me out regularly.'

'Who is he exactly?'

Ben took over. 'He's from a new valley family and they've proved themselves decent and useful a time or two already. It'll be easy for you to check them out, if you have any doubts, Sean. Or you can take my word for it. I too trust their lad. He's another good 'un.'

'I'm sure I can rely on your judgement absolutely.' If Ben trusted this Rahim, could be useful to work with. The old man had been a noted figure locally in his time, leader of this small and unofficial but occasionally useful arm of government security. And he'd headed one or two trips to other countries as well. People would follow his lead in who they accepted in the community.

'I can stay at Lavender Lane and help look after Gramps, if you like?' Norry offered. 'I've not got a steady job because I don't like answering to idiots and this would be something different and interesting to do. I can keep up with my online stuff anywhere without anyone else knowing where I am. It earns me some useful regular money.'

'It'll be useful training to have him there,' Ben said quietly. 'He's definitely one of the people who'll take over from our lot one day in keeping an eye on our valley.'

Sean smiled at the bright-eyed young chap. 'It'll be good to have you around, Norry, and I don't think we employ any idiots so I reckon you'll enjoy the company at the Lane.'

'The lad will enjoy the library at the big house too, if you don't mind him using it,' Ben said.

'No worries about that. He'll be welcome to borrow books.'

'He and I will both enjoy seeing what else is available there to feed our minds. Libraries are wonderful places and, thank goodness, my body might be failing but my brain is still a pleasure to me and an excellent tool.'

Sean didn't say it but he reckoned Ben and Arthur had some of the sharpest minds he'd ever encountered.

'Will tomorrow, just after midnight, suit you as a time to arrive?'

'We'll be there,' Norry promised. 'Then Rahim can

walk home and I'll keep the van in case of an emergency.'

'Do we need to provide carers for the others?' Sean asked.

Ben shook his head. 'No. They'll see to that themselves. Staying at the Lane always used to make a pleasant change for me and my friends. It'll be wonderful to start doing it again. We've always got on well.'

Chapter Eighteen

When Sean went back to the big house, he explained the situation and asked the others' help. 'I need to find a team of cleaners to get the cottages ready for immediate occupation. Do any of you know where I can find enough help to do it quickly? I've not been living round here long enough yet to have made useful contacts in some areas.'

He saw Ilsa glance round and wait a moment to speak. She seemed to tread extremely carefully as to what she said and did, not just because she was settling in but all the time. She didn't complain about anyone or anything, only he was rather good at reading between the lines and he'd guess that she hadn't always been treated well by her employers, or by life in general. And yet she seemed to him to be a hard worker who performed any task she was given extremely efficiently.

'I do know someone, actually, Sean,' she said in her usual quiet way.

'Great. Tell me about them.'

'There are a couple of women in town who organise that sort of occasional cleaning job and they're well respected. I've done casual shifts for them as a cleaner now and then while I was at the shop, especially in recent months when my main work wasn't always full time and I was, well, a bit short of money. Some of the jobs were overnighters and others were on Sundays.'

'They sound perfect. Thanks, Ilsa.'

She smiled reminiscently. 'I've worked with them on some strangely timed and unusual jobs, such as clearing up after rowdy parties held by younger folk when their parents were away on Saturdays. Their stupid behaviour was their loss and our gain, we always said, because it meant overtime for us and double wages for us on Sundays, as well as extra charges for the organisers to pay for any repairs needed.'

'Can you give me these organisers' contact details or would it be better for you to make the arrangements with them? After all, you'll be on site and be able to work out how best to start the task of cleaning out all the cottages. We'll need three of the cottages ready for occupation within the day if that's possible, and the others just want readying for use generally.'

She didn't look worried at the prospect of organising this, but pulled out a little notebook and began scribbling in it.

'I'll go round all the cottages quickly as soon as it's light tomorrow and jot down exactly what needs doing, then set the whole job up with my friends.' She held the pen poised and asked, 'Which three cottages do you want setting up first?'

'The two closest to the house, the ones on either side of the central path between the trios of cottages. If those two can be occupied straight away, these particular patients and anyone acting as their carers can more easily keep watch for intruders coming in from the rear car park. Get the central cottages done next, and the bottom two when convenient. Will it be possible to get them all done quite quickly?'

'Oh, yes. My friends are used to rush jobs and they have a list of people on standby for them. Do you have any idea how many people you'll want her to employ in the cleaning team?'

'No. I'm hoping you'll be able to work out how many will be necessary to get it all done rapidly so your friend should bring in people accordingly.'

She smiled. 'Well, that'll be easy enough. I'm sure my friends will be able to work out how many cleaners will be needed to do that and find them quickly too because they've lived locally all their lives. What about cost? It won't come cheaply. Is there some limit?'

'Pay whatever is reasonable to do this quickly. If they can start by working till the first three cottages are ready, not sticking to certain hours of work, it'd be good.'

'Wow!' she said softly, surprised by this. 'It's going to be expensive, you know.'

'It's urgent.'

Ilsa stood silently for a moment, looking thoughtful. 'Since it's a rush job, the first lot of work will go better if you not only pay slightly above the usual overtime rates but also provide on-the-job meals and snacks for as long as it takes. I could sort out the food quite easily as well as keeping check on the work being done, but what about Ned? All the signs are that he's getting steadily better but do you want me to leave him on his own and nip back occasionally for quick checks on how he's going?'

Nina, who had been listening to their conversation, joined in abruptly. 'I'll be around in the big house for most of tomorrow, Ilsa, so I'll be able to keep an eye on Ned. I can easily get him drinks and snacks as needed now we've got proper food supplies on hand.'

'Are you sure?'

'Oh, yes. I'll just be working on my computer, so I'll be in the library anyway, right next to him, whether you need me or not.'

Ilsa looked at Sean to confirm that this would be all right and heard him heave a sigh of relief, then say, 'That'll be very useful.' He also gave Nina a warm glance.

Ilsa couldn't help wondering whether Sean and Nina were aware of how much even the rapid glances they shared betrayed about their growing feelings for one another. It must be wonderful to have someone to care about who felt just as deeply about you. She'd never had that.

She wondered suddenly whether Ned had anyone special but a few seconds' thought made her realise that'd not have been possible in his line of work.

Sean seemed to be thinking about something else and looked as if he was about to speak, so they all waited for him to tell them whatever was on his mind. He was, she thought, very much a leader.

'I think that arrangement is going to work well. In fact, it all seems to be falling into place nicely, doesn't it? To sum up, firstly, we need to sort out the accommodation in the cottages, then to bring in our oldies who look like convalescent patients so that Ned can just be one person among several.'

'Why did they come here previously?' Ilsa couldn't help asking.

'To socialise and reminisce. I gather they shared a couple of drinks and simply enjoyed spending time with people their own age. And as they stayed one night, if not two, it gave their families a break from caring for them, too. Everyone needs a rest from time to time, don't they?'

Ilsa nodded and saw the others do the same. She liked the capable way Sean was organising this and appreciated the clear way he shared information.

'I've arranged for one elderly gentleman to come in late tomorrow afternoon and another will be arriving shortly after him. Finally, Prue will be coming to join them the following morning.'

Ilsa considered that. 'Will there be someone here to settle them in or do I need to find helpers to do that?'

'They'll be arranging for their own helpers. They're apparently looking forward greatly to starting to do this again.' He grinned as if remembering something. 'They're amazing. Like no oldies I've ever worked with before. I want to be just like them when I too turn into a valuable antique.'

'Valuable antique!' She chuckled. 'That sounds much nicer than a mere oldie.'

'Yes. I've heard them call themselves that for fun. But they have been very valuable members of society in their time and I honour them for that.'

'Anyone would. There's a lot of money and effort going

into this whole situation, isn't there?' Ilsa looked at him thoughtfully as if asking why.

'Yes, there is. I'm semi-retired now and I was intending to take full retirement soon till I was asked to work with Nina and then stay on to manage Lavender Lane.' He smiled. 'It won't be a hardship to spend time with her. As you've no doubt noticed, she and I are getting on rather well, so it's all fitted together nicely as an ongoing project.'

'And on top of that you're trusting the rest of us,' Ilsa said.

He gave her a quick smile and nod. 'Yes. Now that I've met you in particular, I trust you completely. You've already shown that you're very capable, and I'm a good judge.'

'Oh. Well, thank you. That's great to hear.' This man that made her feel good and she was looking forward to working with him.

Ilsa watched him turn his head and glance across at his partner again and saw Nina give him a glowing smile for no visible reason. She sighed enviously.

'To get back to the arrangements, Ilsa, are you all right with everything so far?'

She stared at him solemnly. 'Yes, I am. Very much so. You're trusting me with a lot of the organising yet you've never seen me running a project from scratch before.'

'I hope you don't mind but I checked your capabilities with someone I know in your old army unit. They were very sorry to lose you and the woman I was speaking to assured me that you're not only a really hard worker but highly efficient and innovative in the details of what you do. She said how greatly she'd missed your organisational skills in the admin team when you insisted on leaving after your last term of service ended. How come you were doing such a lowly job as the one in the dress shop?'

Ilsa flushed again, hesitated, then met his eyes and told the blunt truth for once, without trying to gloss over her own stupidity. 'When I wasn't able to re-enlist, I felt really down in the dumps because the army had been my main focus as a younger adult, as near to a home and family as I'd ever got.'

She found it harder to tell even him the next bit, but he said, 'Go on! I won't think any the worse of you whatever you tell me,' in such a gentle tone that she took a deep breath and did it.

'I was seriously depressed for quite a while after being injured as well as damaged physically, and I couldn't be bothered with anything very much outside work hours. I watched a lot of television to try to switch my feelings off. I felt that I'd outlived my useful life – useful for doing worthwhile things, that is – and in the beginning I was quite sure it'd have been better if I'd been killed rather than merely injured.'

'That must have been hard to live through without any family support. I'm glad it didn't drive you to try anything drastic, though. That's a good sign.'

She shrugged. 'I guess I don't have the suicide gene, because I've never seriously considered killing myself even when life was at its worst. I just lived with it all as best I could.'

That made him stare at her sympathetically but he didn't comment directly, only said gently, 'Well, I'm glad you found us, Ilsa. You definitely haven't outlived your usefulness as far as I'm concerned. As a group, we're all benefitting greatly from having you around because you have superb organisational skills even in small things and you seem able to pull the detailed side of a job together with amazing rapidity once you start on it, and without things going wrong.'

She could only gape at that, then couldn't hide her pleasure at such a lovely compliment. Her gratitude came out huskily. 'Thank you.'

'Your former commander speaks highly of you and was sorry she wasn't able to persuade you to take further training to become an officer, only you refused to do it several times and in the end she felt that her insistence was one of the reasons you left the army. Apparently you'd resisted doing anything that involved that sort of studying previously as well.'

'Oh. Yes. She did try very hard to persuade me to stay in the army but I, um, don't like studying, and I'm just not good at it. In the end I decided that I needed to experience a full range of life situations after all those narrow, limited years in care as a teenager and then in the army as an adult. I felt that I'd been shut away from the real world for too long.'

She glanced down involuntarily at her bad leg. 'I was wrong to leave, though. I should have stuck it out and I've certainly paid for my mistake.'

'If it's any comfort, Ilsa, it's my belief that people can learn from everything they experience in this life, good or bad. If you would like, we could discuss your long-term future another time because I think I can help you to find a far more interesting focus for your life after this project is sorted out. However, we need to get on with preparations now because this job is very urgent indeed. Can you take over completely on organising the cleaning team?'

'Sure. I'll enjoy doing that.' To her surprise she realised she was looking forward to being in charge of it and what's more, she hadn't felt at all low in spirits since she'd met these people, which felt like a minor miracle in itself after the dreariness of the past year or two.

When they were alone, Nina looked at Sean. 'Poor lass.'

'Yes. We'll have to find her a better focus. Maybe she can stay on in charge of admin here. It'd give us some freedom to enjoy life and perhaps some travel together.'

'Good idea. Apart from anything else, I really like her. She's a decent person, and that may sound a strange thing to say, but it's one of my highest compliments.'

He pulled her to him and plonked a kiss on the nearest cheek. 'So are you, my darling.'

The endearment made her pause, then she hugged him before stepping back and looking him firmly in the eyes. 'You haven't told me everything about yourself and who sent you to help me with this project, have you? You clearly have some rather interesting connections and experiences.'

'No, I haven't told you everything. Forgive me for that, darling. My security branch background makes it impossible ever to explain fully about my past life. It's not that I don't trust you and I'd like to put it on record that I want to stay with you permanently on a personal level from now on. My feelings for you are *not* feigned. But I have an important job to finish first, after which I'll be semi-retiring.'

'Semi?'

'You never retire fully from what I've been doing, I'm afraid, and the project here will be low key and only occasionally active but it will still need some form of management. Can you live with that edge of uncertainty, Nina?'

'Yes, as long as it includes you.' She eyed him again then said thoughtfully, 'You must be quite an important person.'

'Oh, not all that important.' He reached out for her hand. 'It's mainly in the past, anyway, and once we've sorted everything out here, you're going to be the most important part of my life, I promise you. You do want that, don't you?'

'Of course I do. I don't know why but I've trusted you from the first time I met you.' She took hold of his hand and raised it gently to her cheek in a brief caress.

He gave her one of those warm, loving smiles, the sort you couldn't fake, and she couldn't help adding, 'I fell in love with you quickly too, Sean.'

They stood staring at one another and smiling for a moment or two longer before getting on with the things that needed doing at once.

Sean knew that he'd been doing a lot more smiling since the first day they met and was just as certain that she had too.

She'd lost her husband and had to cope with loneliness. He'd had to choose loneliness in order to do a rather important job. Now they were ready to choose to be together and enjoy their lives. Very ready.

As the rest of the day passed, Sean watched Ilsa more carefully than she probably realised and was impressed all over again by how thoroughly and efficiently she prepared for this task, sitting down later with a few scraps of paper and rapidly making a list of actions and the order in which they'd need doing.

He noticed, however, that she didn't seem to work nearly as well when it came to making the final, neater summary notes to give him.

He'd sneaked a couple of glances at what she was doing as he passed by and didn't think he was wrong when he figured out that she probably had the same problem as the son of one of his cousins. That lad had been diagnosed with dyslexia, which was nothing to do with a lack of intelligence but, if he remembered correctly, dyslexia was a learning disability that affected how people related to written content. Dyslexic people read using shapes and patterns rather than by individual letters so it took much more effort than 'normal' readers.

That might be why she'd avoided serious study because, sadly, dyslexia still seemed to have a stigma as far as some people were concerned, especially people of Ilsa's generation, and those who had it often tried hard to hide their problem. Some people who had to deal with dyslexic employees or family members didn't take the trouble to learn how best to help them.

No time to find out her full story now, but he would look into that aspect later and check out the latest approaches to helping her. After this project was resolved he would help her to find a better way to learn how to deal with whatever it was rather than by avoidance and keeping a low profile.

That decided, he turned his mind back to the matter in hand. For the moment they had to get Lavender Lane open again and people who looked like invalids settled into the cottages to pretend to 'convalesce' or to need 'respite care' till they had got the facilities properly sorted out to help people who genuinely needed to convalesce.

Thank goodness the first three invalids who were about to be installed came from a similar background to himself and could provide their own weapons for protection or else that'd mean more delays while he brought in protection for them!

He'd watched Ned struggle to move normally after being attacked so brutally and had seen the damage inflicted on other people injured in the course of their duties as well, so he wasn't leaving anyone unprotected, not if he could help it. He was even going to sneak a gun to Ilsa. She'd have learnt to handle weapons when she was in the army.

He would move heaven and earth to protect his team here, he vowed grimly. He always had done his best to protect those handling difficult situations, sadly not with a hundred per cent success.

And he mustn't forget the IT side of things. The computers were very old-fashioned and the security system stopped at the doors of the cottages. He and Nina were in agreement that they needed to bring in someone with the expertise to set up a modern, effective system for the whole place, only they'd not had time to sort that out yet.

The following day, Sean made sure that vehicles came in and out of the parking area at the rear of the big house at regular intervals, making bogus deliveries. He was hoping that any potential intruders would be deterred by the busy traffic.

His neighbour who ran the horticultural group that was going to tend the revamped gardens, and especially the lavender bushes, was particularly helpful after he had explained the situation and Elizabeth also enlisted the help of some of her friends.

He explained what he was doing to members of his own team and sent them out too for short drives to various shops or the main post office in town.

It had been his guess that regular traffic might help keep any intruders from coming onto the property itself, though of course he couldn't stop them from hovering nearby. And this strategy seemed to work.

He watched carefully from various vantage points in the big house and though there were one or two people he didn't like the looks of wandering past or loitering nearby there seemed to be no one coming close to the Lane and his staff said the same thing.

But the tension was there among his colleagues as their preparations continued; how could it not be?

And he was on edge, too.

Chapter Nineteen

By noon, the three cottages that needed to be occupied first were immaculate and the cleaners had moved to start work on the others. Arthur was to be brought to Lavender Lane later that afternoon.

A young woman called Glynis was brought in during the early afternoon to act as a general helper for appearances' sake. Nina briefed her about keeping an eye on him and his old friends. She seemed a cheerful sort, which never hurt when caring for people who needed some sort of help, or even when only acting as a watchful companion.

'Yes, I can see to food and cleaning the cottage but I bet none of these particular oldies will want me to do much by way of personal care.' She winked at Nina. 'Well, I've met them before and they don't really need much help, do they?'

'No. But it'll help if you bring meals down from the

big house and generally keep the places tidy. They said they didn't need much personal help but it would look better to have someone else around, keeping an eye on things. You come very highly recommended for your ability to do that.'

She beamed at Nina. 'Thank you. I do my best and I've had one or two of these security jobs before. So this time I don't have to cook for Arthur or the others at all?'

'No. We'll provide the meals for everyone, you as well. And we'll make sure there are snacks available in each cottage too. We have a trolley with insulated compartments for you to bring them to and fro on.'

'Sounds to be a very easy job. I shall feel guilty that I'm not earning my money if there's nothing much for me to do here.'

'Well, we assume you'll keep your eyes open for anyone lurking around or anything that looks odd or out of place. We don't want intruders actually getting in, do we? And if people like you are seen moving around and looking busy that'll help to deter them. You'll be earning your money just by being here, really.'

'I'm glad you think so.'

'I do. But if you could bustle up to the big house occasionally, either carrying something or bringing something back, that'd help too, I'm sure.'

'Good to know. I hope you've got a good cook. He likes his food, Arthur does. I've known him for years, even before I got into this sort of job. Eeh, I envy him. He never puts any weight on either, though he's always been a hearty eater. Talk about lucky.' She looked down regretfully at her own slightly plump body. 'I have to watch what I eat all the time.'

'Well, we have an excellent cook so I daresay Arthur will continue to enjoy his food while he's here but it'll be healthy food so you should be all right too.'

'All right.' But she sounded dubious. 'Where do I sleep, then? I shall need to unpack my own things.'

'There's a small loft bedroom in Arthur's cottage. Will you be all right with that? His bedroom is on the ground floor. The cottages are all different inside. You may as well go and sort out your belongings now, while you're waiting for him to arrive. The stairs are rather steep, I'm afraid, but there's a comfortable armchair for you up there in case they need a bit of privacy.'

'The stairs don't matter. I'm fitter than I look. And if they need private meetings, I can sit upstairs and keep an eye on the street in case anyone tries sneaking around. There are a lot of nosy people in the town, most of them harmless but they still like to see what's going on.'

'Well, there are plenty of books if you have time to fill, and more in the big house if there's nothing here that takes your fancy.'

'And I'll have my fancy new phone that my niece has been teaching me to use. It's amazing what you can do on a phone these days, isn't it?'

'It certainly is. Don't tell anyone you speak to on it where exactly you are, though, or anything about this place.'

'No, dear. I won't. The supervisor put an app on my phone to keep that sort of thing from showing by mistake even. I've worked in similar jobs before and I do have experience in keeping a low profile as well as security clearance, remember.'

'Of course you do. I'm probably fussing too much.'

Glynis patted Ilsa's shoulder. 'Better safe than sorry, eh? I'll go and sort my room out now.'

Later that afternoon, Ilsa waited to see Arthur settled in. Once he was inside, he studied the bay window.

'This is a special sort of one-way glass, so I can watch the world from that nice armchair without being seen.'

'Yes. They won't be able to see anything from outside,' Ilsa told him.

'Good spot to sit. I'll be able to see anyone coming towards the precinct from the car park long before they get here. Not that many people will be coming near the place yet but I'm nicely situated to keep an eye on them when they do.'

Glynis came down to join them just then and Ilsa was pleased to see the two of them chat and laugh like the old friends they clearly were.

His smile vanished abruptly, however, when Glynis asked what time he'd like to take a nap. 'I never did go in for naps when I was younger and that hasn't changed as I've grown older. I told you that last time we worked together. I know you like your naps, so go ahead and take a snooze whenever you feel like it.'

'I will if I can take it in one of those lovely big armchairs in your sitting room, then I'll be close by if you need me.'

'I don't know how you can snooze in such a busy area but be my guest if there's no one else around. I'll spend most of the day in this armchair, if someone will move it into the bay window for me. That way I'll be able to read or watch the comings and goings to the Lane and the big house. I enjoy watching folk. Though I mustn't forget to move about regularly or I'll get too stiff.'

Glynis moved towards the chair. 'I can move this now, if you like. This sort of chair is easy to push around.'

'When exactly will my friend Ben be arriving?' he asked once he was sitting comfortably. 'Do either of you know?'

Ilsa nodded. 'Yes. He'll be coming soon and staying in the cottage at the top of the other trio, on the opposite side of the central path to you.'

'That's good. I'll maybe totter across to visit him now and then, and he can wheel himself across to visit me.'

He sighed and added quietly, 'Who's going to be looking after him? Sadly he needs physical help more than he used to.'

'His great-grandson Norry.'

'Oh, good. Clever lad, that one. He's got excellent hearing and he's a light sleeper when he's on a job, so he'll know if anyone comes prowling round during the night.'

'We haven't put CCTV on the outside of the cottages yet because most people who come here value their privacy, and anyway, all the IT systems need updating properly. I should think such equipment is easily available if you want it installed. It's people with the skill to install it who are in short supply.'

'Yes. It's not urgent at the moment. After all, we want to appear rather helpless and old-fashioned, don't we?' He gave Ilsa a rather wolfish smile. 'Don't look so worried, lass. If there are any major glitches, Ben and I still know how to defend ourselves.'

'I heard you'd insisted on bringing guns. I've been told to emphasise that you'd better have a good reason if you do use them.'

'We know that. If it makes you feel better, since I gather you're staying around, I promise faithfully that we shall only use them if absolutely necessary, which it rarely is. We prefer to fool any observers that we're helpless oldies and have a reputation so far in working for this organisation for managing to do that. It's what the authorities prefer too, I know.'

She shrugged. It wasn't quite as straightforward as that. These oldies were very determined to do things their way and for some reason had managed to get permission, so they must have a very good reputation for success in such ventures. All she could do about it was remain very alert.

He smiled at her. 'Stop worrying. We know what we're doing. Now, tell me about Prue. When is she coming and will someone be pretending to be her carer? I'm really looking forward to catching up with her again.'

'She seemed delighted to be invited to stay here and I gather she feels the same about seeing you two. She has been missing your monthly trips to the Lane, which were sometimes just pleasant escapes and occasionally there were incidents that needed dealing with. She said she'd bring her niece to seem to be her carer for appearances' sake, though just like you, she insists she can look after herself perfectly well.'

Arthur nodded. 'We'll liven Prue up a bit like we used to. She's been a widow for several years now and she never had children, so she's been a bit lonely while the place has been shut down. I knew it'd suit her to join us here this time and you won't need to worry about her having a gun because she's a better shot than I am.'

'I didn't hear you say that.'

He chuckled. 'There are a few other things you won't hear me say, too, as we chat, but I'll tell you all that I can.'

'Well, I hope your friend will enjoy her visit and that none of you will encounter any problems that need drastic remedies.'

'We'll enjoy Prue's company, that's for sure.'

There was a slight edge to his voice that made her look at him sympathetically and she risked saying, 'I was reading in the paper only a few days ago that loneliness is a major disease of old age these days.'

'And boredom too, I've found. You sound as if you understand better than most.'

'I do. Being on one's own more than one would wish isn't restricted to oldies, you know. Not all of us come from large extended families.' Ilsa broke off abruptly. What was there about these people that had made her confide so much in them? She usually kept quiet about her own situation and regrets.

He gave her a shrewd look. 'I gather you don't have any close family at all.'

She shrugged and shook her head. To her relief he didn't pursue the point. She didn't want to seem in need of sympathy, thank you very much. She'd better watch what she said to them from now on. She coped with what life threw at her and enjoyed the rarer good experiences and times, like this assignment. That must be enough.

'When exactly will Prue be arriving?' Arthur asked. 'You must have more specific information than just a vague tomorrow.'

'We don't have an exact time, were only told it'd be whenever her nearest ambulance has a slot free to bring her here.'

He chuckled. 'As if she needs an ambulance! She's still driving her own car the rest of the time. She has a cleaner and someone helps her with the shopping but she manages the rest of her life just fine. Which cottage are you putting her in?'

'She'll be taking the middle cottage of your trio, Arthur, right next door to you.'

'Good. And what about that injured lad? He'll want a bit of company, surely? You can put him in the other middle cottage opposite Prue.'

'They're still wondering whether to do that yet, perhaps not until we have external security here sorted out a bit better.'

Arthur merely smiled dismissively. 'You know we'll be here to keep an eye on him. Is he walking freely again? If so he'll maybe enjoy a bit of company. His scars should be mostly healed by now.'

She frowned at him. 'You're not supposed to know any details about him coming here, let alone what sort of personal problems he's been facing.'

Arthur gave her a cheeky wink. 'Well, now you're aware that I do know quite a bit and that I'll be telling the others all about his situation as soon as they get here. That'll save us all a lot of time and trouble but you'll need to keep us up to date with anything new that's decided or that crops up from now onwards.'

'I will if I can.'

His voice was firm. 'Tell Sean I *need* to be kept in the loop about every single detail that changes and send him to discuss it with me if he doesn't agree to let you do that. Oh, and there's something else I want to discuss with you, but not till tomorrow when the others are settled in here and I've run it past them. Sean dropped me a hint and I like the sound of it.'

'You're going to discuss it with me?'

'Yes. If the others feel as I do about his idea, you will be the next person to find out about it and then you can tell us what you think of doing a little job for us in connection with it.'

She frowned and glanced quickly round. 'Are there some arrangements you don't like and need changing? Because if there are, you should tell me at once.'

'No. It's another strategy that might be worth trying here as well as what you folk have already set up. Tell Sean I like his idea and will discuss it with Ben and Prue first before we ask what you think, and then we'll run it all past Sean again. He's famous for putting interesting little twists into situations. And that's all I'm going to say about it for the moment.'

He changed the subject again and very firmly too. 'I gather that this Nina is a nice woman and folk in the valley who've seen them together reckon Sean will make her a good husband. He's done without family for long enough because of his job, don't you think?'

Ilsa couldn't hide her surprise at this remark but didn't say anything else. She'd never been in a situation like this and was finding it much more interesting than her usual jobs. But what could they possibly want her opinion about? Mostly, she just got told what to do, not even *asked*.

'Come on, lass. Anyone who's seen Sean and Nina together can tell how attracted they are to one another. You can't have missed that.'

'Well, yes, I had noticed but I'd never comment on it publicly. How they feel about one another is their own business as long as it doesn't interfere with this project and I'm surprised you've even mentioned it to me.'

'I didn't want you to think I don't notice what's going on around me – *all* the details, think on – so never try to keep anything from me.'

She breathed deeply and gave him a look of the sort that usually made men back off.

This man merely chuckled again and said, 'Now, remember that we three oldies will need to speak to you on your own after we speak to Sean and Nina so I'd rather you didn't discuss the situation here with anyone else until after we've had another little chat to you.'

He leant back in his chair, staring at her so thoughtfully she wondered what he was thinking. But he was clearly not going to reveal anything else yet and she'd already figured out that he'd be as stubborn as any boss she'd ever met when it came to getting his own way about something he considered important or necessary.

So she went back to the job, making suitable arrangements for the younger chap who would most likely be coming to stay in one of the cottages later.

It was a relief to be dealing with something more straightforward.

Arthur seemed to have been waiting for her to have a think about the situation and she decided to go over everything she knew with him. She'd learnt to recognise people you didn't mess about with so she said, '*If* they think it safe, I gather that Ned will be moving in next to Ben, probably tomorrow, and they may or may not bring a guy here to help look after and protect him.'

He looked thoughtful. 'If they do, he'll be armed, I hope?'

She hesitated.

His voice was quietly emphatic. 'I need to know. I am, after all, going to be in the next cottage, right in the firing line if things go wrong.'

There were times when he had such an air of authority underneath that genial old man pose that she wondered what his background really was, so she went on to finish telling him the simple truth. 'Yes, if they decide he needs a helper, the man will be armed and a strong chap. But I shouldn't be telling you that so please keep it to yourself.'

'I will. But remember that my friends and I haven't survived this long by letting anyone find a way to get at us or our comrades. We try not to give them a reason to even try by seeming old and doddery these days. It's better to prevent trouble than deal with it.'

She compromised by saying, 'Sean hasn't taken any chances with his arrangements, believe me.'

'He has a reputation for being very capable. And anyway, this will mostly be a standard convalescent or respite home. There will only be the occasional hidden extra purpose.'

She shook her head as she walked back to the big house, wondering what Arthur was planning and what they'd want from her before this was over.

She didn't want to let these people down in any way. They not only seemed very special, but had all of them treated her so kindly she wished she could stay working with them for ever.

Chapter Twenty

Ilsa went to greet Ben and check whether anything else was needed for his comfort.

As she had when dealing with Arthur, she quickly decided that this man was another who must have been quite an important person in his time.

And she liked the sturdy independent air of young Norry and his friend Rahim, not to mention the bright, eager expressions on their faces. What's more, the two of them seemed mature beyond their years in the way they interacted with the old man and discussed the situation and he treated them as equals. In fact, it was lovely to see how well the three of them got on.

She wished she'd had that sort of relationship in her younger life, but as usual she didn't let herself linger on the regrets about her own situation because there was nothing she could do to change what had already happened. You couldn't pull relatives out of the sky for the future, either, could you?

As Arthur had done, Ben was studying her as if he could read her nature in her face, and he didn't attempt to hide his interest. He was polite but it didn't take her long to decide that she wouldn't like to try going against anything this man wanted her to do, either.

This wasn't to say, however, that there wasn't an underlying kindness to the way he spoke to everyone, herself included. In fact, he and Arthur were very much alike in that too. They were both really pleasant to deal with as well as having that subtle air of authority in the way they spoke, somehow.

Ilsa had learnt in the army to manage on less sleep when needed and thank goodness! It was her guess that this ability was going to come in useful if this job gave her the disturbed nights she was already half expecting.

She set her alarm for earlier than usual the following morning so that she could supervise the provision of breakfast for the oldies. She'd also need to keep an eye on the work being done to Prue's cottage, which needed a few details finishing off to be sparkling clean and looking appealing.

Prue arrived just after eleven o'clock accompanied by her niece, Zoe. She hobbled slowly and stiffly into her home, using her walking stick, stared round it then turned to smile at Ilsa. 'It all looks fine, dear, thank you. Where are Ben and Arthur staying?'

Ilsa pointed out the two nearby cottages and told her who would be in each.

Prue winked at her. 'I think I can just about manage to totter that far without a wheelchair.'

Ilsa didn't contradict her but something in her expression must have given away her knowledge of these people's actual health condition and a little gurgle of laughter escaped Prue.

'You're aware of the true situation, I see. Good. I shan't need to pretend with you. And since I don't really need help, perhaps you'd show Zoe where to take our luggage then carry on with your day. She'll unpack for me and I'll settle here near the window until the others are ready for a chat and perhaps lunch together. You might call in and suggest they come over to greet me when convenient.'

'How about you have lunch here together at about one o'clock. There is a table with leaves that we can use.'

Prue nodded. 'Yes, the boys and I will enjoy that.'

Boys indeed! Ilsa thought. One guy was in his nineties and the other in his mid-eighties. She went to order them a meal, arranging to have a bland lunch sent in this time with items people weren't usually allergic to. Someone would surely have told her if these people had any serious dietary problems but you couldn't be too careful.

After that she reckoned she'd earned a little quiet time so spent a peaceful hour with an early lunch for herself and yesterday's newspaper to enjoy. She loved finding out what was happening in the wider world.

She helped deliver their meal, gave them time to finish it in peace then went back to check that they were all right, not to mention asking what types of food they liked best so that she could make some more interesting meal plans for them in future. She'd have to check that there were relevant food supplies in the pantry at the big house afterwards. She prided herself on getting every single detail of whatever she was organising correct.

As she reached the first pair of cottages, she glanced through the windows. All three oldies had gathered at Prue's and even before she got to the door she realised that they were speaking so quietly she couldn't even sense their tone of voice, nor was their rather minimal body language any clue to how they were really feeling. It seemed as if they were making doubly sure of their privacy.

As she approached the front door, Prue looked up, saw her through the glass panels of the upper part of the door and tapped Arthur's arm. 'We have a visitor.'

When she opened the door, she smiled and beckoned to Ilsa. 'Do come in and join us. Your arrival is well timed because we were just saying it might be useful to speak to you about something.'

Ben gestured to a chair so she pulled it up and sat down with the group, thinking yet again that not all senior officials were as polite as this to their underlings.

'I hope you don't mind if we ask you some rather personal questions, Ilsa?'

She didn't mind but it puzzled her why they'd bother. People running things didn't usually have the slightest interest in the personal background of their casual helpers and attendants.

'We'd be interested to hear more about your family, if you don't mind us asking. The little I've found out shows that you have a distinct lack of any close relatives, which may mean you'd be both free and willing to help us with something. What happened to your immediate family?'

'I don't mind you asking but there isn't much to tell. My parents died in a car crash when I was ten. No one ever told me the details of how that happened and there wasn't any information about other relatives in their possessions, so I was taken into care and moved from one foster family to another over the years. I didn't remember my parents ever speaking about any relatives and of course ongoing foster parents knew even less about my family than I did.'

Arthur looked at her in surprise. 'There were no birth certificates or other official papers to indicate where you come from?'

'No, nothing at all. Later, when I was older, I asked about that but the foster mother I had then only shrugged and denied knowing anything. Even when I went to the first foster home, I never saw any possessions that might have belonged to my parents, that's for sure, only my own clothes and schoolbooks.'

'How sad. The authorities should have left you some mementoes.'

She shrugged. 'Sad things happen. I was looked after well enough physically, I'll grant the carers that. By the time I was old enough to wonder and make serious enquiries about my family, I was with my fourth foster parents and naturally they knew nothing whatsoever. And the person who'd organised my care originally had left her employment with the local authority and moved overseas, so couldn't be contacted.'

It had upset her, Ilsa admitted to herself, and she still considered it to have been done inefficiently and cruelly too, but it was too late to do anything about it by then.

'When I left school I went into the army, which felt like a family in some ways.'

'What made you think of doing that?' Ben asked.

'I'd been in the cadet corps at school. I wasn't the only one there without close relatives.' That had comforted her. A little, anyway.

'We saw the army service listed in your CV, but we weren't sure why you hadn't stayed in the military if you were happy there. Can I ask you that?'

'I wanted to try a broader slice of life than foster families and the army. And my commanding officer would keep pestering me to train as an officer. I didn't feel ready for that and I don't like studying. Anyhow, I knew I could always re-enlist if I decided the army was the best place for me.'

'And then you were seriously injured in an accident and couldn't go back. Hard luck, that. How are you now physically?'

'All right as long as I don't overdo things that involve that weaker leg taking a lot of pressure.'

'I must say I haven't seen any signs of a limp so the leg must cope all right with normal everyday life.'

'It does. There are no hidden health secrets there, I promise you.'

'Thanks for putting up with our nosiness.' Ben looked across at his friends as if to hand the conversation over to one of them.

It was Arthur who took over, smiling at her. 'Can we consider the present situation here in Lavender Lane now?'

She nodded. This was a rather strange conversation, jumping to and fro in ways that surprised and confused her. She really couldn't see why they were interested in her remote family background. Surely all that mattered now was that she did the tasks they needed her for efficiently?

'We've been discussing an additional strategy for disguising the special work we do here, and making it look like just a convalescent care facility. Would you be willing to do something rather unconventional to help your country?'

She stared for a moment then nodded slowly. 'Willingly. As long as it doesn't involve breaking the law or hurting someone, of course.'

'No, no! Nothing like that. We thought you could pretend to find a long-lost family member here and we'll use that sort of thing in an ongoing way to keep distracting people as to the secondary purpose of this place.'

'I can do that though I can't see how that would help our country.'

'It'd help in a small way here in Lavender Lane, which is occasionally useful to the authorities in ways we'll explain later.'

'Well, it'd be nice to help a bit more than I do now, I must admit, and to do something different.' She waited but they didn't go into further details then and Arthur nodded dismissal with another of his pleasant smiles.

'We'll talk further about this later, Ilsa. Could you ask Sean and Nina to join us this afternoon at about three o'clock to give us time to talk about the details? We'll need to run our basic idea past them now we've spoken to you, then discuss the details of how best to organise this strategy, so we'll get you back in to help us plan things once it's been approved.'

Her puzzlement must have shown because he gave her an apologetic look and added, 'I'm sorry to take so long to sort this out but it's a delicate step and it has to be done just right, so we want to test it out. You know how careful one has to be with red tape sometimes.'

She nodded. Anyone who'd served in the forces was only too aware of that.

'And please don't mention this to anyone.'

As if she would go around blabbing about anything she did at work! As if she had anyone close enough to blab to them!

Ben said, 'Perhaps you could keep the injured guy company while we have our little chat with the others. Ned, he's calling himself now, I believe?'

'Yes, Ned.'

'Recovering well, is he?'

'Oh, yes. He's got the right attitude about his health and is very determined not to remain an invalid. And actually he's very pleasant to be with.'

'Good for him. I'm sure it'd help keep him cheerful if you could spend some time with him, except for when you're getting food and drink for us all, of course. He'll benefit from the company of someone closer to his own age and it'll make him feel more normal.'

'All right.' That made sense though not much else did at the moment. And she was rather disappointed about what exactly they wanted her to do here. It didn't sound as if there would be anything particularly interesting about this new situation.

She glanced quickly round before she left, checking that all the arrangements for their physical comfort were in place because she didn't want Sean and Nina seeing anything, however tiny, that they could find fault with. Then she left the oldies to it. She wished there were more to do to occupy her time.

As she walked slowly back up to the big house to pass on their message, she couldn't help wondering what they were actually up to. They were playing their cards close to the chest, making it hard to guess anything at all, even for her and she was usually good at solving puzzles.

The most baffling aspect of all was how they could wish to involve her in what they were planning if it was such hush-hush stuff. She was such an ordinary person compared to them, compared to anyone, really.

Still, if she could help even something minor to happen smoothly without any hassles, it'd be something worth achieving, wouldn't it? She liked the thought of that.

And in the meantime, she really would enjoy spending time with Ned.

Sean looked up as Ilsa came in to join them in the casual meals area near the kitchen to get a drink of chilled water. He waited till she'd rinsed the glass out and put it to drain then asked, 'Everything all right?'

'Yes. But the oldies want to run something past you and Nina this afternoon and wondered if you could join them later.' She looked at the clock. Just over an hour to go till then.

'Only Nina and myself? Not you as well this time?'

'No, not me. They suggested I go and chat to Ned.'

'We're free now and could go down to talk to them straight away.'

'They're not quite ready for you yet, though. I think they need to discuss the details of their idea first.'

'What did they want to talk to you about? Do you mind me asking?'

'They were asking me about why I left the army and what I wanted to do with my life.'

He thought about this for a moment then shrugged. 'They've got a reputation for shrewdness and for working out quirky solutions to difficult problems, so I'm certain that if they have a suggestion about our situation it'll be worth all of us listening to their ideas. They probably wanted to pick your brain about some of the practical details. Details can make such a difference to the success of small jobs and you're good at getting them right.'

That compliment pleased her. 'Yes. I suppose that'll be it.'

She hesitated then risked commenting on the three oldies, since he had done so, 'They're an incredible trio, aren't they? Very sharp and alert. That stands out a mile.'

Nina stopped working on her laptop, looking down at it with a sigh. 'No word from my sons. Their idea of keeping in touch is usually a two-line email or text.' Then she shrugged and went back to the previous topic. 'As to the oldies, I've only just met them, but that was my impression too. I wonder what exactly they're planning to do?'

By that time Ned had set down the book he was flicking through to join in the conversation. 'I've been wondering about that as well ever since you told me about them.'

Ilsa glanced at him. He was sitting in a far more normal and upright position now, and seemed to be looking more alert all the time, every hour or two even. But he was still clearly wary of what was happening around him even when it didn't sound like it included him. And who wouldn't be when they'd escaped death so narrowly?

His question was aimed at her. 'They just want to chat to Nina and Sean next? Did they mention seeing me at some stage?'

This was clearly worrying him but she could only tell him the truth. 'I'm afraid not.'

He stared at the other two. 'If the plans concern me, I shall want to know more about the situation before I agree to do anything else. I'm sick to death of being kept in the dark and then expected to jump in at some deep end or other when ordered.'

He was looking distinctly grumpy now, Ilsa thought, and hid a smile. That was a good sign that he was recovering. He was probably fed up to the teeth of being an invalid, and it'd hit an active person harder than one who lived a sedentary life. Hanging round doing nothing would drive her mad.

When she turned back to look at Sean, he too was frowning, then he stared at her and said abruptly, 'I hope they're not making too detailed a set of plans for doing whatever it is before they've run it all past me to check that it will be allowed.'

'They sound more like the sort of people who make the rules than meekly obey ones set by others,' Nina said.

Another pause, then Sean said, 'Look, it's a bit unorthodox to ask this, Ilsa but did you overhear anything that might hint at what sort of an idea they've come up with?'

'No. And I'm still wondering why they were asking me about my family background at one stage. It surprised

me because I don't really have one. They said they liked
to know about the people they worked with, but it still
seemed a bit strange to need to know details about
someone in as unimportant a position as me. As I was
only ten when my parents were killed I don't remember
much about my family background at all.'

'That must have been hard,' Nina murmured.

Ilsa shrugged. What could you say? Done was done,
and she always tried to focus on the future, not the past.

'Is Prue in on this secrecy as well as the two men? I've
met her before and always considered her a particularly
level-headed person,' Sean said thoughtfully.

'Yes, but I could tell from her expression today that she
too thought whatever it was to be a good idea.'

'I think I'd better go straight down and tell them
it could be a waste of time to discuss the details till
they've run the basic idea past me. I am still in charge
of running this place, after all, and if something goes
wrong it'll be my head on the chopping block.' Sean
stood up abruptly, pushing his chair back so that it
nearly fell over.

Ilsa moved to hold her arm out and bar him from
leaving. 'I was hoping I wouldn't have to say this, sir,
but I think they must have been expecting you to get
a bit annoyed about the situation because they said to
remind you that if you go marching down there straight
away they may not be ready to share their ideas with
you yet.'

He stopped dead and scowled at her.

She spoke coaxingly. 'Also, we've got this place
particularly well protected from scrutiny by outsiders, but

I was taught that you can never be 100 per cent certain and if anyone is watching, we don't want them to wonder what's upsetting you. It shows in your face that something is.'

'Damn you, you're right. I was reminded of the same thing by an expert only last year at a refresher course. She said 99 per cent secure is possible for a new building – perhaps – but nothing in life is ever 100 per cent perfect or secure.'

Ilsa didn't move, watching as he turned away from the door. 'And this house was built a long time ago so it has a lot more nooks and crannies than a modern one would have,' she pointed out softly.

'Bringing it into the digital age and upgrading security are on our list of things that need doing,' Nina said.

He'd stopped moving and was standing motionless, breathing deeply. She guessed he was forcing himself to control his anger at being excluded from these preliminary discussions, but from what she'd heard, these oldies had in their time been both famous and highly respected in the upper echelons of national security and she'd bet they went their own way once they'd decided on something. She was good at reading where the real power lay in situations, she knew, and that ability had helped keep her out of trouble at times.

Now looking calmer, he turned back to her. 'I apologise. I'm really sorry to have put you in the difficult situation just now of having to stop me, Ilsa. But the fact that they've now gone into a huddle and are planning something in detail has still got me worried. We're in a very delicate situation here and at a crucial stage too in sorting things out at a higher level for the future, I suspect.'

'It won't hurt to wait an hour or so to speak to them, Sean,' Nina said gently.

The two of them might have been alone in the room for a few seconds, the way they looked at one another, Ilsa thought enviously. If that wasn't love sparking between them, she didn't know what was. Lucky them!

Then he confirmed her guess by reaching out to give Nina's hand another of those quick but still intimate squeezes. 'No, I suppose not. I'm a bit on edge about it all, perhaps not thinking as clearly as usual. Look, I might as well use the time till I go and meet up with the oldies by getting back to Elizabeth next door and sorting a garden matter out with her.'

'Oh?' The two women stared at him with even Nina looking a bit puzzled now. Ilsa was glad when she asked bluntly, 'How is Elizabeth involved in this?'

'She isn't yet. But she's a gardening guru, apparently. I've not been talking to her about what those oldies are discussing but I've been told that if I can, I should foster the lavender plants that give this place its name. It's a minor matter and apparently fairly straightforward, but they're well known in this valley. Anyway, it'll make a nice change from what I've been doing lately.'

They all looked a bit confused now, so he explained. 'The authorities have promised to let her and the gardening group sort the outside out for us. I told her she could come round for a quick look as soon as I could slot the visit in. She's worried about the lavender bushes because apparently these are a rather rare old species and she and her gardening friends will be happy to help preserve them. They apparently need regular attention to trim them and plant replacements of the same sort because they're not long-lasting plants as individuals.'

Ilsa couldn't see how this minor detail mattered, especially at the moment, and exchanged mystified glances with Nina.

'They assure me that the bushes look spectacular when they're in bloom and they attract horticulturalists from all over the area.'

Nina was still looking at him in bewilderment. 'Are you sure that's worth dealing with just now?'

He shrugged. 'I know nothing about gardening so I may as well pick her brain and it'll only take a short time to nip next door. There's nothing happening at the moment and you and I are going to be responsible for the maintenance here once we've sorted this mess out so it won't hurt to make a start.'

When he'd gone, Nina said, 'We haven't been together all that long but I know him well enough already to understand that when he gets that look on his face, it means he has to do something active or burst with frustration. My older son, Brandon, is a bit the same.'

'Men!' they both said at once and smiled at one another.

'Want a mug of coffee while we wait for His Majesty to return from next door?' Nina asked.

'I'd love one.'

As she waited for Nina to make the coffee, Ilsa thought again how much she liked these people. And she felt as if she'd grown closer still to Nina in this brief exchange of views about men.

She hoped that lasted. She didn't have any real women

friends at the moment and there weren't many other staff here to mingle with. She'd cope, of course she would, but she'd rather not have to endure total loneliness outside working hours.

Sean walked slowly along the path that ran down the edges of the gardens, staring at the lavender bushes that gave the facility its name. He also glanced at the other plants, trying to remember their names. He was no gardener and wouldn't have known any but the most common ones of all if his neighbour hadn't pointed out one or two to him.

Elizabeth had insisted it was his duty to make sure these heritage plants didn't come to any harm, and he supposed she was right.

They looked OK to him at the moment, not wilting or anything, but what did he know? He'd have them checked by an expert as soon as things settled down and in the meantime she sounded to know what she was talking about. She might even *be* an expert.

'I like to make sure it doesn't need any special attention, just a quick check,' she'd said. 'After all, the garden has suffered a couple of years of neglect. We did replace one or two dying plants last year, though. We didn't think anyone would mind.'

'Definitely not. Very public spirited of you.'

He strolled down to the little-used front gate, which was the quickest way to go next door on foot. He'd suggest to Elizabeth that today might be a good time for her to take a preliminary whizz round. A rapid one, strictly no more than twenty minutes and it'd have to be done at once or not till another day.

He smiled, amused that he was the keeper of a heritage garden when he'd never done any grubbing in the dirt in his whole life. Good thing he had a neighbour who knew what she was doing because even Nina didn't know much about English plant species since most of her gardening had been done in Australia.

Chapter Twenty-One

Elizabeth looked out of the side window of the kitchen while she waited for the kettle to boil so that she could make cups of coffee for herself and her friend Selina.

She'd been staring out much more frequently since the new people arrived and the place next door began to re-open. And if that made her a nosy parker, too bad. She was sick and tired of living quietly here, even if she was getting older.

Her son might think she should stop wasting her energy fiddling around with her own and other people's gardens, but her interest was more than just a way of keeping things looking nice. She'd saved a few rare species in her time and was proud of such achievements. There was even one flowering plant named after her.

Anyhow, like many widows, she was glad to have something interesting to do with her days. Her husband had died a few years ago, poor love, her children had grown up and moved away from the area and no, she wasn't going to leave her beloved garden and buy a flat near either of them. She'd rather babysit plants than young children any day, far rather.

She continued to watch Sean, hoping he was coming to see her because she'd been feeling a bit down and she was hoping this charming newcomer would liven things up for everyone nearby.

He came through the ramshackle gate at the street side of his garden, turned right and started striding across towards her home. Oh, good!

'It's my new neighbour and he can only be coming to see me,' she told her friend. 'He's looking rather miffed. I wonder what's upset him.'

Selina came to join her by the window. 'He's rather dishy for a man his age, isn't he? Is he married?'

'I have no idea.'

'Well, we'll have to check his background socially, but you're right: he definitely looks miffed. Do you want me to leave? Or can I stay to meet him and watch the fun?'

'No need for you to leave, but it may not be fun. And I keep telling you that I'm *not* looking for another husband, or even a toy boy. I wonder what has upset him. We'll have to learn to manage him if we want good access to the unusual collection of plants growing at his place.'

'You're on. That sounds like fun.'

Elizabeth didn't open the door until the knocker sounded. 'Sean! Lovely to see you. Do come in.'

He followed her inside but said, 'I can't stay, I'm

afraid,' and made no effort to sit down.

'How are things next door? My friends and I are really looking forward to helping you to get your gardens properly sorted out.'

'I'll be really grateful. I have neither the time nor the knowledge to deal with them myself, that's for sure.'

She grinned and added cheekily, 'Well, you'll not get rid of us easily in that case because there aren't a lot of other heritage gardens nearby for us to play with, so we'll be happy to continue borrowing yours.'

He nodded then looked towards her guest, so she introduced them properly. 'This is Selina. She's looking forward to helping me with your garden.'

'Thank you in advance for that, Selina. It's very kind of you.'

'We're both excited about your garden. It'll be lovely when it's brought up to scratch.'

'Do sit down, Sean,' she said again.

'Sorry but I can't stay.' He glanced out of the window then down at his watch. 'I wanted to ask if you'd seen anyone hanging around nearby behaving suspiciously? We shall want to keep our guests safe from unwanted attention. Some burglars target oldies, seeing them as easier targets.'

Selina frowned. 'Well, we didn't get nearly as many passers-by hereabouts till you came to live here, so there are certainly people wandering about. I can't say whether they're connected with the re-opening of the convalescent centre, though.'

'Oh. Thank you for telling me. Could you let me know if you see someone you think looks particularly suspicious or out of place, or who's been here a few times? I'll give you my private phone number.'

'Yes, I'd be happy to do that.'

Selina looked puzzled and asked, 'What do they think you're hiding there?'

'Who knows?' He turned back to Elizabeth, looking a bit upset. 'If we go on at this rate the whole town will be treating watching Lavender Lane as a spectator sport.'

She could see that he was upset by it, so spoke soothingly and changed the subject. 'What exactly do you want us to do to the gardens?'

'Since I have no experience whatsoever of gardening, I'll be relying on you completely to tell me what needs doing, and even to explain what these various procedures will entail.'

He stopped because she was chuckling. 'What's so funny?'

'You make it sound like a medical situation with doctors operating on plants instead of people. Have you any idea when we'll be allowed to start work on the gardens?'

He ran one hand through his hair. 'Not yet.' Then he glanced down at his watch. 'Sorry if I'm not explaining things very well. I'm just trying to tell you something quickly because I have another appointment shortly.'

'No, I'm the one who should be sorry for interrupting you. Do go on.'

'I can provide money for plants or whatever else you may need and there are some tools in that shed at the far end of our rear car park that you can use or else bring your own. But apart from that, it's up to you what jobs you do and in what order. I must try it sometime, digging my fingers in the soil, I mean. Or building sandcastles at a beach. People are always going on about how satisfying doing that can be.'

He stared down at his neatly manicured hands, which made the two women study them as well and exchange quick glances. They had clearly not been used for manual labour.

Elizabeth goggled at him. 'Did you never even try digging in the sand as a child, Sean?'

'No, never. I grew up in a flat in London with an ultra-neat mother and was never allowed near a sandpit.' He'd been sent to a school for gifted children, but wasn't going to brag about his mental abilities, because he was sure now that this special education had been started too young. If he'd ever had children, he'd have given them time to play before putting their noses to a non-stop grindstone.

'Go on,' Elizabeth said gently.

'After I left university, I went to work for the government and was sent here and there in the world, moving on from one project to another, so I continued to live in flats or rental homes in between these forays. I've rarely stayed anywhere for long. I suppose I've just used the places I've lived in as temporary staging posts.'

To his surprise, Elizabeth gave him a sudden hug. 'You poor thing. You've missed a lot. Nothing eases sadness like a stint of grubbing in the soft earth or pruning a shrub or two.'

'Or stroking the soft petals of a beautiful flower.' Selina smiled across at a plant on her friend's windowsill.

'I'll have to take your word for that till I've tried it myself. I'm hoping to be able to settle down here eventually, once we've sorted everything out. I don't know why, but I like the feel of the place.'

'You don't sound to have ever had a real home,' Elizabeth said.

He glanced out of the window towards Lavender Lane and murmured, 'No. But I'm hoping perhaps I've found a permanent one now.' He didn't know why but his voice came out rather choked. He didn't usually let his emotions get the better of him.

She noticed, of course, and tactfully waited a minute for his feeling to subside before asking, 'Have you any idea how much money there will be available to do the work needed at your place, Sean? It'll cost a fair bit to do things properly, so perhaps we'll need to prioritise the jobs.'

He shrugged. 'There will be as much money as is needed to do a decent but not lavish job. It's not exactly *my* place, though. It was my partner who inherited it and I happened to have a connection to the charity it's legally and permanently linked to so I came with her to see it and we both fell in love with the place. And with each other.'

This was the story they'd agreed on and actually quite close to the truth, but it still filled him with wonderment and joy that it had happened so quickly. The mere sight of her lifted his heart in a way no other woman had done.

'So do we need to discuss any suggestions with her as well?'

'Not necessarily. Especially now. She and I have both got other things going on so we're a bit busy at the moment.' He stared at Elizabeth, his expression suddenly stern. 'But keep all this to yourselves. I don't want what you're doing to be talked about widely at this stage, if you don't mind.'

After another of those thoughtful pauses, he added, 'Can you please play down the funding we're providing for your group as well, and not chat about anything else you see going on at the Lane – not to anyone at all, even if they're your very best friends? If you can't guarantee that reticence, our mutual arrangements will have to be terminated.'

He waited for their reply, his expression very solemn. There was no doubt he meant every word.

Elizabeth shrugged, hoping she'd hidden her surprise at this vehemence. 'You said that when we first talked about this, so I've been very careful which friends I've invited to help look after this garden, Sean. I can assure you that, like Selina here, the others will be totally trustworthy. Lavender Lane has always been a rather secretive place, my mother told me, and if you think I didn't notice that you and Nina seem to be carrying on that tradition, you're wrong.'

'I did feel almost immediately that I could trust you to stay quiet about what's going on here, and I want to reiterate that both Nina and I very much appreciate your help.'

He held out his right hand and they shook on that, then he pulled a credit card out of his pocket and held it out to her. 'Nina inherited a gardening fund and this card draws on it. You can use the money for whatever you need to purchase in connection with the gardens next door – but for nothing else. We expect you to be sensible and not go for outrageously expensive or difficult-to-look-after plants, but do please buy whatever you need to make things look cared for as rapidly as you can. The emphasis at this stage is on speed of getting the garden tidied up rather than cost. We want to enjoy living there and for the place to show the world that it's inhabited again and back to its former use.'

'You can't make plants grow to your timetable, only choose them carefully and encourage them to grow. They usually start off small then do their own thing about how fast they grow bigger, however hard you encourage them.'

'I know that but it looks such a mess at the moment, though I did wonder whether someone had been trimming the lavender plants.'

'I plead guilty. They needed it desperately, poor things. I couldn't let them die, so I've nipped across every now and then, to give them a helping hand.'

'Thank you. You'll be able to tidy the rest up as needed and perhaps buy a few bigger plants of other sorts to help give things a kick start on looking good? The only things we don't want changing are the lavender bushes, as we've already agreed. The place is, after all, named for them. I looked them up online and they did seem rather lovely.'

Elizabeth beamed at him. 'I shall enjoy organising it all. You probably don't realise it but those bushes are of a particularly rich blue colour and they smell heavenly too.'

'I shall look forward to seeing them for myself. And any time you want, you can take some cuttings with our blessing.'

'Wonderful.' She got out her purse and put the credit card away in one of the inner slots. He looked so weary, her heart went out to him.

'Anything else I need to know or do urgently in connection with the gardens?' he asked.

'Not at the moment. I'll get back to you on that once we've done our survey and made proper plans.'

'Good.' He glanced at his watch again, then moved

towards the door. 'I'll let you take a very quick look round now so that you can make a start with your planning, but you won't be able to come back very often until I've sorted out a few other things.'

'You look tired. Why don't you sit down again and at least have a cup of coffee?'

'I'd love to do that another time but there's too much to do setting things up, not just today but all week.'

He moved towards the front door, where he stopped to say, 'One other thing. You should only come round to work in daylight hours when we can keep an eye on you and your safety.'

She patted his arm. 'Yes. So you've said. And we'll do that. Now, give us a couple of minutes to change our shoes then we'll follow you round and take a quick preliminary look at the gardens.'

'Very well. I've someone coming to see me later so you really do need to do it very quickly.'

After he'd left, Selina went out to get her gardening boots from her car and the two women sat down to pull on their sturdy footwear, beaming at one another.

'That project is going to be fun,' Elizabeth said. 'I've never had such a generous budget before.'

'And to add to the pleasure, it's money that we didn't have to provide ourselves and fundraise or beg to obtain. I'm so glad you included me in this project.'

'We always work well together. Let's go next door and whizz round our blank canvas then come back and make a rough start on the planning.' She smiled and made a triumphant fist in the air. 'Yeah! We'll be sensible but there's clearly no need to be frugal this time.'

'That'll be such fun, buying the best plants for the various positions.'

Elizabeth had absolute confidence in Selina. She'd known all the people who would now be involved in this project for years and felt sure she could trust them to keep quiet about the details of what they were doing as the project got under way. Well, they'd kept quiet about one another's marital ups and downs over the years too, hadn't they?

Sean hadn't told her exactly what this was all about. It must be something very important if the government was throwing all this money at it. How intriguing it all was. But if a man as savvy as him was worried about danger after dark, then she'd have to make sure from now on that she locked her outer doors and windows very carefully and switched on her perimeter security system at night, even if Selina was staying over.

Thank goodness she had an excellent security system. She wasn't stupid enough to live alone as a single older woman without taking precautions. Her son had helped her set that up after his father died.

Maybe she'd find out the full details of what was going on next door one day and maybe not. Even if she didn't, she'd enjoy her part in it because creating new gardens could be such a wonderfully rewarding activity in its own right.

She smiled as it occurred to her that Sean had another focus to his life now apart from his work, and it seemed to have happened quickly. But from the way he smiled at the thought of Nina, it was making him very happy. Well, good luck to the pair of them. Everyone deserved a loving partnership of some sort at least once in their lives and he was a bit of a late starter.

She passed a new notepad to her friend. 'Here. You're better at sketching than I am. Can you do a rough sketch as we go round of where the flower beds are with an estimate of their size? This is going to be fun but we'd better hurry. We only have about fifteen minutes left to whizz round this time.'

Selina nodded. 'I'll pace it out roughly as we go to get a general idea of size then we'll go back to your place and start planning.'

'I wonder when we'll be allowed to start the real work.'

'We may have to wait to do that. But it'll make a great excuse to have a preliminary wander round the plant nurseries in the area, won't it?'

'Several wanders.'

'Of course. But first, do we want a cottage garden look or more formal borders of flowery annuals?'

Selina considered this, head on one side as they walked along the first path. 'Flowers galore, for sure. They lift just about everyone's spirits and if this is any sort of convalescent home that will be a particularly good thing. But not too formal. And the plants will have to fit in with the lavender around blooming time.'

'Yes. I agree.' With matching blissful sighs, they began work.

Chapter Twenty-Two

Prue stood by the window, looking round her temporary home while her niece went upstairs and unpacked their things. She'd stopped using the walking stick once they were alone but still felt it necessary to carry the dratted thing round with her in case someone she didn't know came to the door.

Zoe came down to join her, smiling happily. 'It's very cosy here. Thanks for offering me the job, Auntie Prue. The money will come in very useful indeed and I can do some of my studying online from that bedroom and stay out of your way. This place has a really good internet connection.'

'Just make sure you don't tell any of the friends you're online with about what you're really doing here, *not anyone at all*. And the fact that I pretended to need a carer must stay buried afterwards. Only for Ben and Arthur would I be pretending something like that.'

'They're a great pair of guys, not old in the head at all.'

'That as may be but don't change the subject on me. You must never, ever talk about what my friends and I have been doing here even after we've sorted everything out. If anyone asks, just smile sweetly and say you don't know because you were studying and only here in case I needed help, which I don't and won't need,' Prue warned her.

'You've said that about six billion times and I did understand you on the first iteration.'

Prue's smile vanished. 'It could be life and death, Zoe, if we don't take care, it really could, so you'll excuse me if I go on about it.'

Zoe looked at her aunt very seriously. 'I do know that. I have some idea about what sort of things you've done in your working life because Dad gave me a broad outline, and I admire you greatly. I'll keep my promise never to speak of it, believe me.'

She relaxed visibly and smiled as she added, 'And I'll also keep quiet about the money so no one wonders where I got so much from. It'll go straight into my savings for the holiday in Australia and New Zealand that I'm planning to take once I've finished studying for this degree. I shan't waste a penny of it on frivolous stuff like fancy coffees and the latest fashion in clothes, believe me.'

'Good for you.'

Zoe gave her aunt a big, rocking hug and whispered, 'I won't let you down, not now and not ever. I want to be just like you when I grow up.'

Which led to another longer hug, something Prue didn't mind at all.

A short time later, Sean and Nina came down from

the big house to welcome Prue and make sure she had everything she needed, then she settled into the comfortable armchair placed temptingly near the window. She had chosen a book to read from the small set of shelves that had greeted her from one corner of the room, but would still keep an eye on what was happening outside. Well, who wouldn't be tempted into dipping into their favourite author's latest book straight away. As she'd found in recent years, you were never alone when you could dive into a good story.

It had been agreed even before she set off for Lavender Lane that they'd not meet till the afternoon, on the pretence that she needed to recover from her journey here. She did tire more easily these days but not that easily, for heaven's sake. Only in this little charade, like others they'd been involved in, you had to make sure every detail fitted the picture you wanted to project.

Her niece settled down at the other side of the sitting room looking out to the rear. She was fiddling around with her phone, as she often did, to check it was working OK. That might be more important than usual while they were here.

They had now, Prue hoped, covered all possible problems and she could have a little rest. She had decided she'd rather hold the meetings here than be wheeled to and fro in such a humiliating way. And if that was vanity, too bad.

Later, when the three friends were settled in Prue's living room, she waved Zoe away and Norry went to sit outside at the back with a book. Prue had already arranged with her niece that she would go and sit outside under the tiny patio to the rear when Prue's friends arrived. Good thing it was a sunny day.

This would serve a dual purpose, not only preventing Zoe from hearing the details of what they were planning to do next but also having someone placed to keep watch for any stranger lurking near the two trios of small cottages.

However, Norry didn't go back outside to join Zoe. He hovered by the door, clearly reluctant to leave them and return later for his great-grandfather. In the end Prue watched him take a deep breath and say, 'I'd rather stay here with you, if you don't mind. I'm physically useful to help my great-grandad move around and I'm also interested in how you're planning to proceed. I'd like to see in detail how you work out your tactics. And you know you can trust me not to reveal anything that's discussed.'

After another deep breath and he added, 'You see, I'm definitely going to do this sort of work one day myself and you can't start too soon to get a feel for it.'

'You're right about starting early and I think you'll do well at it,' Ben said with quiet certainty, then turned to his friends. 'Would it be all right for Norry to stay for this and for most of the other meetings from now on? We can trust him absolutely, I assure you.'

'You didn't need to tell us that,' Arthur said with a smile at Norry.

The three oldies exchanged smiles with one another and Prue answered for them all by gesturing to a chair. 'Of course we feel sure we can trust him. You didn't need to tell us that. And it's been obvious for a while where he's heading long term. We watch out for likely younger folk. We need to keep an eye on our country, and on our little valley, not only now but for the future.'

She smiled at the younger guy who was looking in doubt about whether to join them for the rest of the discussions. 'Why don't you bring that chair forward and join the group properly?'

Norry did that, looking happy and alert. 'Thank you for your trust. I won't ever let you down.'

'As we already said, we know that or we'd not have let you even linger this long,' Prue said.

They settled down to discuss a suggestion Ben wanted them to consider very seriously indeed. He outlined his idea in more detail than previously and even though it surprised them at first, they were soon murmuring agreement.

'Do you think Sean will agree to do it?' Arthur asked. 'If he will, so will others and that could be the main key to its success.'

'It might take a little persuasion,' Prue said, 'but not much or I'd not try to do it. He's ripe for a change of lifestyle, if a man ever was, and he could continue doing useful work here for our operatives.'

'Does he get on well enough with Ilsa?'

'Oh, yes. He couldn't have done that sort of job for this long without being able to get on with just about anyone. But actually, I think he really does like her already – well, I've been keeping an eye on her and most people do get on well with her. She may be quiet but she's highly intelligent and has a very decent way of interacting with the world.'

'Yes, that shows clearly,' Arthur agreed. 'If you can't recognise decent people by our age, you haven't done much with your life, I reckon.'

They all nodded.

'I'm quite certain she'll not let us down,' Ben said. 'She doesn't show her deepest feelings to many people and I'd guess she's kept her own secrets for most of her life, probably since she was first taken into care. I'm pretty certain she's dyslexic and that's one of the main reasons why she didn't want to study. I have a relative with that problem. But now that she understands the group better, and has shown her belief in what we do, we'll be able to let her participate in other things after this project ends.'

Prue sighed and shook her head sadly. 'She wasn't treated well as a child by those who should have looked after her, was she? Imagine a ten-year-old child having to cope with a major bereavement then being shuffled from one place to another without much care for her feelings, only the care of her body.'

'Well, we'll make sure she benefits from our group's contacts after she's helped us with this project and help her make a more fulfilling life for herself. It's one of the joys of my old age, helping youngsters who need a bit of extra help.'

'Who's going to tell her the details of this little project and ask whether she's willing to be involved?'

'It won't matter which of us does that,' Arthur said. 'I'm sure she'll agree. But first we need to check that Sean is on side for it – and I'm thinking that perhaps Nina needs to be included in the planning for this as well, now.' He chuckled softly. 'From the way they look at one another, she and Sean are well and truly together as a couple already and fortunately she seems to get on well with Ilsa too.'

'I think you could be right there. Great to see, isn't it? Nina is another good lass and is a credit to our group already. Laura was right: she was an excellent choice to inherit, don't you think?'

'I agree.' Ben turned to the boy. 'Now, back to you, Norry. We'll still need to use you as a messenger lad at times, if you don't mind, as well as involving you in what we're doing and why. Could you please go and ask Sean and Nina to join us again now?'

'Yes, of course.'

'Promising lad, that,' Arthur said again once he'd left.

'We've fallen lucky with our younger folk, haven't we? Looking at the future, I think we have some really good people on our side getting ready to take over one day when it becomes necessary. That makes me feel that good has an advantage even now over evil, both morally and practically, now and in the future. I don't know about you, my friends, but I feel it's particularly important in our sort of job to keep an eye on the succession planning.'

Ben sighed. 'We give up a lot to do this sort of work, don't we, and I wouldn't have been part of it for all these years if I couldn't have believed in it wholeheartedly.'

Prue said quietly, 'Our group is fighting a minor part of the bigger war, but fighting evil with good has been an ongoing battle throughout the history of humankind, not simply counteracting evil with weapons and, sadly, the spilling of blood but replacing it with more worthwhile beliefs, however you dress them up.'

He suddenly stopped and looked embarrassed. 'Sorry. I didn't mean to batter the ears of the converted.'

'I've always admired the way you've stayed enthusiastic for all those decades about what we do,' Prue said quietly.

They nodded, then waited quietly for Norry to re-join them. Quiet times were important too, in renewing the spirit.

Norry came back shortly afterwards and was soon followed by Sean and Nina, who didn't seem to realise they were holding hands as they approached the cottage.

Prue and Ben were both betrayed into sentimental sighs at the sight.

When everyone was seated, Arthur said quietly, 'I think I have a good plan for the future use of Lavender Lane. As I hinted last time, this will need your involvement, Sean, and to a lesser extent, yours, Nina.'

'I'd be delighted to hear more about that and to help as needed,' Sean said at once.

Nina nodded. 'So would I.'

'What if we were to become a place where the personal and family backgrounds of our senior staff are sorted out and not just ignored after they finish their service? I should think lost family members could sometimes be found and whole families reunited. Or at least the odd distant relative located. Or even, perhaps, adoptive families created and helped get together.'

He waited a minute for that to sink in then said, 'It'd be a good thing to do, surely, before people leave active service to go into retirement and need to pick up a mainly private personal life once again. There have been too many cases of PTSD in people who've left the service.'

'Why would our officials suddenly divert their resources to doing that?' Sean asked bluntly. 'We're not exactly lavishly funded as it is.'

'To find improved ways of helping our people ease into retirement, which isn't always an easy thing for those who've had our sort of active life.'

Nina joined in. 'I think it'd be an excellent service to set up. I've read quite a few articles recently that finding their way back into civilian life can be a problem for some of the people who leave the armed forces.'

Sean nodded. 'And perhaps we can sell it to the senior echelons that how the game ends should not only morally be a part of pastoral care but will save money in the long run. Ned's case is a good example of the rehabilitation of physically injured operatives who need longer-term attention. But there can be a social and psychological need too as you can see with him.'

'He seems to be starting to find his way. He relates well to Ilsa, as if they're on the same wavelength, and if a man like him can accept the sort of sympathetic input she's offering, then others will value it too, I'm sure.'

'Do you have someone in mind to organise this?' Sean asked.

'We have someone in mind to set a shining example as the first person to join in, and that's you, Sean. After which we'll look into how best to organise it with your expert advice.'

'But I think we're going to have to deal with the technology side of things. We're way out of touch here.'

'It's a pity my elder son isn't here,' Nina said sadly.

'Brandon would be perfect for that job. I came to England originally to live near my sons and then both moved away. The other son, Kit, didn't plan to leave but he was headhunted and couldn't resist the offer made to him about a job in New York.'

Arthur looked at her. 'Give me his details. I'm not promising anything but if your son is as promising as you think, we might be able to do some headhunting ourselves.'

Ben looked at them. 'In the meantime perhaps we can go back to our little experiment in pulling families together. What do you think, Sean? Would you give it a try, as an experiment?'

He sat quietly contemplating the proposal for several seconds then looked across at Ben. 'But I don't need rehabilitating. I've managed perfectly well. And I don't have any lost relatives I need to find and cosy up to, either.'

Nina intervened, taking his hand. 'Let them tell you all the relevant details so you can understand all that they are proposing, and then you can decide if you want to go along with the idea. I think everyone is better for having a family of some sort and it is a lack in your life.'

He looked at her in shock then back at Ben.

'We thought you might pretend you've found a lost cousin or niece or whatever relationship you think best,' the older man said quietly. 'We're at the stage where we'll probably learn a lot more about how to manage this sort of interaction by observing it in action rather than by merely talking about it and reading articles in psychology journals.'

There was dead silence and Sean didn't speak till Nina nudged him again.

'Why use me to play the part?'

'Because you're here and about to retire, and because you really have lost touch completely with most of your relatives. It's all very convenient and would help us enormously if you would agree to participate in this project.'

Sean leant back in his chair, arms folded, scowling. 'And where are you going to find a lost niece for me?'

'We have someone right here: Ilsa.'

He looked stunned for a few moments, then protested. 'But she and I aren't related.'

Nina grabbed his hand and gave it a little warning shake. 'They know that. Shut up and let them tell you how they're planning to do it. And I might say that I personally would like to see something done to help people like that brave young woman find a way into a happier life. I wish we *could* find her a relative. And I wish you had a relative or two as well.'

He scowled at her. 'What makes you an expert on families?'

'I know what it's like to lose touch with people I care about because both my sons went off to lead their own lives, and all I get now is the odd email. I might as well be alone in the world most of the time. But at least I've experienced family life and am hoping against hope that my family will come back together again, that my sons will eventually settle down.'

He stared at her, surprised at her vehemence, then noticed the tears in her eyes and gave her a sudden hug. 'Sorry for snapping at you, love.'

'It's all right. The idea took you by surprise.'

'It certainly did. Ilsa is a nice lass, I'll grant you that.

And she's making a big difference to Ned. But—'

'But she's one of the loneliest people I've ever met when it comes to friends and family of her own, and she's so brave about coping with it. She never complains but she's had a lot to endure that it'd be quite reasonable to complain about in the way the system has treated her emotionally.'

He nodded slowly as this sank in. 'I don't think I ever saw that as clearly. You're right.'

'People aren't able to make good long-term relationships when they're moved about so often, as she was in both foster homes and the army. Or as you have been. Life was particularly cruel to her, though. You've had it much easier. That accident jerked her suddenly off her preferred path as an adult.'

She let that sink in and noticed that everyone else was looking thoughtful so continued, 'I like her and I'd already begun to wonder whether anything could be done to help her, and maybe *should* be done, even if it was just me keeping in touch, acting like a sort of aunt.'

She gave a little nod as if to say that she'd finished and fell silent, folding her arms and staring round at them with an air of defiant challenge as she waited for her remarks to sink in.

'I've not had much to do with her,' Prue said thoughtfully. 'I must get to know her better after hearing how well you think of her, Nina. What's more, I don't like to think of one of our people being called *loneliest* and *bravest* at the same time. It doesn't seem fair that those officers managing her have let that happen.'

'I've chatted to her a few times recently,' Nina said. 'She's been on her own in the world since the age of ten – *ten!* –

and although she was taken into care, from what she says they only looked after her physically. She found a sort of family substitute in the army, though that's not like having a real family, and then that accident and the resulting injuries took even that path away from her.'

She looked across at the three oldies. 'I'd been hoping but now I'm *intending* that when this project is up and running I shall find her some niche that will give her the equivalent of a home. I'm sure we could do it better as a group for people who have been detached from family contacts if we set our minds to it.'

'I agree. And I too have begun to hope that we can find somewhere Ilsa can fit in permanently, possibly helping to run this place, or some other job that suits her skills.' Arthur smiled happily round at his companions.

After a moment or two, Sean nodded slowly. 'It's inconceivable that we wouldn't want Ilsa to stay on here after this project ends, and as an important part of the team because she's so efficient.'

'I agree, Sean,' commented Nina. 'So perhaps you and she can pilot our experiment. You'll have to be genuinely sympathetic if you get close enough that she reveals underlying sadness. And of course you'll give her a hug or two as part of getting closer. Unless you have some objection to hugging people other than me?'

'No. I don't. It's a natural human reaction to some situations.' Sean said. He hesitated then added, 'Though unlike some people who seem born multi-huggers, I don't do it often.' He smiled across at Nina as he added, 'Only when my affections are genuinely and deeply engaged.'

'There you are then. You seem to be halfway there in

your understanding before you even get into building a new relationship between yourself and Ilsa. Which you are going to do, aren't you?'

He hesitated, looking thoughtful, then nodded.

After a few moments of silence, Nina lifted the mood by saying, 'I can vouch for how skilful he is when he sets his mind to hugging someone. See.'

She gave Sean a big hug and plonked a kiss on first one cheek then the other.

'I dare you to hug me back in front of them all,' she whispered.

'You sneaky devil,' he muttered back but returned the hug with every appearance of pleasure, then stepped back and looked at the group of oldies. 'All right, then. You've caught my interest. When do I start and what exactly do we start with?'

Arthur winked at Nina and then at Sean. 'Let's move on with our plans, shall we?' he suggested.

There was a lot of nodding.

'We need to find ways to start doing some normal social activities that people enjoy with relatives they care about,' Ben said quietly. 'We thought at first we might find Ilsa a project at one of the bases reasonably close to here but actually, why don't you just ask her to go for a walk with you so that you can chat without interruptions?'

'She won't mistake that for me propositioning her?' Sean asked, suddenly sounding anxious.

'She'll know exactly how things stand because of course we'll be briefing her as well as you on the possibility of forming a sort of adopted relationship before you actually go for the walk. And she'll have seen you and Nina. There's no mistaking how you two feel about one another.'

'Just so that you know,' Sean said sharply, 'I don't have any close relatives at all, so how are you going to explain our connection to others? I can't see people accepting that she's a niece – maybe some sort of cousin would be more credible?'

Arthur nodded. 'I think you're right there. There are all sorts of cousins; you could even take your pick about which level of relationship to call it.'

'Hmm. Yes, that'd definitely be more flexible.' Sean was still looking worried. 'There's another thing.'

'Go on.'

'However hard I try, I may not do this as well as I'd like to. I'm not brilliant with small talk, never have been.' He looked sideways. 'Except with Nina.'

She shot him a quick sympathetic look then turned to the group of oldies. 'I could go with him and help. I'm good with people and as I've already said, I'd be genuinely happy to get to know Ilsa better. I already like what I've seen of her. She won't mistake us for genuine lost relatives if she's been properly briefed, I'm sure. Nor will she think Sean is propositioning her if I'm part of it all.'

She turned to her partner. 'If you're struggling for the best way to do something, I could either nudge you into action, Sean, or you could simply follow my example in the small ways people behave towards strangers. Just think: if we could do this properly, we could make a big difference to future generations of retiring personnel. Stop them getting depressed and feeling lost and alone in civilian life.'

His tone was mocking and perhaps just a little too acid.

'What? Set up a lonely hearts club?'

Her voice was calm and quiet. 'Loneliness isn't good for people, Sean. And Ilsa has had more than her fair share. You have too.'

He ran one hand through his hair, leaving it tangled. 'Well, I'll give it my best shot and perhaps with your help I can manage not to put my foot in it too badly. I've always considered losing touch with family as the price people like me have paid for the privilege of serving our country.'

'And maybe this new project would set an example so that we could help people like you to come out of the shadows afterwards and form new relationships. After all, that's what you've been doing with me, isn't it? Making a new relationship? And doing it rather nicely in my opinion.'

As she took hold of his hand and gave him one of her beautiful loving smiles, he stared at her as if that hadn't fully struck him before, then said, 'You're easy to care for. I feel very lucky to have met you, my darling, and I hope and pray you feel the same.'

'Don't look so worried. I'm extremely glad we did meet and I do feel the same way about you, have done right from the start. But as I've learnt more about your sort of life, I have worried at times that the army is creating people who don't seem able to connect closely with anyone after they retire.'

He frowned, listening to her carefully. She was good with people, better than anyone he'd ever met. He was so lucky that she cared for him.

She seemed to understand when he was ready to continue their conversation. 'I watch people all the time, you see; they're so fascinating. I'm going to write novels one day.' She flushed slightly. 'I've had a few short stories published already. People-centred stories with warm, happy endings.'

'And I reckon you'll do it well, lass,' Ben said. 'I don't know how young folk write novels; they've so little experience of life compared to someone like you.'

She nodded and beamed at him.

There was silence and Ben looked at Nina. 'You go with him, lass, guide him and Ilsa both.'

It was such a fragile bubble they were creating, looking for a better way of treating the operatives who were about to retire. Ben prayed it would work, even if it wasn't perfect. He couldn't imagine life without his family, especially young Norry. And although he supported the lad's ambitions, he didn't want Norry to end up a total loner either. It was too high a price to pay. He could see that so clearly now.

Sean cleared his throat. 'So, how are we supposed to go about this?'

'We'll just ask her to come for a walk with us, then we'll tell her about this discussion and see what she thinks. No need to complicate matters, is there? The simple truth of the situation may be enough to make her want to form a personal connection with us.'

'Ought we to hold our discussion in the library or somewhere?' Sean worried.

'No. I'm sure she'll think better out of doors. And so will you.'

Ben smiled at her. 'You're right. We hadn't planned for you to be part of it but I'm beginning to think that you can help our venture in several ways, Nina.'

'There's just one other thing,' Sean worried. 'What if Ilsa doesn't want to get involved?'

'She will,' Nina said confidently.

Sean was startled. 'Can it be as easy as that to make a start?'

'Yes, it can. Let's go and find Ilsa, take her out for a walk up the hill and speak to her about it now. The oldies will probably have said something to prepare the way.'

When Nina and Sean had left, Prue and Arthur both looked at Ben. 'You're a cunning devil, Ben, far more than most people realise.'

Norry opened his mouth to ask what they meant but Ben shook his head at the lad and mouthed the word 'Later', so he didn't say anything.

Ben shot Prue one of those boyish grins and said, 'I think this is important in several ways.'

'I do too. And I've no doubt whatsoever that it'll all work out as you've planned. Things usually do when you set them up. And we have Nina as well this time. She really is superb with people. No wonder Laura left Lavender Lane to her.'

He put one finger to his lips. 'Let's pour an early glass of wine and enjoy a chat. I think we can leave the natural human instinct to bond with other humans to take over from us now and win the day.'

Chapter Twenty-Three

Sean and Nina went up to the house and found Ilsa in the kitchen, setting the trays for the evening meal.

They walked across to join her and she looked up with one of her calm smiles.

'All work and no play isn't good for anyone,' Nina said. 'We're going for a walk and would like you to come and join us.'

'Are you sure?'

'Very sure. We both enjoy your company and there's a national park with hiker paths at the top of the hill that I don't think you've visited yet.'

'I've been as far as the car park and the woods are down on my mental list of places to visit properly when I have time. I love going for long walks.'

'Well, going for a walk there has just reached the head of our list so are you coming?'

To Sean's relief Ilsa said simply, 'Yes. I'd love to join you.'

He was surprised at how nervous he was feeling, knowing what they intended to do, and was glad when Nina gave his hand a surreptitious squeeze. 'It's a lovely sunny day, shame to waste it,' he managed. He couldn't think of anything more interesting to say.

After they'd gone a little way along the hikers' path, Ilsa said casually 'We've been watching that TV programme about finding long lost relatives. Have you seen it?'

'Yes. It's very touching at times, makes me wish I'd found some lost relatives,' Ilsa said quietly. 'Only I'll never know, will I?'

'Oh, you may find some one day with the improvements in checking DNA and linking it to other people round the world. Never give up hope.'

Sean suddenly found the courage to join in. 'People really benefit from having relatives, I reckon. People who're connected to you are more likely to watch your back if necessary, and would do it more carefully than mere acquaintances might. And I reckon' – he paused for a deep breath before continuing – 'I reckon the next best thing would be to adopt some relatives and make a new family for yourself deliberately.'

Ilsa gave him a rather sad smile. 'It's a bit of a big ask, don't you think? Wanting someone to treat you as if you were connected to one another?'

'Not really. And actually, that's why we've brought you here, to ask you whether you'd consider starting to form a family with us. I've completely lost touch with any close family I ever had and Nina's sons are in a phase where they're gallivanting round the world, working at high-powered jobs.'

'So for the time being I have Sean here and no one else in my family within reach,' Nina said.

Ilsa stared at them in shock, then saw Nina wink at her, which made her feel less tense. When she looked back at Sean, his nervousness was so clear it made her feel more confident. 'Do you mean that, sir?'

'Oh, for goodness' sake don't call me sir. My name's Sean, as you very well know.'

'Sean, then. Did I hear you correctly? Are you and Nina wanting to – to . . .' Her voice faded away and she gulped.

'To start adopting one another and you too as a family. Yes.'

Nina gave him a poke in the ribs. 'You're expressing yourself badly, my lad.'

'Sorry. I meant I didn't have any close blood relatives, and now I've got Nina. She's made me understand that I *need* a family.'

'I think my sons are more interested in making money and will be late starters on the family front. And I – well, I need people too, not just Sean. I'm not a solitary person by nature.'

'So yes, of course I mean it.' He gave Ilsa a rueful look. 'Though I've had to pull all my courage together to ask you about joining us.'

He waited again but she still couldn't quite believe this, let alone find the words to accept as she wanted to.

He filled the silence by saying quietly, 'Ilsa's a pretty name. Where does it come from?'

'I looked it up once. It's a form of Elizabeth, apparently, but more often used in Germany.'

'I might have know you'd have checked. You're good at details.'

'I do my best.'

He felt Nina let go of his arm and give him a poke, as if to tell him to continue, so he did.

'I'm sorry for one thing,' he said suddenly.

'For what exactly?'

'My awkward behaviour today. Nothing to do with you, but I've never been the best at talking about my emotions.'

'I can understand that. Neither have I.'

They exchanged rueful glances and both seemed to have forgotten Nina, so she took another furtive step backwards and stepped out of their line of sight, hoping they wouldn't notice if she opted out of the conversation for a while. They had to find their own way into this as well as both of them getting together with her.

'Nina approves of this idea. And of you,' he said in a near whisper.

Ilsa looked at him as if she found this hard to believe. 'She does?'

'Oh, yes. Very much.'

'I like her. She's very easy to get on with.'

'She likes you, too.'

Ilsa could feel herself flushing. 'Does she really?'

'Yes. And I do too, have done from the start.' After a pause and a deep breath, he muttered, 'And why I'm so nervous about doing this, I have no idea. Only – well, I haven't had a lot to do with relatives and I feel at a disadvantage about how to deal with people on a close personal level.'

'I've no memory of any relatives, Sean. But I'm used to situations where I don't really know someone and I just – you know, go with the flow and try to be pleasant. I don't think you'd be able to force a friendship even if someone really was a real relative, but you and I have always got on well and – and I admire you, so I think we may be able to muddle through if we do the adopted family thing.'

His voice was husky as he said, 'Only if you want to, of course.'

Behind them Nina crossed her fingers in the air at each side of her head, hoping this would continue to go well, but neither of them noticed.

Ilsa nodded and said in a little gasp of sound, 'I do want to try it. Very much indeed.'

He beamed at her and some of the tension seemed to leave his body. 'That's great. And I think you're showing more self-control than I am today, Ilsa. In fact, you're handling me rather well.'

She could feel herself blushing at that. 'I'd love to have a family,' she said softly. 'I've always wanted one. I know what it's like *not* to have any relatives at all. And it's not good. And – and I know you well enough to understand that you'd not be saying these things if you didn't mean them. Can I ask what made you think of it?'

'That trio of oldies. They're very wise. The idea took me by surprise but I liked it. And Nina approved too.'

Ilsa forgot that Nina was standing nearby. 'She's nice, so easy to get on with.'

'Yes. I fell in love with her very quickly. You and I could learn a lot from her. But I have to warn you that though I can run big organisations or cope with dangerous situations, I'm not all that good at making small talk on a personal level. You may find it rather boring to chat to me unless she's around as well to oil the wheels of conversation.'

Ilsa couldn't help smiling and her reply was out before she could prevent herself from commenting honestly, 'I had noticed that, sir – I mean, Sean.'

They stared at one another, then she saw him give a faint smile, which widened into a genuine smile then a rich, deep chuckle.

'Neither are you,' he said in the end. He didn't know why but he suddenly felt more comfortable with her.

'I know.'

She was still smiling. He liked her smile, liked a lot about her.

'I shall enjoy having an extra relative,' he admitted. 'What level of relationship do you think we should make it so that outsiders don't misunderstand the situation? Not a granddaughter. I definitely do not feel old enough for that.'

'Cousins?' she suggested tentatively.

'Cousins would be perfect. Cousin Ilsa. It sounds good.'

It was the name that got her. *Cousin Ilsa.* She gulped and stared at him, then tears started welling in her eyes and rolling down her cheeks and she couldn't stop them. Her voice was little more than a croaky whisper as she echoed the word, 'Cousin. Cousin Sean.'

He looked at her in near panic as the tears continued. 'What have I said? If you don't want to do this, I won't let them force you.'

He couldn't bear to see her pain and moved to pull her closer, in fact right into a proper hug. 'What is it?'

'I – have been lonely all my life, so very lonely. And that's the first time I've ever called anyone cousin.'

He pulled out his handkerchief and dabbed at her face, then said, 'Oh, hell!' and pulled her closer, letting his own tears slip out for the first time in years, feeling for her pain and *caring* for her personally.

He hadn't realised until now, hadn't let himself admit even to himself how utterly lonely he'd been at times. Nina had breached the careful wall he'd built around himself and now Ilsa had crept closer to him as well. He had no doubt her tears were genuine. And to his surprise, his were too.

He couldn't have borne a woman who acted upset but he could care for a young woman who was, as Nina had said, one of the loneliest and bravest people she'd ever met.

And he could let her care for him as well.

Nine judged it time to step forward and put an arm round each of them, pulling them into a triple embrace, and keeping them cuddling one another closely.

'What a lovely thing to happen!' she said. 'We are going to have such a loving family. I'll introduce you to my sons when they pop across to England again. Though I don't think Brandon is enjoying his job in America so I wouldn't be surprised if he makes another move, hopefully back to England.' Then another thought suddenly struck her and she said, 'Ned!'

Her companions looked at her in puzzlement.

'He doesn't have any family either.'

'Hey, slow down,' Sean said. 'You can't adopt the whole world.'

'Why not? He's lonely too.' She grinned at her beloved's panic. 'I won't bring a houseful of people home, but one more person won't hurt and anyway, he and Ilsa get on really well. We can at least give them a chance to see if the feeling that's starting between them lasts.'

She let that sink in, then said quietly, 'Let's do some walking now. Come on. Chop, chop!' And she tugged them into walking at a smart pace but stayed in the middle and kept hold of their hands till the path narrowed too much.

And as they walked, she said, 'We have to have a party, for ourselves and for those delightful oldies.'

Sean and Ilsa looked at her in surprise.

'Just a little party,' she said coaxingly. 'I love throwing surprise parties.'

Sean rolled his eyes at Ilsa. 'When she gets that look on her face, I've found out already that it's best just to say yes to whatever she wants to do.'

'Fine by me. No one has ever thrown a party for me before.'

'Are we going to tell Ned what we're celebrating?' Ilsa asked.

'Of course we are. And we'll ask him to join us. In fact, becoming a family is well worth a happy hour together today as well as a party tomorrow, don't you think?'

When they joined him in the library, Ned was sitting in an armchair with a book lying open but face down on the small table beside him.

He listened to what they were celebrating, beamed at them and had no hesitation in raising his glass to their future happiness.

'We'll have a proper party tomorrow,' Nina told them all.

Epilogue

Nina went shopping the following morning and brought back several bottles of champagne plus lots of luxury nibbly foods. It took her a long time and when Sean and Ilsa both protested that she'd bought too much, she merely flapped one hand at them. 'Trust in me. I'm good at throwing parties.'

Which made the other three share anxious glances. What was she planning now?

By late Saturday afternoon, the feast was ready. Nina had directed operations and hired Ilsa's friends as servers. The others had simply done as they were told.

'It makes me feel happy to see this,' Ned confided in Ilsa at one point.

'Why?'

'Because these are signs of a happy life, something I want to build for myself once I'm fully better.'

'I'm sure you'll succeed.'

A short time later, Nina clapped her hands and gathered them round her. 'Time to change into your party clothes.'

'I don't have any,' Ilsa said.

'A few things happened to fall into my shopping. Go and look on your beds and then change quickly. Come back here as soon as you've changed and everything will be ready for you then.'

The three of them looked at her in puzzlement.

'You'll see.'

Ilsa found a wonderful trouser suit on her bed, made from a material with glittery bits. She'd never owned or worn anything half as frivolous in her life but when she put it on, it fitted and was very flattering.

When she went downstairs, the others were waiting for her, also smartly dressed, and four glasses were filled with some pale gold liquid that was bubbling gently.

'Three of us took a wonderful step yesterday, becoming a family, and we're going to celebrate it for the rest of our lives, starting today. But first I'd like to invite you to join our family as well, Ned.'

He stared at her in shock, his mouth literally dropping open.

'Want to take a chance?' she asked him.

He didn't hesitate. 'Yes. Oh, yes, please.' But then he gulped and had to fight to stay calm.

'No hesitation?' Sean asked gently.

'None whatsoever.'

'We'll celebrate that, just the four of us, and then I've invited a few others to join us,' she said. 'Now, raise your glasses. To our new family.'

Inevitably as they waited for the other guests to arrive, Ilsa found herself chatting to Ned while the other two whispered to one another.

'I still haven't got used to the feeling of being a real part of all this,' Ilsa admitted, waving one hand around to indicate the whole scene.

'But it must be making you feel good because you look happier than I've ever seen you before.'

'Do I really?'

'Very much so.'

'You look pretty happy yourself.'

'When you've been as close to death as I have and then come through it, you don't hesitate to seize anything joyful that happens to you, both small and large – and today is very large.'

'Isn't it?' She held out her glass to his and they clinked, and sipped again.

As she was finishing the glass, Nina turned to them. 'Would you mind if I just rang the oldies? It's time for them to join us. And also I need to admit I lost my bet.'

They looked a bit surprised at that. 'Prue bet me we'd get on well and adopt each other as relatives really quickly, and the others agreed with her. I thought it'd take longer but it's one bet I'm happy to lose.'

There was silence as they took this in, then Sean gave them a smile. 'It was their idea, wasn't it?'

'Yes, of course it was. And I think they'll be including Ned too, in some way.'

'They'll deserve to win the bet and to celebrate with us as well, then.'

As Nina passed to pick up her phone, she paused to give

Ilsa another big hug. 'I'm so glad, so very glad to have you in the family.'

'I'm over the moon about it. In fact, I've never been so happy in my whole life.'

The whole room was soon full of happy people. It was almost as if the air sparkled with joy.

ANNA JACOBS was born in Lancashire at the beginning of the Second World War. She has lived in different parts of England as well as Australia and has enjoyed setting her modern and historical novels in both countries. She is addicted to telling stories and recently celebrated the publication of her one hundredth novel, as well as sixty years of marriage. Anna has sold over four million copies of her books to date.

annajacobs.com